"...they emerged from the big spa, and wrapped themselves in white fluffy robes from the wardrobe and lay on the small patch of grass between the rose bushes, and watched the night-time display of the endlessly shifting cosmos.

'We don't have stars in New York City,' she said softly in the darkness, her head on his shoulder, gazing upwards. An owl hooted somewhere close by and the old windmill squeaked as a lick of wind coaxed it into motion. 'We have stars on the ceilings of stretch limousines and we have stars above the beds in posh hotels to remind us that they're up there somewhere, but we don't have stars.

At least, nothing you can see. Nothing like this.'

'Maybe it's true what they say,' he said, drawing her closer.

'What do they say?'

She felt his lips kiss her hair. 'You can't have everything.'

She said nothing for a while, just lay there thinking. She didn't want everything, if that's what he was suggesting.

She just wanted to be back in her apartment with Carmen and for things to settle down and be normal again.

And she wanted to get that promotion.

But most of all she wanted this tangled heavy feeling in her chest to unravel itself and go away.

As she lay beside him feeling the steady drumbeat of his heart beneath her ear, she thought, what was so wrong with a girl wanting a few stars?"

ALWAYS ON MY MIND

TRISH MOREY

ebook ISBN 978-0-6488359-2-9

In memory of my darling Dad,

Max Duffield.

*Whose Cornish ancestors sailed into Port Adelaide in 1854 on
board the barque, David Malcolm,
and whose grandfather was born in a dug out in a creek at Burra
in 1859
and grew up working alongside his father
in the Moonta mines.*

*Thank you for riding shotgun while I was writing this baby.
This one's for you, Dad.*

xxx

PREFACE

Pip Martin saw her life as being made up of two distinct parts.

There was the before, when summers were long and hot and the days filled with girlfriends and the cute guy next door or chasing after her irritating little brother, with her mum and her gran whipping up cupcakes or a roast in the old wood stove. Days when her dad would come home tired and cranky after another long session in the paddocks bringing in the harvest on their Yorke Peninsula farm.

Then there was the *after*, where there was only Pip, and her ailing gran, and a bone deep sense of betrayal, for everyone it seemed had known or suspected the truth.

Everyone but Pip.

But by then it was too late to find out who she really was. All she knew was that she didn't belong and that she needed to be as far away from her lying past as possible.

CHAPTER 1

*A*delaide Airport had grown up while Pip was away. There was a shiny new terminal with air bridges now, and disembarking the plane had the same generic feel it had worldwide, so she could almost have been anywhere – if not for the unmistakeable line of hills to the east, with the three towers marking the highest point in the Mount Lofty Ranges.

That, and the twisting of her gut that told her she was nearly home.

Home.

After almost a decade and a half living and working in Sydney and then New York, she wasn't even sure what that meant any more.

Her recently turned on phone burped up the messages that had come in since last checking her phone during her connection in Auckland, and Pip held her breath as she scanned them. She smiled at the 'Missing you' message from her friend, Carmen, and frowned at the three from Chad but didn't bother with those now. She was relieved to see there was nothing from her gran's nursing home. No news was good news, although it didn't stop her calling as soon as she was inside the terminal.

'How is she?' she asked, to be told there was no change. She checked the wristwatch she'd already adjusted to Adelaide time and did a mental calculation – one hour at most for the formalities of immigration and customs and to collect the keys to her rental car, and another two for the drive to the town of Kadina – and told them she'd be there by lunch.

Too easy.

Her business class ticket meant a short queue at immigration, so she beat her luggage to baggage collection, the carousel still stationery. It wouldn't be long once it did kick into action, she knew, courtesy of the priority tag her suitcase was wearing. But still she felt impatient to keep moving, her stomach wringing itself tighter and tighter the longer the wait continued. Feeling conflicted. Needing desperately to see her gran, but knowing that visiting her home town for the first time in almost a decade was going to shake things up, things she'd sooner leave right where they were.

Like questions from the past she didn't know the answer to.

Like other stuff.

Like . . . *Luke.*

God, she didn't want to think about any of that, least of all Luke. That was history. So ancient, it shouldn't even figure. And then a siren sounded and a light flashed and the carousel kicked slowly into motion. A few bags in, her suitcase appeared through the rubber strips. She almost sighed as she hauled it from the carousel. She'd still be out of here within the hour. Thank god she had nothing to declare. Another ten minutes or so and finally she'd be free.

It was when she turned that she noticed the sniffer dog, trotting its way between legs and luggage. It was a beagle and cute as a button and for the first time in hours she managed a smile. Until it took one sniff in her direction and plonked itself down in front of her, and cute as a button turned into the incoming passenger's worst nightmare.

'I don't understand,' she pleaded, as the dog's handler asked to see an incoming passenger card that clearly stated she was carrying nothing that should be of any interest to a sniffer dog or its handler.

'Are you sure there's not something in your bag?' he asked, as curious heads craned around her. 'Some food from the plane, perhaps?'

She shook her head, the cold sick fear of what-if curdling the aeroplane breakfast in her stomach. What if someone had stashed something in her luggage en route? What if any one of a thousand other scenarios had happened? But she had done nothing wrong. She knew she had packed nothing that was contraband. She tried to smile. Tried to look confident. Tried, and failed. 'Nothing. Absolutely nothing.'

Of course, there was nothing else for it but to search her bags. As her hopes of a quick getaway faded, her sigh of exasperation didn't win her any friends.

'This won't take long,' said the stony faced official.

'I'm sorry,' she said, trying not to aggravate the man any further. Not that anyone seemed fussed about not aggravating her. 'It's just, I'm kind of in a hurry.' She licked her dry lips and wondered if she'd they'd give her a break if she explained why she needed to get through customs and immigration as quickly as possible. 'You see, my grandmother's dying and I promised to be at her bedside by lunch.'

The official paused, latex sheathed hands poised over her suitcase, and for one moment Pip thought that maybe he might actually let her go. 'That's too bad, miss,' he said, deadpan but with a glimmer in his eye that told Pip she'd probably made the biggest mistake of her life by playing the dying grandmother card. He looked convinced she was trying to hide something now. 'And now, if you'll kindly unzip your bag?'

After twenty minutes of rifling through her things, twenty minutes of excruciating embarrassment as his big hands sorted through her knickers and her bras and the stuff she hid in her toiletries bag specifically so it wouldn't spill out if her suitcase came undone en route, twenty minutes of questions during which the official found nothing before finally conceding that the beagle had likely smelled the banana she admitted taking most days to work, she was free to cram her belongings back in and go hunt down her rental car.

She sighed with relief at the agency as she gave her name and the attendant pulled out the paperwork. Finally something was going right. Soon she'd be on her way.

Or not . . .

'Hang on,' she said to the car rental agency attendant, who seemed to be having a lot of trouble with her booking. 'I don't want a sports car!'

The man rolled his eyes and glanced meaningfully over her shoulder at the queue of mums and dads and kids and luggage already building up behind her. 'But you booked a cabriolet. It says so right here on the form.'

She shook her head, knowing that the last thing she wanted was a sports car. Her plan was to get in and out of Kadina making as few waves as possible. There was no way on earth she'd have asked for a damned sports car – or for that matter, any car that might draw attention to herself. 'I want an ordinary car. Something nondescript and plain. Haven't you got something boring? A Toyota or something?'

The attendant smiled. If you could call it a smile. More a baring of his teeth. 'That's actually a little awkward right now. We're fully booked with the Christmas holidays start-ing. And after all, you did book the cabriolet.'

Pip sighed. Clearly someone had stuffed up. 'Martin,' she said again for good measure. 'M-A-R-T-I-N. Can you check again please? There must be some mix up.'

'There is no mix up.' He didn't even pretend to smile this time, all attempts at the pleasantries over. 'This is your name on the rental document, yes?'

She glanced at the papers. 'Well yes,' she conceded, 'but for the last time, I didn't book –'

And with a cold shiver of realisation, it hit her. She hadn't booked it at all. While she'd been in a panic about packing, Chad had offered to do it for her, using his firm's corporate code because it offered a better discount than hers. 'Just a car,' she'd told him when he asked what kind she wanted. 'Any old car.'

Shit . . .

'Hang on,' she said, reaching for her phone, scrolling through the messages she'd ignored earlier, clicking on the first.

Figured you would have landed by now.

She deleted that and moved onto the next.

Thought you might be missing me.

Weird. She frowned and sent that one to the trash as well. It was the third message where she hit paydirt.

So surprise! Enjoy the wheels. Think of me every time you put your foot down.

What the hell? She'd think of him, all right. She'd imagine pushing him under her pedal and pressing her foot down hard. Dammit, why the hell had she ever trusted him with her booking?

She sucked in air and looked back at the attendant and gave a weak smile. He had no trouble lobbing a wide one right back, and she knew that whatever expression had been on her face when she'd read those messages might as well have been ringed with neon lights. He was loving every minute of this. 'All sorted then?' he asked smugly, and without waiting for the answer pushed the rental agreement closer to her. 'So maybe we can finish off the paperwork. If you just sign here . . . and here.'

Pip sighed. 'Okay,' she conceded, holding up one hand. 'Apparently someone did book that car in my name. But it was actually a misunderstanding. Are you sure there's nothing else available? Nothing at all?'

He blew air through his teeth and gestured to the queue behind her that was growing longer by the minute, full of fractious kids and their exhausted looking parents. 'Not a sausage. I'm sorry, these people have booked all our *boring* cars.'

Ouch! She glanced over to the other agency desks, wondering if she should threaten to take her business else-where, but those desks looked just as crowded.

'So there's really no alternative?'

'There's always an alternative,' he told her, and when she looked back at him, halfway interested, he continued. 'There's always public transport.'

All the way to the Yorke Peninsula? In what – a bus? And meanwhile she was supposed to be halfway there already, at her gran's bedside. Oh god, Gran! Two hours after landing she was still stuck here at the airport. 'Okay,' she said, scrawling her signature on the paperwork. So much for trying not to be noticed. 'I'll take the damned convertible. Please just tell me it's not red.'

The attendant looked studiously at the papers and didn't say a word, but still she caught the curve of his lips. She could only hope it was because he was happy to be finally seeing the back of her.

Five minutes later she knew it wasn't the only reason.

She surveyed the car. Her nondescript rental designed to fly under the radar and go unnoticed in her home town.

It was all kinds of red.

Look-at-me red.

Trouble-on-wheels red.

Sex-on-wheels red.

Enough!

Whatever the colour, she would have to deal with it. She would just have to cope. She wrestled her bag into the trunk – boot, she reminded herself – and opened her door, staring blankly for a moment at the missing steering wheel before she realised.

'Damn!'

She slammed the door, disgusted with herself as she rounded the car and found the driver's seat.

She was in Australia now. Driving on the other side of the car, and the road. She'd better not forget that again.

CHAPTER 2

*T*he last thing Luke needed in the middle of harvest was to have to head into town. But the fuel filter had clogged in the harvester he'd been nursing and the whole thing had finally sputtered and died, and there was no putting off a visit to the local John Deere dealership any longer. Besides, it wasn't like he had nothing else to do while he was in town. The running repair he'd made to the back sheep paddock fence wouldn't last forever, so he might as well get those extra droppers he was short of, not to mention pick up the mail and grab a few groceries into the deal. A pre-Christmas ham in the fridge made meal preparation easy, sure, but even he was getting sick of ham sandwiches.

By the time he'd talked himself into the inevitability of it, he was almost happy to forget the inconvenience of leaving the harvest unfinished and load up Turbo alongside him. For a couple of hours they'd leave the troubles of the farm behind. Just the thought of chicken and chips for lunch for a change improved his mood. And god knows, he could do with a bit of company.

The dog whimpered and laid its head on his paws where

he was sitting on the seat beside him, and Luke almost wondered if he'd spoken out loud. Then again, his dog had always been uncanny in picking up on his moods. 'Sorry Turbo,' he said, curling the fingers of one hand around his ears. 'Nothing personal, but a bloke needs a bit of human company every now and then.'

Turbo snorted his disagreement and sulked into a restless doze as the ute headed down the back roads towards the highway to Kadina.

Luke smiled. The dog was right. Turbo had seen him with human company – of the female variety at any rate – and hated every mismatched minute of it. And most of the time he had no need for two-legged companionship anyway. Turbo was a better companion than just about any friend he'd had. Honest, hardworking and loyal to a fault. If only the dog could learn to rustle up a steak sandwich or a feed of chicken and chips for them every now and then, he'd be just about perfect.

Luke changed his plan of attack as he drove by the local agricultural supplies dealership. The Ag store car park was in gridlock, a combination of harvest needs and pre-Christmas shopping. Forget waiting in line, he'd come back after lunch when there might be more chance to catch a minute with his mate Craig, the manager. He needed to check the details for Sunday's christening – it wouldn't do to turn up late, not given he'd agreed to be Chloe's godfather.

The supermarket welcomed him with air-conditioned comfort, canned music and the occasional nod from other customers, none of which he minded as he made his way around the aisles filling his basket. Until Sheila Ferguson bailed him up in the frozen food section, her trolley blocking the only part of the aisle her ample body didn't. And damn it all, she was between the Potato Gems and him.

'Did you hear the news?' she crowed, bright eyed and

delighted, holding her ground after exchanging the usual pleasantries. Luke raked fingers through his hair, scratching for a clue. Sheila headed the local native animal rescue network and was famous for her work adopting orphaned wildlife. There was hardly a week went by where Sheila and the latest orphaned babies weren't featured in the local newspaper. Maybe she'd finally been awarded an Order of Australia for her efforts and he was the only one who hadn't congratulated her for it?

His seeking fingers gave up, drawing a blank. 'Sorry Sheila. I've been busy with the harvest. What did I miss?'

The woman's eyes widened, as if she'd just hit the mother lode. 'You really haven't heard? Then it's lucky I found you. Priscilla Martin is coming home.'

He blinked. A really slow blink. To give his gut a chance to deal with the shock and move on before any hint of surprise might show in his eyes. Before any hint could be transmitted that he might actually be interested in the news. Because he wasn't – interested, that is – he just had to get used to the concept.

And he was glad he'd taken his time, because when he opened them he found Sheila Ferguson examining him much like he imagined she'd examine one of her marsupial roadkill victims. Closely. Intently. Studying them for any signs of life before she plucked whatever newborns were hanging around the pouch waiting to be rescued.

He grimaced. Lucky for him he wasn't brandishing a pouch. The woman did good work, it was true, but he wouldn't fancy Sheila's gnarled hands rummaging around his nether regions.

'That's nice,' he lied, as nonchalantly as he could. And, after all, why shouldn't he be nonchalant? It was long since he cared what Pip Martin did. So long ago it was ancient history. 'So, what brings her back?'

'Violet Cooper is fading,' the woman continued, nodding sadly, her fingers tightly wound around her trolley, still blocking the aisle and any chance of escape. 'They say she's not long for this world.'

It shouldn't have come as a surprise. Pip's grandmother had managed to hang on for so long she was almost part of the furniture at Kadina's nursing home. She had to be pushing ninety years old. But the bigger surprise was finding that her granddaughter actually cared enough to leave her highly paid job in New York City to come. As far as he knew, she hadn't visited for nigh on a decade. Why bother now?

Not that he was about to ask Sheila that, because then she might think that he cared. And then everyone Sheila spoke to might think he cared. And that would be wrong.

Because he didn't care.

Not about Pip, at any rate. Long ago she'd more than severed any connection they'd had.

'I'm sorry to hear that,' he said instead, because it was far safer territory and he truly was sorry. And because he felt guilty. He'd loved Pip's grandmother like his own once. But his had been taken out by a sudden stroke while Pip's had lingered through the slow decline of Alzheimer's. And while he'd meant to pop in and say hello from time to time – and had, once or twice, in the beginning – the visits had tapered off as Violet's disease had taken hold. 'Thanks for letting me know, Sheila, but Turbo's waiting in the car. I better get going.'

PORT WAKEFIELD ROAD was even more chaotic than she remembered. It had always been busy, sure, but now it seemed more frenetic than ever, its sides heaving with businesses hawking the likes of caravans, boats and prefabricated houses. As Pip passed mile upon mile of new suburbs backed up against the highway, she found herself wondering if the expanding city would ever end.

Norah Jones singing on Pip's phone did her best to soothe her fraying nerves, and for all its showiness, the Audi ate up the bitumen with ease, but still the sprawling city seemed interminable.

This had all been open paddocks once, the highway nothing more than a long straight ribbon of asphalt heading north-west through flat, drab countryside.

Not that it had been any more inspiring then.

But at least it had been familiar.

Finally the long belt of city fell away and broad paddocks opened up either side. Flat and brown, this was how she remembered it – just about as different from Manhattan as you could get. The tallest things around her now were the B-Double trucks hurtling along the highway, and there wasn't a yellow cab in sight.

It should have felt wrong after so many years living away, the first five years in Sydney, the last nine in New York. She should have felt like a stranger. But it didn't feel wrong and she didn't feel like a stranger.

Instead, it felt – *she felt* – sad.

It was a long flat road back to nowhere. Nowhere she wanted to be, at any rate. Nowhere she would be heading now, except for . . .

'Oh, Gran.'

And maybe it was mad, rushing home to be with a woman who hadn't recognised her the last two times she'd visited and wouldn't know she was here now. Except that Violet was her grandmother and she had no other family.

None that she knew of anyway.

Damn.

Pip swept a stray tear from her cheek. She'd known

coming home would stir up all kinds of questions from the past, but right now she couldn't afford to let herself think of anything besides Gran.

The Audi rolled on, past the oddly named towns of Dublin and Windsor and the more fittingly named Two Wells and Wild Horse Plains. Weariness dragged at her. She'd bought a business class ticket in the hope that it would give her the comfort and space to sleep, but she'd been kidding herself. She'd been too worried about her Gran to get anything more than patchy sleep, and once she'd landed in Auckland, the knowledge that she was nearly home had been too powerful to let her rest. Now the time wasted at the airport hung heavily on her. By rights, she should already be there.

The town of Port Wakefield appeared before her, a cluster of bakeries and crowded fuel stops, and then disappeared before the road split and suddenly it was quieter, the bulk of the traffic traveling north while she swung west, the low domes of the Hummocks rising before her, the range that had always signalled the divide between Adelaide and the Yorke Peninsula.

The range that was the final barrier to her former life. She shivered, and not only because she was worried about her Gran.

Not long now ...

CHAPTER 3

The groceries safely stashed in the esky in the back of the ute, Luke pulled up outside the post office. He didn't bother turning off the engine, he'd only be here a minute. He was pulling out the wad of mail curled tightly inside his letterbox when the post office door opened beside him.

'Luke Trenorden!' he heard. 'Fancy meeting you here.'

He groaned inwardly, even as he recognised the voice and turned to greet his high school English teacher. Jean Cutting liked nothing more than to talk. And talk.

'Hi, Mrs Cutting,' he said, a habitual greeting forged through three years of classes and somehow never shed. No matter how long ago his school years were, she'd never be anything but Mrs Cutting. 'How's it going?'

Her eyes were bright and her ruddy cheeks were lit up like a pair of red delicious apples, and for a moment his stomach tightened and he wondered . . . But no, there was no reason to panic, because his old high school English teacher was always glad to see him. It didn't have to mean anything.

'So what brings you into town today?' she asked, studying

the pile of mail in his hands and nodding knowingly. 'Looks like you haven't been in for a while.'

'Got to pick up a part for the harvester. Figured I might as well grab the mail while I'm here.'

'Oh,' she said. And then gave a lilting girlish laugh. 'And here was me thinking you'd come in to see Pip.'

Good grief.

So much for those ruddy cheeks and bright eyes not meaning anything. The bush telegraph was clearly alive and well. 'Pip?' he asked, and was grateful his voice didn't squeak.

'Pip Martin. I hear she's coming home today to see Violet Cooper before she goes. I thought maybe you'd come in to catch up with her.'

'Uh, actually, no.'

'Because you two were so close in high school, of course.'

He scuffed an imaginary clod of dirt from his boot against the concrete verandah. 'Yeah, well, that was a long time ago.'

'And a lot of us were hoping that one day you might end up as more than just friends.'

'It's funny how things turn out, for sure.'

Her eyes turned sympathetic as she shook her head. 'I know. It was so sad about you and Sharon not working out.'

He scratched his head, wondering how long he was going to have to stand here while she prattled on about all his past failures. Any minute now and she'd launch into a blow-by-blow critique of every miserable essay he'd ever written. 'Yeah, well –'

'Do you think you'll look her up?'

'Who? Sharon?'

'No. Pip, of course.'

He looked towards his car where Turbo was sitting panting in the driver's seat, the engine still running. The dog looked like he was ready to reverse and drive away, and Luke had never wanted to change places with him more. 'I really hadn't thought about it. I imagine she'll be pretty busy with her gran 'n' all.'

'Well, it's not a very big town, is it, really?' And then she did that lilting laugh that had always set his teeth on edge. 'You're bound to bump into each other somewhere along the line.'

Not if he had anything to do with it. In fact, as soon as he was done with the Ag store, he sure as hell wouldn't be setting foot anywhere near town again until he knew she was gone. 'Anyway, I probably should be getting on. Get those parts, you know. Nice seeing you, Mrs Cutting.'

'Call me Jean.'

'Sure, um, Mrs Cutting. Catch you later.'

PIP'S EYELIDS grew heavier and heavier. She'd imagined when she'd scaled the Hummocks that she was nearly at Kadina, but she'd been kidding herself. Forty kilometres to go. Forty kilometres that had never seemed so long. She felt a pang of guilt passing the turn-off to Melton, the tiny collection of farmhouses clustered around the one-time railway siding where she'd lived what seemed a lifetime ago, but she'd make time to visit the old place later. Turning off now would mean passing those three black markers on the side of the road, and she wasn't ready for that. Not yet. She had the living to think about first. Her gran needed her more right now.

Besides, Luke lived down that way, and she had no desire to meet up with Luke just yet. No desire to make small talk and learn he and Sharon had a clutch of kids by now. She wasn't fooling herself, in a community as tightly knit as this one, and with mutual friends, it was almost inevitable their paths would cross sometime during her stay. But she was in no hurry for it to happen.

So she'd go and visit the old place another time. But for now the long straight road to Kadina stretched out in front of her and all she could think was that she wanted to be there already. Already parked. Already at the nursing home at Gran's bedside and not battling weariness.

She turned up the stereo so Norah Jones could keep her awake, but 'The Nearness of You' came on, and she wasn't going to go there. Hearing it while she was half a world away had been one thing, but that had been *their* song and the last thing she needed was a reminder. Especially now she was so close to where they'd both lived.

She picked up her phone, flashed through her collection, settled on Muse and 'Starlight' – she could belt out the words and stay awake – and too late realised she was going through a town and had missed a speed sign. Her foot hit the brake. But not before the world behind her lit up in flashing red and blue.

Shit!

She pulled over, her head flopping against the headrest as the police car pulled in behind her. Could this day possibly get any worse?

She saw him coming in her wing mirror, tall and lean in his navy blue uniform, dark glasses hiding his eyes as he pulled on his peaked hat, and she wound down her window, ready to hand over her New York State driver's license.

'Afternoon, miss,' he said, as he drew alongside, his fingers at his cap. 'Do you realise –' And then he paused, his brow puckering above his glasses. He took her license and examined it. 'Pip Martin, it is you. I heard you were coming home.'

'Do I know you?' she asked, searching for a clue. He had a voice that was pure Aussie country and a jawline that could have been chiselled from the limestone of which the peninsula was hewn, but still she drew a blank.

He peeled off his wraparound sunglasses. 'You don't remember the man who played Prince Charming to your Cinderella in the Kadina Primary Year Seven school play?'

And realisation jolted through her. 'Oh my god, Adam Rogers? You're a policeman?' She blinked, her mind going a gazillion miles an hour trying to remember. 'Isn't your father a policeman as well?'

'Yeah, like father, like son. Though he retired a few years back. I hear you've got some high powered job in New York?'

'I'm a market risk analyst for an investment bank. It pays the bills.'

'Wow.' He took his hat off, her license still locked between two fingers on that hand, and ran the fingers of his other through thick, sandy hair. 'I don't even know what that is.'

'Less exciting than your job, that's what it is.'

'And so I guess,' he said, tugging his hat back on, and turning hazel eyes upon her, 'you've got yourself a fancy New York type husband or boyfriend to go with it?'

An image of Chad flitted through her mind for all of about a second, mostly because she was still pissed at him for hiring her this show-pony of a car. 'Nope,' she said, taking direct aim at Chad and firing with both barrels. 'Still footloose and fancy free.'

Adam huffed. 'Always knew there was something wrong with those Yankees.'

She laughed for the first time in what seemed like forever and it felt good. 'What about you? You married?' He had to be. He was too good-looking not to be.

Something skated across those hazel eyes and he gave an all too brief smile. 'I was married. Marnie Smith from Moonta, her folks had the deli on the main street. Remember her?'

She searched her memories, but could pull nothing out. She shook her head.

'Yeah, well . . . Anyway, she died a few years back. Breast cancer. There's just me and Jake now. He's eight next month.'

'Oh, I'm sorry to hear that. That's rough.'

'Well, there's a lot of rough going around. I hear you're back to see Violet.'

She nodded. 'Just flew in this morning.' Her teeth found her bottom lip, scraping it, thinking he hadn't pulled her over merely to talk about old times. 'Look, Adam, I'm sorry if I was driving a bit fast. I was changing the music and must have missed the sign.'

'Yeah.' He tapped her license against the thumb of his other hand. 'You were going almost twenty k's over the speed limit.'

'That much? Oh god. I slowed down as soon as I realised I was in a town.'

He looked around at the empty street and the row of buildings set a block back from it. The place might as well have been deserted. They'd been passed by all of one car since he'd pulled her over. 'Well, it's not like you were in too much danger of hitting anyone. How about this time I let you off with a warning, seeing as you've just stepped off the plane? Wouldn't be a good look to welcome you home with a speeding ticket.'

'You mean it?' she asked, as he handed back her license.

'Yeah, but only on one condition.'

'Don't do it again?'

He smiled. 'That goes without saying. I actually meant something else.' He rested a hand on the roof of her car and leaned closer to the window. She could see the play of muscles under the tanned skin of his arm. It was a good look – Adam Rogers worked out and it showed. 'Come out with me for a drink sometime. We can talk about Cinderella and Prince Charming and how the fairytale could have ended.'

Her eyes flicked back to his. He was flirting with her? Seriously? 'Look, I'm not sure –'

'Yeah, I know you'll be busy with your gran, but you'll probably need a drink sometime while you're dealing with the rest of it.'

Wasn't that the truth? And why shouldn't she have a drink with Adam for old times' sake? It wasn't like she was planning on marrying him. She wasn't planning on marrying *anyone* from out this way.

She smiled. 'Okay, you're on. That'd be nice.'

'All right!' His knuckles rapped out a rhythm on her roof before he pulled out a notebook and pen and handed them to her. 'Give me your number,' he said, 'and I'll give you a call.'

'Sure,' she said, writing it down. 'And otherwise, you can always reach me at Tracey and Craig's. I'm staying in their B&B.'

'I know.'

'You do?'

'Mum's one of the cooks at the nursing home. I reckon there's not a soul in Kadina that hasn't heard about the return of its most successful export.'

'Oh.' She looked down at the steering wheel and blew out a breath. So much for flying under the radar. 'Great.'

'Just make sure you drive carefully, okay.'

She smiled up at him and nodded. 'I will. And . . . thanks.'

'Anytime.' He rested his hand a moment on the sill of her window. 'It's good to see you again, Pip. You're looking good. All glamorous and New Yorkified.'

He didn't look so bad himself, but it was one thing to agree to a drink, another to start something that could have no ending. 'Um, thanks. I'll be seeing you then.'

'You will,' he said, and nodded before heading back to his

car, her eyes following his progress, wondering how she'd never noticed that tight butt before. But then, she'd gone to college in the city for her high school years and only seen him occasionally during that time. Besides, she'd only had eyes for Luke back then. She'd probably missed all kinds of stuff while she'd been wasting all her time on him.

More fool her.

Adam pulled out and waved before doing a U-turn, heading back to his speed check hidey-hole just inside the town limits. She turned the ignition and took a few deep breaths before easing carefully back onto the highway. There was one good thing about being pulled over by the cops, she mused. Suddenly she wasn't tired any more. After that little heart starter, she was wide awake.

CRAIG WAS JUST FINISHING up with another customer when Luke walked into the Ag store. Craig didn't smile, Luke noticed, just looked decidedly sheepish as he came over to greet him, and he gritted his teeth, knowing what was coming.

'Don't bother,' Luke bit out, before his friend could utter the question on his lips. 'I already heard.'

Craig raised his eyebrows. 'Trace reckons she'll be here this afternoon. Her flight was due into Adelaide this morning, apparently.'

Luke turned aside and made a show of inspecting a display of gumboots that held absolutely no interest to him at all while he cursed the harvester's fuel filter for choosing today of all days to give up. 'That's nice.'

'You don't mind?' his friend asked.

'She's a grown-up. She can do what she wants. Why should I mind?'

'Luke –'

'About that part I need . . .'

Craig regarded him levelly. Took a deep breath. Huffed it out before taking another. 'Well, given you don't mind, you might as well know – she's staying at our place while she's here.'

His head whipped around. 'Your place?'

'Jesus mate, you know Pip's not my favourite person. But Trace invited her to stay in the B&B – seeing we're doing it up and it's free and all – and I have to live with Trace.'

'Sure.' He turned back to the display. The gumboots were on sale, he noticed. How long since he'd bought gumboots? He picked up a pair, tested the weight in his hands, checked the sole and the height of the heel. All the things he'd never bothered about with gumboots that seemed vitally important right now. If only because they distracted him from the knowledge that not only was Pip coming home, but that she was staying at his best friend's place and he'd been too bloody gutless to tell him. 'These come in any other colour?'

'Luke!'

He stopped scrutinising the boots long enough to look over. 'Hmm?' And suddenly wondered at the weird pallor to his mate's skin. 'What is it?'

'There's more you should know.' Craig licked his lips and Luke was reminded of the last time he'd seen him use that exact gesture – right after he'd got the call to say his wife was in labour for the first time. He'd been here in the Ag store buying his goddamned header when Trace had called Craig to tell him her waters had broken. Luke had watched him turn a deathly shade of pale right before his eyes. And suddenly he wasn't sure he wanted to hear what his mate had to say. I just need to warn you, okay. I really hope you don't mind, but Trace is planning to invite Pip to be Chloe's godmother.'

Luke blinked. Put the boots down. He could always come into town later. Much later. Maybe the year after next. 'I should be going,' he said, sickened that the mention of someone he hadn't seen for nigh on ten years – someone he'd been done and dusted with for a decade and a half – still had such an impact on him.

'What about that fuel filter you wanted? It won't take long –'

'Nah, can't wait. Get that young bloke – Jacko? – who lives up the road to drop it off on his way home. I'll get those droppers I need while I'm here. Fix the fence while I'm waiting.' Fix anything that needs fixing and then find something else to do. Anything to keep busy, to avoid coming into town again in a hurry.

'You'll still come to the christening, though? Still be godfather to Chloe?'

Oh yeah, that.

He sucked in air. Craig was his oldest friend. They'd started kindy together. Gone through school and a dozen footy and cricket teams together besides. He could hardly blame him for his wife's random acts of madness. 'I said I would, didn't I?'

'I'm really sorry, mate. If it's any consolation, Pip might still say no.'

'Two chances of that,' Luke said, certain of the maliciousness of Murphy's Law. 'Buckley's and none.'

CHAPTER 4

The town of Kadina emerged from the golden paddocks one slow kilometre at a time. The grain storage site on the right. More paddocks before the Ag store on the left. And then she was there. Finally. Relief battled with hunger, Pip's stomach rumbling loudly as she negotiated a roundabout. No wonder, given it was two o'clock and she hadn't eaten since breakfast on the plane, hours before they'd landed.

But there had been a cafe not far from here, she recalled, and indeed there still was, even if it had experienced a makeover or three since she'd been gone. She pulled up outside, stretching her travel weary limbs as she climbed out. A salad sandwich and a takeout coffee would go down a real treat. And then she'd be ready to go see Gran.

LUKE PULLED into a space outside the café, right next to a low slung red convertible that looked like it belonged anywhere else but here. His lip curled. Not a local then. Clearly someone from the city with loads of money and a lot less sense. There were plenty of them around these days, people looking for a sea change on the coast and finding it hereabouts. He couldn't blame them. He wouldn't trade where he lived for quids.

But it didn't make him like their poncy city cars any more.

He patted Turbo's head with the promise of chicken and chips on his return and was almost at the door when the plastic fly strips buckled and parted with someone attached to a takeaway coffee cup coming the other way. Someone who looked as preened and polished and high maintenance as the car out front. He snorted. Figured.

'Sorry,' he said, stepping back out of the way to let her through. And then he saw her face and it hit him like a punch to his gut and he knew it for a fact, that Murphy was indeed a bastard.

PIP SENSED the man before she saw him clearly, her first glimpses coming through the gaps between the strips as she focused on not spilling the coffee that was filled to the brim in her hand, glimpses that built a picture of long legs encased in denim and finished in dusty boots, a look a million miles from Manhattan and one that could still stir her womanly senses. Nothing at all wrong with a man in jeans and Blundstones.

Or a policeman in uniform for that matter, she thought, remembering Adam.

Maybe coming home might have its compensations. She loved her life in Manhattan, but it had been a long while since she'd felt herself stirred by a pair of dusty boots. Why not enjoy the view while she was here?

And then he stood back and she heard him say sorry as scalding coffee sloshed over her fingers. Burning skin was the least of her worries though, as her brain hurtled her back a decade and a half to the last time she'd heard that voice utter that word.

No!

She stopped dead in her tracks as the last of the fly strips fell into place behind her, and then she saw his face and realised her brain hadn't lied. It was Luke all right, all six foot four of uncompromisingly gorgeous looking male, and she realised a bitch of a day wasn't done with her yet.

'You!' she said, her voice as flat as the paddocks that surrounded the town, and that told him everything he needed to know right there.

Luke wondered at the coffee he'd seen spill over her fingers, but she either didn't feel it or didn't care. She didn't even flinch. She just looked as shocked and unhappy as he was.

'Nice to see you too, Pip,' he said automatically, and it might have been halfway to the truth too, if she'd been anyone else. In any other circumstances he might almost have enjoyed bumping into a woman who looked like her. Because whatever she'd been doing these last few years, it sat well on her. She was as slim as he remembered, her bare arms smooth and toned, the rest of her tucked neatly under a sleeveless shirt and slim fitting pants, and she'd grown her hair long again, just the way he'd always liked it. She'd had it coloured too, or frosted or highlighted or whatever it was that women did to their hair to make it catch the light and make it look even better than nature intended.

Damn.

'I'm sorry, Luke,' she said. 'That was rude. I just . . . got a shock to see you, that's all.'

Her accent sounded different to how he remembered. More American. Grating. 'Yeah, I guess you'd hardly expect to see me in the town where I've lived my entire life.'

This time she did flinch, her blue eyes frosting over, cold as what he imagined a glacier would be like, and he was almost sorry for sending her to that frosty place. Almost. Except this was Pip and she'd sliced him into pieces and thrown them away once before.

And he was never laying himself down on that particular altar again.

Someone tried to duck between them into the cafe, between her still coming out and him still going in, and both of them shifted and made way. And while he was tempted to cut and run, damn it all, he still wanted that chicken and chips, so he didn't. He stood his ground and when the plastic fly strips stilled again she was still right there, looking up at him.

He wished she wouldn't do that.

God, she had gorgeous eyes. She'd always had gorgeous eyes. So blue you could take a dip and drown in them on a summer's day.

Those eyes cast a longing look in the direction of the Audi and escape.

And suddenly, madly, contrary to everything he'd felt the moment he'd set eyes on her, he was glad she hadn't gone. Not before he'd said what he should say, regardless of what she'd once meant to him and what she'd done to him. Because that was history, and right now should all be about Violet.

He licked his lips. 'I'm sorry to hear about your gran.'

She blinked, and the ice melted and turned her eyes watery. 'Thanks. I'm just going to sit with her now.'

'Give her my regards.'

'I will,' she said, even though they both knew it was pointless, that Violet Cooper hadn't recognised anyone or anybody for years and wouldn't remember who he was, even if she was still capable of hearing.

The logical thing to do next would be to say goodbye and walk right on by. That was what a normal person would do. A normal person who'd run into someone they'd known long ago but really didn't give a shit about now.

He wanted to be that normal person, not this lunatic whose blood was spinning furiously around his veins and whose stubborn feet remained bolted to the floor.

Turbo barked from inside the car, impatient for lunch. Luke's dog had got him out of plenty of scrapes in his time, but he'd never been more grateful than in this moment. 'Well, I better get going. Feed the dog. You know how it is,' he said, and immediately wanted to sink through the verandah with the lameness of his words. But at least they'd done what he'd needed them to do and broken whatever spell had rendered them both immobile.

'Me too,' she said quickly. 'See you 'round.'

'Sure,' he said, thinking, not if I see you first.

Inside the fly strips the air was cool and Elvis was crooning something from a speaker in the corner near the ceiling and the woman who'd gone in before him was just being handed her milkshake and passing over a note to a woman he didn't recognise.

'Be with you in a moment, lovey,' said the woman, as she turned to the cash register to fetch her customer's change.

He looked over his shoulder, telling himself he'd better check to see the dog wasn't getting up to any mischief, but it was the red car next to his that drew his eyes. The red car with the driver who looked like she'd just stepped out of a fashion magazine.

Pip in a convertible. She sure had changed. She'd always hated flashy cars. Well, she had once upon a long time ago.

Though that'd been then.

'Can I help you?'

He turned back. Help him? He wished somebody could. Because suddenly he'd forgotten what he'd come in for. He studied the blackboard menu but the words might as well have been written in Sanskrit for all the sense they made. He blinked and now all he could see were the words of a song. A sad song. And then he realised it *was* a song. The song coming from the corner near the ceiling.

'Hello?' The woman was still staring at him and waiting, one hand perched on hip and the expression on her face saying she thought he was being a time waster or just stupid or both. 'No rush,' she said, 'Anytime this century'd be good.'

He shook his head. Suddenly he didn't feel hungry anymore. All he wanted was to be away from that song.

'Sorry,' he said and turned for the door. As Elvis sang 'You were always on my mind' one last time, he made it through the fly strips in time to see the red car disappearing into the distance, and he cursed Murphy all over again that he'd picked today of all days to come into town.

He climbed back into the driver's seat. 'Okay, fella, let's go home.'

Turbo whimpered and pawed at his leg, and it took Luke a moment to work out why and remember. He sighed as he started the engine, curling his fingers around his dog's ears with the other hand. 'I'm sorry, mate,' he said, jamming the ute into reverse, 'but it's not like there's anything actually wrong with ham sandwiches.'

CHAPTER 5

*C**rap!*

Pip drove away with her heart still thudding in her chest and her palms slippery on the steering wheel. She rubbed them one at a time on her pants as she accelerated away. Of all the dumb luck, she had to pick that particular cafe on this particular day.

Crap! Crap! Crap!

Luke Trenorden was not who she needed to bump into today. Or any day for that matter. But definitely not today.

Especially not when he looked so good. He'd looked good back then, sure. Lean and long-limbed and drop-dead gorgeous. But the eight years since she'd last seen him at Fi and Richard's wedding should have made him look older than he did, surely. They should have turned him into more of an old married man, with hair greying at the temples from too many kids driving him nuts.

If there was any justice in this world, that's what should have happened.

Instead the years only seemed to have enhanced what had already been there – the residual softness in his face turned to lines that added ruggedness and character. The cast of his shoulders broader, stronger. And every change, every discernible difference where boy had turned into man she'd noted with her seeking eyes while her disloyal feet had been rooted to the spot outside the cafe.

Not even the start of a beer belly under that work shirt. And she should know. She'd damn well searched for evidence of one.

She swung the car through one last roundabout and pulled her thoughts back into line at the same time. She would not think about Luke a moment longer. He was history. He was her past. And dammit to hell and back, he was married.

And since she was committed heart and soul to a career in New York City, he was irrelevant to boot.

But couldn't he have tried to look a bit less like he'd just walked out of an R.M. Williams catalogue?

He could have at least made an effort.

Her mental rant took her past the turn-off, and she had to wend her way back through long forgotten streets until finally she was there, parked outside the Kadina Nursing Home.

She sighed a grateful sigh of relief which lasted all of a second before she felt a sudden surge of fear at what she might find inside.

Gran.

Her gran.

Dying.

This day had been coming ever since she had been admitted into the facility. Pip had known then that no matter what happened inside, whether Gran shifted from low care to high care or to the secure dementia unit, there was only one way out, and that one day the call would come – to come home quickly, or that it was over.

She'd known, and yet . . .

Oh god.

She took a moment to steel herself, resting her head on the steering wheel, before grabbing her coffee and sandwich and heading for the door.

Inside the air was cool and controlled, the scent in the ward a combination of cleaning solution and air fresheners. About as good as it could be, she figured, under the circumstances. Pip wrote her name in the visitor's book by the door and let herself into the secure area. She'd barely reached the nurses' station when she was spotted. 'Pip! You made it, you're here!' And then Molly Kernahan's sturdy arms tugged her into a tight embrace. 'You, girl, are a sight for sore eyes.'

It was a struggle to hold onto her coffee and sandwich, but Pip felt the beginnings of a watery smile against Molly's ample welcoming girth. Molly Kernahan had been a fixture at the nursing home since Gran had been admitted. It was Molly who had emailed her to say, 'Come now, if you can.' And now, after thirty plus hours of luxurious but ultimately soulless travel, a hug from someone she knew had been here forever was enough to bring her undone.

'Is she still . . .' she started with a sniffle against her shoulder. 'Is Gran . . . ?' But the words stuck in the back of her throat. She couldn't bear it if Gran had slipped away already, when she'd come so far and been so close.

Molly took her shoulders and held her at arm's length, her round face breaking into a broad smile, but still she didn't miss the moisture filming the other woman's eyes. 'She's made of stern stuff, that one. Nothing surer. Come on, I'll take you to her.'

She swept her down a corridor done out in fresh pastel shades some time since she'd last been here, every now and then negotiating her around another shuffling old dear on a walking frame, and always with a pat to their shoulder and a gentle word.

Molly Kernahan was a treasure, Pip thought. Every nursing home should have a dozen of her at least.

And then they entered a room with windows overlooking a garden filled with flowering bushes and plants. It was a gorgeous light-filled room dotted with small pieces of furniture she remembered from the old farm house, small side tables covered with crocheted doilies Gran had made long ago, when her eyes were clear and her fingers still nimble, and a mahogany dressing table with her silver backed mirror and brush still lying on top, ready for Gran to climb out of bed in the morning and use.

Only she wouldn't, because there – barely a bump in the bed – her gran lay dying.

'Look who's here!' Molly announced as she plumped pillows and adjusted the head of Violet's bed to raise her up a little. 'It's your Pip come to visit. All the way from New York City. Isn't that nice?'

Gran blinked watery eyes and smiled a gummy smile that lasted barely a fraction of a second before her face slackened again.

Molly stroked her hair. 'Ah, your gran is such a love. Always a smile. Even at a time like this.' She turned away, but not before Pip saw the moisture sheening her eyes. 'Here, Pip love, come say hello. I'll fetch you a chair.'

Pip deposited both coffee cup and sandwich on a table and came closer. Gran was like a bird, shrunken and tiny, her limbs no more than skin over bone and corded sinew. Her hair was totally white and cut short around her gaunt face, her once familiar long hair and bun sacrificed for comfort and the staff's convenience.

'Gran,' she whispered, swallowing down a catch in her throat as she kissed the old woman's forehead. 'It's me, Pip.'

There was that sideways stretch of her lips again. The hint of a smile that Pip knew didn't mean I remember, but was just a recognition that someone was there, talking to her. It was something. It was enough.

She sat down in the chair Molly had brought and gently placed a tiny, claw of a hand into her own, stroking the old woman's palm with her thumb. 'I missed lunch, Gran, I'm sorry. I got held up.'

Molly rested a hand on her shoulder. 'She's not eating anything now, lovey,' she shared quietly. 'Not even custard and sweets that she used to love even up until a few days ago. She doesn't need it anymore, do you Molly?'

Tears pricked at her eyes as Pip stared hard at her gran – precious Gran who had once been as strong as an ox and milked the cows every day and tended a garden that stretched all around the farmhouse and beyond. Gran, who was all the family she had left in the world. She suddenly wondered why the hell she'd stayed away so long. And for what? It was all so difficult to remember.

'I should have done more,' she said.

Molly clucked her tongue as she opened a window to let in the fragrance of the rose garden on the warm breeze. 'Don't start going down that path, Priscilla Martin, or you'll never find a way back. You've done more than some families do, and you've had far better reason to do nothing at all, given how far away you live.' She gestured towards the floral arrangement on Violet's desk. 'You've sent new nighties and dressing gowns and bedsocks the moment we suggested she needed new ones, and you've sent flowers every single week your gran has been here. She's loved them all, though she hasn't a clue who sent them – even when we tell her every time. And the rest of the residents have loved them too, when the new bunch comes in and the old one goes out in the

lounge for another week. Don't you dare tell me you should
have done more.'

Pip still sniffed.

'You were dealt a rough hand,' Molly continued, her voice
softer as she put an arm around her shoulders. 'Nobody but
you left to care, and you played it the best way you could.
Never feel bad about living your own life. Not when your
gran's was already gone for all intents and purposes.' And
with a final squeeze of her shoulder, she checked if she
needed anything else to eat or drink, and left her in peace,
closing the door after her to shut out the sounds of the trol-
leys clattering down the hallways.

Pip sat there a while, her sandwich and coffee forgotten
while she held her gran's frail hand in hers, and told her all about
life in New York City, of the tall buildings and yellow cabs and
wall-to-wall people, and how it was so different to be home, but
good to be home too. She told her of her apartment in an old
brownstone building near Central Park that she shared with
her friend, Carmen, and then she started telling her all about her
job before she ran out of things to say. So she picked up the book
she'd spied on her Gran's bedside table, a familiar book that had
graced her gran's bedside table as far back as she could remember. *Not Only in Stone* had been her gran's favourite.

And she opened the book at the bookmark and began to
read Phyllis Somerville's fictionalized but so true to life story
of the Cornish families who had settled the Yorke Peninsula
– as Violet's own family had done – when it was copper, not
wheat, that had made the region's fortune. She read the pages
she'd first read as a teenager because she'd been told she
should. She read them now and this time their stories
seemed more than words. Now, it seemed, she was reading
what could have been her own family's life. Their struggles.
Their victories. Their losses.

She read as her gran lay still on the bed, her breathing intermittent, her blue eyes filmed with grey, and her mouth twitching every now and then as if she remembered, while the fragrant scent of roses carried on the breeze that stirred the curtains and perfumed the air . . .

SHE WAS in a plane and being pulled over by the police again, and this time he was prodding her, except he didn't look like Adam, he looked like Luke. And that wasn't right because it sounded like a woman . . .

'Pip?' Another shake. 'Pip?'

Pip came groggily to through a thick fog of confusion to find two women, Molly and another she didn't recognise, but who smiled down at her and clearly knew who she was.

'You should go home, lovey. You're dog tired.'

She blinked and put a hand to her spinning head. The book had fallen onto the coverlet and her neck ached from lolling at an angle. She looked at her gran, eyes shut and seemingly motionless, until her tiny bird shape fluttered and the covers shifted as she took one more breath. 'Gran.'

'She's resting. Like you should be. Where are you staying?'

She rubbed her aching neck and glanced at her watch. Barely five o'clock. Too early to sleep just yet. 'Out at Tracey and Craig's place.' There was no need to bother with surnames. Everyone knew Craig from the Ag store, and by extension, his wife Tracey.

Molly frowned. 'Are you sure you're okay to drive out there?'

'I'll be fine,' she said, and reached for her coffee. Bleh. It was stone cold.

I'll bring you a hot drink,' Molly said, 'and you say your goodbyes for now and then go and get some rest,' Molly commanded gently. 'That's an order.'

'But Gran? What if . . .'

'Nobody knows, lovey. Death has its own timetable, but your gran's surprised us enough times already to suspect she'll still be here waiting for you tomorrow. And if she's not –' she shrugged as she smiled sadly '–then she'll be in a better place. Just make sure you tell her you love her before you go. That's all you can do.' She bustled towards the door. 'Now I'll get you that coffee. How do you like it?'

Pip told her and then said, 'Oh, and Molly?'

The older woman paused.

'Do you think Gran could have some music playing? You know, something to keep her company when she's alone.'

Molly smiled. 'I think that's a very good idea. What does she like listening to? Classical music? A bit of Slim Dusty?'

'Hymns,' Pip said with a frown, suddenly thinking it odd – their family had never bothered much going to church. 'She always loved listening to *Songs of Praise*.'

Molly smiled. 'I've got just the thing. Don't know why we didn't think of it before.'

She was back in less than five minutes with a CD player, a selection of discs and a hot coffee for Pip. Pip set up the player, popped in a disc and sipped her coffee while she listened to the York Minster choir sing 'Amazing Grace'. Then she said goodbye to her gran, and even though she was asleep she told her she loved her, and gently squeezed her claw-like hand and kissed her brow again, and managed to hold herself together while she exited the building.

But once in the car, it was a full five minutes before the tears slowed and she could see clearly enough to drive.

CHAPTER 6

The Maitland Road was long and straight, with only an occasional dip or crest, not that the crests provided any surprises when the view from the top was more of the same – a long straight belt of bitumen lined either side with strips of bush. And not that it was boring, for beyond the scrubby gums lay the inevitable fields of gold, some rippling in the summer breeze, waiting to be harvested, some already bearing the geometric lines and patterns of the harvester's progress. She could see where they were working, the clouds of dust puffing up on the horizon signalling where the headers were busy bringing in the grain.

But she was dog tired and as she pulled off the main road onto the dirt side road that led to the farm, Pip half wished she was staying in town, rather than having to drive the fifteen kilometres out and back. A room nearer the nursing home made a lot of sense right now.

Or maybe Tracey and Craig having a house somewhere nearer the nursing home made more sense right now. Because it wasn't like Craig actually farmed anymore. Within a season of taking over the family farm he'd decided he was far better at retail than farming. He'd employed a manager for the property and had gone and bought the Ag store.

But then she saw the farm come into view, the old stone house and metal sheds and the windmill standing guard over it all, and she thought, *yeah, they'd have to be crazy to give all this up*, and pulled into the long farm driveway. Tracey all but exploded from the house when Pip was only halfway along it, running out to the big vehicle and machinery turnaround area, the two farm dogs barking and spinning in circles around her, and Pip felt a pang of homesickness and knew she'd done the right thing by coming here.

She pulled the Audi to a stop next to where Tracey stood with her hands clasped together, her grin a mile wide, and then she was out of the car and they fell into each other's arms, laughing and jumping and crying as the dogs continued to party around them.

'Welcome home, girlfriend! It's so good to see you!'

'And you, Trace.' She squeezed her friend tight and breathed in the smell of friendship that spanned the decades. 'It's been way too long.'

'But hey,' the other woman said, holding her at arm's length, 'just look at you! I love your hair straight like that. You look like you've just stepped out of a fashion shoot, especially with the flash car. You look fabulous.'

She was too happy to apologise for the car right now. She was too excited just seeing her friend again. Wearing shorts and a sleeveless shirt, her blonde hair pulled back into a ponytail, Tracey didn't look that much different from how she had as a teenager. 'So do you.'

Tracey laughed. 'Sure I do, with a mess of hair that hasn't seen a hairdresser since Chloe was born and mashed banana smeared all over my shoulder.'

'Hey, you look amazing. Nobody would believe you had a three-month old baby,' she said, and Tracey smiled and pulled her into her arms and hugged her tight again, before her eyes shadowed over and her smile slipped away.

'So how's your gran?'

Pip sucked in air and remembered the shock of seeing her, such a tiny bundle under the bedclothes, and felt herself frown at the memory. 'Fading. You should see her, Trace. She's so tiny and fragile. They say she's not eating but somehow she's still manages a smile. I don't know what's keeping her going.'

'Maybe she's been waiting for you.'

Pip's hand went to her mouth, her eyes misting over. 'You think?'

'Oh god, listen to me,' said Tracey, putting an arm around her shoulders. 'I'm sorry, Pip, I don't know. But it's good you're home to see her. It's good to be able to say goodbye.'

'Sure,' she said, though it didn't feel good right now. It felt like the last living piece of her family – her last link with the past – was being slowly but inexorably torn away, leaving her more alone than she'd ever been. Not even in the midst of New York City's eight million souls had she ever felt so lonely. Every man was an island there. In New York City it was normal to be alone. Everyone seemed to have a life somewhere else. A home somewhere else. A family.

She swayed on her feet, the panicked rush of the last forty-eight hours, the stress of having to remember to drive on what felt like the wrong side of the road, the sight of her gran, shrivelled and hollow-cheeked, catching up with her. 'Whoa.'

Tracey caught her by the elbow. 'Are you okay?'

'I think maybe I should just go to bed.'

'No way. It's too early for that. You'll only wake up bright-eyed and bushy-tailed at two in the morning. Come on inside,' Trace said. 'I've got a lamb roast on with an apple pie to follow. Then and only then you can crash. I'll get the boys to drop your bag over to the B&B.'

As if on cue, two boys emerged from the house, tall and lean and with legs that looked like they'd been stretched on a rack. 'You are kidding me,' said Pip, with a laugh, perking up. The last time she'd seen them, the youngest had been a toddler, the eldest not yet in school. 'Tell me these aren't your boys.'

Tracey grinned. 'Sure are. They grow like weeds at this age. Ben, Callan, come say hello.'

They approached her warily, and Pip suspected that if not for the attractions of the Audi behind her, they'd be even more tentative. Ben at age twelve was already the height of his mother, his younger brother by three years a scant six inches behind him but more solid in build, his hair with the reddish tinge of his father. 'G'day,' Ben said with a shy smile, dragging his eyes from the car for a moment, all colt-like arms and legs, but with the makings of a future lady-killer in his square jaw and big blue eyes.

'Hi,' said the younger brother more boldly. 'Is this your car?'

'It's a hire car, bozo,' said his older brother, rolling his eyes.

'All right,' he said, not fazed in the least. 'So tell me, how's things in New York City?'

Pip laughed. 'Cold when I left. Not hot like here.'

'Any snow?' Callan asked hopefully.

'Not yet. Maybe for New Year's.'

'I've never seen snow,' he admitted wistfully. 'Never snows here.'

'You should come visit me when it snows then. Not that it's a heck of a lot of fun to get around when it does.'

'Cool!' He looked hopefully at his mum. 'Can I?'

'Sure,' his mother said easily. 'When you're twenty-one.'

'Aww!'

'Take Pip's bags to the B&B, you two, and then come wash your hands for dinner. Your dad will be home any minute.' She took Pip's arm in hers. 'Come on inside and meet the newest addition to the family.'

Pip followed her friend past the enticing sizzle of roasting lamb coming from the Weber on the covered patio, into the cool interior of the old stone house and through to the big country kitchen, where the sprawling timber table and the smell of baking pie almost brought her undone. How long since she'd had an honest-to-goodness lamb roast followed by apple pie? How long since she'd sat in a big country kitchen like this one and shared a big family meal?

Eight years, that's how long. The last time she'd been back, for Fiona's wedding that time. The three friends had been born the same year, Tracey and Pip only three weeks apart, and had been inseparable all through playgroup to primary school, remaining close even through their high school years when Pip had boarded in Adelaide. Then they'd spent the school holidays together at the beach or helping out in Fi's mother's florist shop, or picnicking out on the stone mounds behind Pip's family farm, dreaming about boys. Well, only one boy in Pip's case – God, she'd been so naive. And then she'd been a bridesmaid for both Tracey and Fiona and they'd been bridesmaids for each other, telling her it was her turn next. And the last night, before she'd flown out, she'd stayed here with Tracey and Craig and their two young boys, not knowing it would be such a long time before she returned.

Eight years.

Zoom! Where the hell had that gone?

Being busy, she told herself, before she felt a stab of guilt about that too. Getting established in a new home. Making a name for herself and carving out a career in one of the most energetic cities in the world. Proving she was committed to that career by volunteering to stay on during holiday breaks when others took leave to visit family - loyalty to the job that was paying off for her now.

No, she had no reason to feel guilty. Even if she hadn't kept up with everything that was happening back here.

'Have you heard from Fi?'

'Oh yeah, I meant to tell you,' Trace said over her shoulder as she skirted around the long timber table that took up the centre of the big country kitchen. 'She wanted to come out tonight and say hello but she had to go into Wallaroo for some day procedure thing at hospital – fibroids or something – sounded ghastly. But she'll be back in the shop tomorrow and she said she'll try and come out tomorrow night, if that suits you.'

'That'd be great. I still have to meet these twins of hers.'

'Oh, you are in for a treat, they are a real pair of ranga ratbags, that's for sure. Fi's so excited they're finally at school. She says the last five years felt like fifty and she's finally getting her life back.'

Twin boys and redheads into the deal. God, Pip couldn't begin to imagine what that would be like. But then, given the work she did now and the long hours, she couldn't imagine having a baby at all. 'I might drop by the shop tomorrow after I see Gran and get some flowers for the cemetery. I'll catch up with her then.'

Tracey stopped then, just before the door to the lounge room, and turned to her friend, her expression half smile, half frown. 'Fi'll get a kick out of that, for sure. But hey, are you okay to go out there by yourself? Do you want company?'

Pip shook her head. It had taken her years before she'd been able to deal with ordering a headstone, and the last time she'd been back, Tracey had gone to the cemetery with her.

The big headstone she'd ordered had been put in place and the stark presence of the big granite slab with its bold lettering had made her loss seem more real. It had been good to have a friend there then, someone to hold her hand, a link to the living when so many of hers were gone. But that was almost a decade ago when she'd still felt battered and raw, and seeing the names and dates carved into the recently installed headstone had felt like someone pressing their finger into a bruise and asking if it hurt. 'Thanks, but I'll be fine. Just need to spend a little time with them by myself, before . . . well, before I need to go out there again for Gran, you know.'

Tracey put her hand to her arm and gave it a squeeze. 'Sure, but if you change your mind, you know where to find me.' 'Thanks. Appreciate it.'

Baby noises came from the next room, happy gurgling sounds interspersed with the ring of bells, and Tracey smiled. 'That's my girl.'

The bassinet sat in the middle of the large high-ceilinged living room, and from the door Pip could just make out chubby hands swinging at the brightly coloured toys strung across it.

'Hey Chloe, look who's here.'

Chloe grinned up at her mother and stuck her fist in her mouth as Tracey lifted her and swung her up onto her shoulder. 'Pip, meet Chloe. Chloe, meet Pip, my best friend from the States.'

Chloe rested her cheek on her mother's shoulder, surveying the visitor with big blue eyes while she gummed at her fist.

'Oh, she's gorgeous, Trace.'

'Yeah, she's a poppet all right. But she has to be good. Her father threatened to sell her on eBay if she didn't start sleeping through the night.'

'He did not!'

'Yep. It worked too. Four weeks from the day she was born, she slept till six o'clock in the morning. I woke up and thought my boobs were going to explode.'

The baby blinked up at Pip innocently.

'Anyway, I better get the gravy sorted or we'll never eat. You take her for a minute, will you?'

'Me?' Pip's throat tightened as she instinctively pulled back.

'Sure. She won't bite. Of course, she might always gum you to death.'

'Hang on Trace –' She'd always wanted kids when she'd been young. Always imagined she'd have a clutch of kids by the time she was thirty, and already she was two years beyond that. But that had been before – and everything had changed since then. Even the last time she'd been here, she'd found excuses not to hold Tracey's baby. A sniffle from the plane, a cold - she'd used every excuse not to hold baby Callan. And so, the last time she'd held a baby she'd been all of six years old and it had been her baby brother in her arms. She still had a picture hidden away in a closet somewhere of the two of them in the hospital room, Pip sitting in a chair with a goofy grin on her face and cradling one day old Trent in her arms. Gerald had taken the photo, and every time she went looking for something and came across it, it still had the power to tear her up.

Trent would have been twenty-six this year, a man probably married and with his own kids by now. She'd be an aunty.

Mum would have been fifty, and a grandmother.

And Gerald...

Only everything had changed on that December night almost exactly fifteen years ago.

The all too familiar prick of tears stung her eyes and she

forced it back. Oh god, she really was strung out if she was crying at every little thing since arriving home. 'Trace, what if I drop her. I haven't held a baby for –' But her friend was already handing the bundle over and telling her that of course she wouldn't drop her, and there was nothing to do but take it. It felt awkward at first, a wriggle of squirming baby who was both stronger and heavier than she'd been expecting, and the baby knew she was a rank amateur, fussing at first with the shift from her mother. But somehow Pip got a hold under her bottom and Chloe managed to do the rest. She found her own balance and plastered herself against Pip's chest, clutching at the ends of her hair and pulling it to her seeking mouth.

'Hey,' she said with a laugh, teasing the ends from the baby's firm grip and flicking it back over her shoulder out of reach. Chloe gurgled and smiled, thoroughly delighted with herself, and somehow it didn't feel so wrong.

The baby still felt heavy but it felt kind of good.

'She's gorgeous,' she said, swaying a little and rubbing Chloe's back, the way she'd seen her mother do.

'I know. All you have to do these days is threaten to sell them on eBay. Works like a charm. Anyway, come into the kitchen and you two can get to know each other while I get dinner on the table.'

Craig arrived home soon after, kissing his wife before greeting Pip and his baby daughter, and then the boys bowled back inside and set the table while Craig carved the lamb and Tracey served up the sides and Pip sat there, entertaining the gorgeous Chloe while being entertained by all of them.

And if she'd been close to tears of anguish before, this time she was close to tears of joy, because it was so good to be back here, in a busy kitchen filled with conversation and the clatter of plates and cutlery and a world away from her life in New York City. A kitchen filled with love.

She looked at Tracey, and looked at her husband and her growing boys and the plump, happy baby she was cradling, and envied her friend.

Tracey had it all, a good home, a loving family and a great marriage.

Could this have been her and Luke fifteen years on, with kids of their own? So obviously in love and with a family of their own?

No. Not a chance.

Because Craig was a good man. A solid man.

She'd bet her last dollar he wasn't the kind of man who'd keep secrets from the woman he loved.

CHAPTER 7

$\mathcal{L}$uke fixed the fence and let the sheep back in the paddock and looked at the westering sun, before heading back towards the house, Turbo trotting behind him. With any luck, Jacko from the Ag store would have dropped off the part for the harvester by now and he'd soon be back in business. The weather forecast was promising – no rain predicted for the next week – not that he put his faith in the weather bureau. He'd been stung more than once before and he took every forecast with a grain of salt, but if they did manage to be right this time, he'd have a fighting chance of getting the harvest finished before Christmas.

It wasn't like he had big plans for Christmas though. His folks were expecting him to join them for lunch at their place in Stansbury, and then it would be nice to kick back and do something else for a couple of weeks. It was about time he took himself and his swag and Turbo down to Corny Point and dropped in a line or two.

The sun slanted lower, turning the sky purple and the golden paddocks molten, while high in the sky to the east, a pale moon heralded the coming of night. His favourite time of day.

Usually.

Usually he headed back to the house knowing he had twelve to fourteen hours of good solid work behind him and a solid seven or eight hours of sleep to come.

Usually he felt satisfied, even knowing he was facing another twelve to fourteen hours of work again tomorrow and every day after that until the harvest was in.

But today he didn't feel satisfied. Today he felt restless. On edge. All because of running into a woman who'd dumped him and walked away fifteen years ago.

A woman who looked a million bucks even after spending what must have been the better part of an entire day in a plane. A woman who looked a damn sight better than she ever had, and she'd looked bloody good back then.

And now he was going to have to endure a christening standing right next to her. He snorted. Well, he could do that. He'd been blindsided today, mostly because Craig hadn't bothered to tell him she was coming, let alone that she was staying at his place.

But forewarned was forearmed. He wasn't about to be sucker-punched again. He could do cool. He'd be so cool, she'd think he was Frosty the Snowman.

And then she'd know he didn't give a damn.

He pushed open the house garden gate and picked up the box Jacko had left on the verandah by the front door. And he felt like howling at the moon with the unfairness of it all.

Because he *could* do cool. But still he looked at the small box in his hand and cursed a harvester that had chosen today of all days to do a fuel filter.

He swung the front door open and Turbo scooted in, already anticipating dinner. Then Luke paused, suddenly remembering.

Bugger.

He'd been so blindsided by running into Pip that he'd completely forgotten to tell her about the furniture. Which he probably should check now, so his precious time tomorrow could be spent fixing the header instead of worrying whether it was okay and what she might find.

C'mon Turbo,' he said, backing out of the house. The dog stood his ground for a second before realising that dinner was delayed and giving up and padding back out the door to his master.

THE CORRUGATED IRON shed had seen better days, but it was still watertight and the best place to store anything that didn't need to be in the house. Which is why he'd agreed to store the stuff from the old house next door here.

Five years he'd kept it as a favour. Five years he'd been waiting for someone to claim it.

Waiting for *her* to claim it.

Was it any surprise he'd forgotten to mention it, when she couldn't even be bothered coming home? He didn't come out here much these days – there wasn't much point since TV had gone digital and the old telly was useless. But that wasn't really the truth. He hadn't come here much since Sharon had left. He hadn't needed a shed to escape to since then.

The big rolling door squealed in protest at being opened, revealing the room at the end of the machinery shed that he'd first set up as a teenager's escape too many years ago to count. The man-cave had later become his haven when Sharon was on the warpath and anything and anyone in her path was a target.

The old familiar guilt bubbled up that maybe he should have tried harder. But no, he had tried at first, tried to placate her and fix whatever it was that was hurting, whatever it was that made her mad. He had tried, until he'd worked out that there was no fixing it. That *he* was the problem and that she didn't want him trying. Didn't want him full stop. It was then that he'd taken to spending his evenings out here in the shed.

He breathed in air that smelled of hay and diesel and grease as dust motes swirled and danced in the last of the sun's fading light. Two ancient overstuffed leather sofas formed a corner of the room he'd made out here, even older carpets lining the floor. An old gramophone and the useless telly he should throw away sat in the corner. And there, against the opposite wall, stood the tarpaulin clad furniture he'd agreed to store because it would have been churlish of him not to when he had space aplenty. He didn't have to peel off the covers to remember what was underneath. A kitchen dresser. An old Singer treadle sewing machine and a writing bureau.

But he did lift a corner of the tarp from the base of the dresser to see how it was faring.

All good. No swelling from moisture. No stink of rodents, the farm cats clearly having done their job.

The furniture was fine. All that remained was to tell her about it.

She was staying at Craig's. He could call her there, tell her what he had and ask what she wanted done with it. It need only take a minute. He could do it right now.

'What do you reckon, Turbo?' he said, his dog looking up at him expectantly, ears pricked and ready for action. 'Should I give her a call?'

Turbo cocked his head to one side and whimpered.

'Yeah,' he said. 'Maybe you're right.' Right now probably wasn't the best time. Tracey would be getting dinner for the kids and someone would have to run and get Pip from the B&B, and he'd be left clutching the phone, waiting.

He didn't fancy waiting on the end of a line for someone who'd once thought nothing of dumping him and walking away. He knew all too well the feeling of being left hanging and he was in no hurry to go there again.

Chloe's christening, he figured, as he pulled the rolling door shut on his way out. She'd be at the christening.

Why go out of his way now? He could tell her then.

CHAPTER 8

*P*ip was so full of lamb roast and apple pie, she was bursting, but a good meal and good conversation had given her a second wind and vanquished that heavy feeling of being pulled under. She'd sleep well tonight, and wake with a fighting chance of getting her body adapted to the time difference. With Chloe perched on her shoulder, Tracey walked her the short distance across the wide yard to the B&B where the boys had left a light on under the porch. It was barely nine o'clock but the sun had set and the heat was disappearing from the day, the air filled with the sounds of creatures settling for the night.

'Oh my god,' Pip said, looking up at the sky above her and suddenly stopping. She wheeled around, trying to take it all in. 'I'd forgotten this. I'd forgotten all about this.' For there it was, spread above her, the Milky Way in all its undiluted majesty. Nature in high definition, without the aid of electronics. Millions upon millions of stars lighting up the velvet sky, a gift for anyone who cared to lift their eyes.

'They're just stars,' Tracey said with a laugh. 'They're always there.'

Pip shook her head and spun around some more. 'Do you know how long it is since I've seen a single star? And you have millions, ripe for the picking.'

'Maybe you should come on home, then. You can have all the stars you want and more.'

Pip stopped spinning. 'Yeah sure. And do what?'

'I don't know,' her friend said, as they started towards the B&B again. 'What do you actually do over there?'

Pip shrugged in the darkness and fell into step alongside her. 'I analyse markets and what's happening in them. I check out what's happening on and offshore and why, and then make predictions about what that might mean for international money markets and the risk for the bank's investments.'

Tracey stopped at the door to the cottage and looked at her like she'd been speaking gibberish. Above her head moths spun and whirled around the light. Somewhere in the home paddock a baby goat bleated. 'And you actually enjoy that?'

'It's a great job! I'm going for a promotion to Executive Director when I get back. It's a fantastic opportunity.'

'So no chance of moving back home on a more permanent basis anytime soon, huh?'

She shook her head. 'I can't see it happening. More and more my future seems to be tied up with the bank and the sky's the limit with how far I could go. I could get a transfer to London if I play my cards right.'

Her friend just smiled at her and said, 'Well, I can't say I don't wish you'd come home for good, but it's great you're doing something you really love.' Tracey pushed open the cottage door. 'I don't know if you remember what this looked like before,' she said as she put on the lights in the tidy kitchen, 'but we've done a bit of work on it since then.'

Pip looked around. The plastered walls had been recently painted a soft grey, and there were new lace curtains over the sash window and a breakfast table for two. Along the opposite wall, a kitchenette had been installed. 'You're kidding me, right? This was just a storeroom last time I was here, wasn't it?'

'Yeah, it was originally the old workers' quarters, but we were using it for storage. But then I read an article about the popularity of farmstays and got the idea to turn it into a B&B. It's not finished yet – I'm still looking for some pieces to fill up a few blank spaces here and there.' She gestured to the empty wall to her left, before crossing to a doorway. 'But check this out.'

She flicked a switch, illuminating a traditionally tiled black and white bathroom with a very untraditional corner spa. Pip's eyes popped. 'You've got a *spa* out here?'

'Yeah.' Tracey grinned widely. 'We're hoping it might appeal to people who like their serenity with a touch of decadence. Birthdays, anniversaries, dirty weekends – we've got it covered.'

'I'll keep it in mind,' Pip said, 'for when I'm about to embark on my next illicit fling.'

'Attagirl,' said Trace, flicking the switch to the last room, which was as big as the kitchen and bathroom combined. 'And here's your bedroom.'

'Oh wow.'

Pip stepped inside, blown away by what her friend had achieved. When Tracey had told her about her plans to create a B&B on the farm, Pip had imagined something far more modest, rustic even. But this was like a step into yesteryear. At one end was a bed – big and wide with a plump mattress and lace pillow shams, and at the other was a sitting area with a sofa and coffee table and wardrobe. But the pièce de résistance was the grand fireplace, regal and imposing in timber and iron and topped by a gilt framed mirror. And all around the room were little traces of history – an old kerosene lamp on the mantelpiece, a bed warmer hanging on the wall. 'It's gorgeous, Trace. You've done a beautiful job.'

She smiled. 'Yeah, it's come up a treat, all right. I had to slow up a bit when Chloe put in an appearance, but finally we're getting somewhere. And you get to be the guinea pig before we go live with bookings.'

'I love it,' Pip said, as she unzipped the bag the boys had left on the bed. 'Thanks so much for letting me stay.'

Chloe started to whinge, feeling neglected. 'Uh-oh, it's someone's dinnertime. Do you mind if I feed Chloe while we talk?'

'Of course not.'

'Okay, baby,' Tracey said, as she sat on the sofa and unbuttoned her shirt, the baby soon latching onto a nipple. Pip was so struck with the ease with which Tracey attached baby to breast that she couldn't help but stare. Nobody she knew in New York did that. And it wasn't just that nobody she knew over there had a baby. She had just never seen a woman breastfeeding before. 'Wow,' she said, as Chloe suckled, her tiny fingers curled into the cotton of her mother's shirt. 'You make that look so easy.'

'Most natural thing in the world.'

'I guess.'

'You'll find out one day. Best job in the world aside, you *are* planning to stop climbing the corporate ladder long enough to have babies one day, right?'

'Sure,' she replied with a confidence she didn't feel, wishing away the lump that had suddenly re-emerged in her throat. She'd have babies one day. Of course she would. But she'd made her choices for now. She had a good career – no, a *great* career – and it wasn't like thirty-two was *that* old. And one day, maybe, she'd meet someone special and . . . 'Hey,' she said, pulling a cellophane package from her case, happy to find a distraction. 'I got this for Chloe at Bloomingdale's. Didn't have time to wrap it, sorry.'

'Ooh, show me,' said Trace.

And Pip slid the garment free, a soft pink top with a tutu skirt and matching leggings with bows.

'Oh, that's gorgeous, thank you! She's going to look adorable in that.'

And Pip was feeling all relaxed again when Tracey had to go and ask, 'So is there someone special back in New York?'

She screwed up her nose. She knew where her friend was headed. 'Kind of.'

'Yeah? What's he like? Are we talking marriage material?'

Chad, marriage material? She laughed out loud. 'It's not really serious. We just keep each other company, you know, when we want to go to the movies –' *or we need a shag* '– or something.'

'What? Like a boyfriend of convenience or something?'

Pip thought about that. It was convenient, for both of them. And it came without the complications of a normal relationship and having to work out if it was going some-where or going nowhere and getting all twisted up in knots when it wasn't going the way you wanted. 'Something like that, I guess.'

'So you're sleeping with him, then?'

'What kind of a question is that?'

Trace batted her eyelashes. 'A perfectly fair question for a prying friend to ask, given the subject matter. So, are you?'

She shrugged. 'Well, sometimes. We're grown-ups. Consenting adults and all that. It is allowed.'

Tracey frowned. 'But you wouldn't marry him?'

Pip pulled the last of her stuff out of her case and carried a few pieces to the closet, hanging the dress she'd brought for the funeral and a few other bit and pieces inside. 'We're just friends really.' Although even the word *friend* was probably overstating it. If they'd been true friends, if they'd been more than convenient bed partners, they might actually have spent more time talking about their likes and dislikes and he probably would have known not to book her a big fat red in-your-face sports car. But she'd sure tell him that, as soon as she got home. 'It's just nice to have company sometimes.'

Tracey sighed and unlatched Chloe to switch her to her other breast, giving her time to burp in between. 'I dunno, Pip, I can't see the point of spending time with someone you're not serious about. It's not like you're getting any younger.'

'Ahem, thirty-two is not old.'

'Maybe not, but there must be millions of eligible bachelors in New York. Why waste time with someone you wouldn't want to marry?'

Because it was safe.

Non-threatening.

And she had someone to share the lonely nights with if she needed.

But there was no way Trace, who'd met her soulmate in high school and now had three perfect children with him, would understand.

'Hey,' she said, heading back to her case and looking for a way to change the subject. Because the subject of Chad was too awkward. Too difficult to explain to anyone who didn't know what it was like to live in a place like New York City, putting in too many hours during the day to feel like going out at night and hoping to meet someone new. 'I was engaged once, you know.'

Trace looked up. 'When? Who to? You never mentioned that before.'

Maybe because there wasn't a hell of a lot to tell by the time she put her brief Christmas email together. 'It was two or three years back. A guy I worked with – well, he was my boss at the time actually.'

'And?'

'There's not that much to tell. We never set a date for the wedding. We never got that far.'

'So what happened?'

She turned and sat down on the bed. 'You know, that's the funny thing. I still don't really know. He took me home for Thanksgiving to meet his folks and the next week it was over. But then they didn't seem too happy to meet me, although they were awfully polite of course.' She pulled a face as she remembered. 'Painfully polite. About as warm and welcoming as crocodiles, come to think of it.' She shook her head. 'He never said anything, but I wondered if they'd threatened to disinherit him or something. I suspect they had plans for him to marry the homecoming queen or something.'

'Idiots.' Tracey sniffed. 'Their loss.'

'And all of a sudden I found myself moved sideways to a different department and a different boss.'

'Jerk! He didn't deserve you.'

'So you see, Trace, I have been trying.'

Tracey lifted a now dozing Chloe upright on her shoulder. 'Well, you'll just have to try harder. You're way too good a catch to be left sitting on the shelf.'

Chloe burped loudly this time, and Pip laughed. 'Amen, Chloe,' she said, and then yawned, tiredness catching up with her.

'I'd better leave you to get some sleep. But hey, I've been

meaning to ask – seeing as you're home for a few days. I was kind of wondering if you might do me a favour?'

'Sure. Name it.'

'It's Chloe's christening next Sunday. And I was really hoping you'd agree to be her godmother.'

'Me?'

'Yeah. You.'

'Wow. That's so sweet. But Gran . . .'

Tracey nodded. 'I know. And I know you're here for her and you need to be with her.' She tilted her head. 'Does anyone, um . . . Do they have any idea how long?'

Pip shook her head. 'It could be anytime. But nobody can say when.'

'Yeah, I thought that. But if it is at all possible, I'd love it if you could.'

'Wow, I'm honoured. I really am . . . But even if I can, are you absolutely sure about this? It's not like I'm such a great role model when it comes to matters spiritual. The only time I'm ever inside a church is for weddings or funerals and it's not like I even live around here. I can hardly be some great support to Chloe while she's growing up.'

'I know. And I understand how great your job is, but what's to say you're going to live in the States forever? You never know, you might come home one day. And even if you don't, I bet Chloe will be only too happy to come and look you up in New York City when she's old enough. We probably all will. God, Callan's busting to visit you already! Will you do it, Pip?'

Pip blinked, those damned tears hovering right back there on the brink again. 'Of course, I will.'

Tracey jumped up as fast as she could with a sleeping baby plastered to her chest, and wrapped her free arm around her friend. 'Oh, Pip, that's so great! Thank you!' Then she leaned back on her heels. 'Um, in that case, there's probably one other teensy tiny detail I should warn you about.'

'Oh, hey,' she said, shaking her head, 'if I have to read something churchy and religious, I'm probably not your girl. We don't do that in our family.'

'Oh no! It's dead easy. All you have to do is stand there, really, and say that you've agreed to be her godmother. No, it's just that Craig's asked someone to be Chloe's godfather.'

'O-kay.' Why did she have a bad feeling about this? She didn't know a lot about modern day christenings, but surely it was normal that there be both a godfather and a godmother? Why was Tracey making out like it was such a big deal? Unless . . . The hackles on the back of her neck stood to attention. 'Does this someone have a name?'

'Well, it's Luke, actually.'

'Luke.' She knew it. 'As in Luke Trenorden, you mean.'

Tracey's lips pulled tight over her teeth, her eyes more than a little worried. 'That won't be a problem, will it? I mean, it's been ages, after all.'

Pip shook her head, not to say no, but because if she shook it long enough, something might shake loose that could make sense of all this. Because nothing was making sense so far. 'You seriously want me and Luke to be Chloe's godparents. Me and Luke. The two of us. Together.'

'Well, yeah. Luke's Craig's choice, and you're mine.'

'What about Fi? Why not ask her?'

'She's already godmother to both Ben and Callan. I could hardly ask her again. And besides, you're here and it would be so nice.'

Nice.

Pip had an idea about what comprised nice and Luke Trenorden didn't feature anywhere in it. 'I was really hoping not to bump into Luke while I was here.' And already she had. Already she had to cope with the discovery that he wasn't looking middle-aged and porky. The thought of having to rub shoulders with him again . . .

'Maybe it's time you two buried the hatchet. You used to be so close.'

'*Used to be* being the operative words there, Trace.'

'Yeah, but all that was a long time ago.'

'And I'm still angry with him! Besides which, I don't think Sharon will be too impressed if I do it. I still remember her glaring at me at Fi's wedding, like she was worried the ghost of girlfriends past was going to snatch away her prize catch from under her nose.'

Trace looked up. 'Oh. You didn't hear?'

'Hear what?'

'Sharon's gone. Left Luke a good three or four years back.'

'What? Why?'

Her friend shrugged. 'Who knows? Apparently she started seeing this guy while they were still married and now she's shacked up with him in Adelaide somewhere.'

'The bitch!'

'Yeah, well, Luke seems to be blessed with women who cut and run.'

Oh, no. She wasn't about to let herself be shoved in the same box as a woman who had been unfaithful to him. 'Come on, Trace, that's a bit harsh.'

'Is it? You left him high and dry too. You walked away and left him.'

'It's hardly the same thing. I wasn't being unfaithful. I didn't just walk out on him for no reason. He let me down too.'

'Pip, it was hardly his fault.'

'He knew, dammit. He knew and he never said.'

'I know. But would you really have wanted to hear, even if he had told you?'

She shook her head and this time it was to deny her the

reply she knew her friend was looking for. Because she *would* have wanted to know. Anyone in the same position would have wanted to know.

Tracey didn't wait for her to answer, just gathered up Chloe in her arms and said, 'God, I'm sorry, Pip, I shouldn't have said anything and now I've gone and upset you on your first day back. And that's the last thing I wanted to do. I'm really just so glad you're here. Truly. You decide what you want to do and let me know.'

She gave Pip's shoulder a squeeze and Pip listened numbly while she told her about the provisions in the fridge and the rudimentary pantry if she wanted to have breakfast and get away early to the nursing home. 'But you're welcome over in the house if you want to eat with us.'

Pip smiled and leant against her friend for a moment in the doorway before she left, breathing in the sweet smell of baby and a woman that smelled of apple pie and friendship. 'I'm sorry, Trace. I'm tired and jet-lagged and cranky. I'll be better tomorrow, I promise.'

'And I promise not to upset you.' She kissed her friend on the brow. 'Sleep well, sweetie.'

'I will. And Trace, I mean it. I'd love to be Chloe's godmother. I'll be there, subject to Gran. Just so you know.'

Tracey smiled and pulled her into a goodnight hug.

'Pip's agreed to be Chloe's godmother.'

The baby was sleeping in her bassinet, the boys were feeding the dogs and the animals in the house yard, and Craig was helping Tracey load up the dishwasher. He frowned a little as he rinsed out a saucepan and found a place for it in the bottom rack. 'I saw Luke today. He came into the store.'

'Today? Did he know Pip was coming?'

'He did by the time he got to me. Wasn't too happy about it either.'

'Did you tell him I was going to ask Pip to be Chloe's godmother?'

'I did. Didn't look too thrilled about that either.'

'But he's still coming Sunday? He'll still do it, won't he?'

He shrugged and reached for a plate to put in. 'He reckons he'll be there.'

Tracey sighed. 'You'd think after so many years, it shouldn't be such an issue.'

'I don't know. If you'd walked out on me when I was eighteen and I only saw you when you came back every few years looking more successful and more beautiful every time, and the one chance I'd had since to settle down had ended in disaster, I'd probably hold a bit of a grudge too.'

Trace smiled as she turned to him. 'You would? You'd really care that much?'

'Hell yeah. I'd want you to come back looking fat and frumpy and unhappy. Then I wouldn't mind seeing you one little bit.'

'Craig Dalgleish, that's a terrible thing to say!'

'Is it? If I'd walked out on you and turned up fifteen years later, what would you want?'

'I'd want you to be fat and bald and miserable.'

Her usually mild-mannered husband surprised her then, as he put down the tea towel and grabbed her by the waist, lifting her bodily to the benchtop. 'You see? Lucky you didn't leave me fifteen years ago or you'd be feeling pretty disappointed right now. Instead, you're probably feeling pretty damned smug.'

'Ha. Who's feeling pretty damned smug?' But she put her arms around his neck and pulled him close anyway. 'Yeah, that would be me,' she said, and pulled him into a kiss.

The back screen door opened and slammed shut and two boys slammed to a halt with it. 'Oh gross,' said Callan.

'Get a room,' said his older brother, before they both fled.

'We have successfully embarrassed our children,' Craig said, patting his wife on the hips. 'Our work is done.'

'Not so fast,' said his wife, pulling him back in. 'I was hoping our work tonight was just beginning.'

CHAPTER 9

*T*he bed was wide and soft and blissful. But that wasn't the best thing about it. The best thing was that it didn't come with the drone of aeroplane engines or the muted sounds and lights of NYC outside her window.

The best thing was that it came with the sounds of silence.

Which was perfect for an entire ten minutes before the silence suddenly sounded deafening.

It was a relief when she heard the car. It was definitely a car. She heard it coming, and coming, and still coming – and then she heard it go, and keep going.

One car.

And not even on the dirt road, she realised, but on the sealed highway between Moonta and Maitland that was the best part of a mile away.

And then there was nothing again. Silence, as thick and dampening as a winter cloud.

Silence.

Nothing to hear but her thoughts.

He wasn't married.

She rolled over onto her back and stared upwards into the darkness. How ridiculous her thoughts would toss that gem up first?

Because what did that matter?

It wasn't like she was interested. She'd breathed a sigh of relief when she'd first read the news he'd married. He'd moved on. Everyone was moving on. It was how it should be.

So what that his marriage was over? They'd all had failed relationships.

She rolled over, punched her pillow and got out of bed to open the curtains. She was exhausted. She should have been asleep by now, but if she couldn't sleep, she might as well look at the stars.

All she needed to do was think about all those gorgeous stars.

He'd looked so damned good today.

Not that she'd been looking. Well, it had been hard not to. Still didn't mean anything.

She gave up on the promise of the stars and rolled over again, wishing she could roll away from her thoughts, and cursing a man she'd had no intention of meeting up with, cursing the bastard fates that hadn't let her get through even one day back without running into him and now promised a second encounter. What was with that?

Luke Trenorden was nothing to her, and she had more important things to think about.

Like her tiny, shrunken gran.

No. Her amazing gran.

Yes, that's what she should be thinking about.

Amazing Gran, who'd shown her how to milk cows and separate cream from milk in a separator, and then how to churn that cream into butter and pat it into blocks with wooden paddles.

Amazing Gran, who'd taught her to use a treadle sewing

machine so well that she'd won the sewing prize at high school – even when everyone else had been using electric machines.

Amazing Gran, who could make a wood stove do her bidding, whether it was cooking a roast or a batch of her famous fairy cakes.

Ninety years ago she'd been born, in a time when the fortunes of the Yorke Peninsula were already moving beyond the glory days of the rich copper mines of Moonta and Kadina and Wallaroo. Since then the trains had come and gone, and towering silos had risen high above the golden paddocks where mine shafts had once been dug.

Ninety years between then and now, and still the silence of the night hung heavy on the land. Still the same stars twinkled down upon the earth.

So many changes in all those years, she thought, as she drifted. So many changes.

And yet so much stayed the same . . .

Morning came with such a blast of sunshine through the open curtains that it was impossible for Pip to roll over and ignore it. There was no going back to sleep.

So she rubbed her eyes against the glare and found her phone and new messages from Carmen.

How's your gran?

More importantly - how are you?

The third one made her smile.

So tell me about the wildlife

Pip lay back against her pillows as she texted back. She knew exactly what kind of wildlife her flatmate was referring to.

Gran's holding.

I'm fine.

She bit her lip at the sudden flash of memory of a man in jeans and Blundstones and texted instead,

And there's a guy called Adam. A policeman.

A reply came back almost instantaneously.

Love a man in uniform!

He pulled me over. Flashing lights, the lot.

Lucky you! Cute?

Pretty much.

Jealous!

Pip sent her back a smiley face and hauled herself from the bed. One night she'd treat herself to a spa, but for now the shower was hot and strong and Pip lifted her face into the stream and luxuriated in the flow. Daylight and hot showers had a wonderful way of putting things into perspective, she thought, letting the water sluice away the overblown concerns of the night. Luke was an inconvenience, that was all. She'd seen him once and she'd survived the experience and so she would again.

Now she'd slept and felt almost human again and it was a brand new day. And from now on there would be no more shocks, no more feeling sorry for herself and no more of those damned tears.

Case closed.

. . .

IT WAS STILL WAY TOO EARLY to bother anyone else when she slipped away, although the morning sun already felt hot to her winter skin. And unlike the drive out, when she'd been battling fatigue, the drive back to the nursing home this morning was a pleasure. The rising sun turned the golden paddocks brazen and bold, and there were details she'd missed last night, details she'd forgotten about in her time away, like the clusters of paddy melons every now and then along the highway, and the callistemons with their brushes of vivid red. She smiled as a car passed her the other way, because she'd also forgotten about the country salute, the two fingers raised while the palm stayed on the steering wheel.

By the time she reciprocated, the car was well past, but that didn't matter. They wouldn't think her rude as such. They'd have taken one look at the Audi and assumed she was some ignorant city chick.

Which made her smile, because she kind of was.

'Morning Gran,' she said a few minutes later when she arrived at the nursing home, kissing her gran's papery brow before sliding into the seat alongside the bed. Aled Jones was singing 'How Great Thou Art' on the CD player and her gran's eyes were closed, but there was that momentary twitch of the lips, that flicker of recognition that someone was there, and Pip smiled and gently put her fingers into her cool palm and chatted a while about the farm and Chloe and the dinner she'd had last night that had reminded her of dinners around their own kitchen table so many years ago. She reminisced about the treats Gran used to make for her and Trent – the butterfly cakes and thickly cut corned beef sandwiches they'd take out to the stone mounds with a flask of cordial to keep them fuelled for another day's construction work hollowing out their hidey hole. And how, when he could slip away from his chores, Luke would join them. Sometimes they'd pretend they were deep inside a pirate ship and Luke was the captain. But more often than not the stone mounds would be their fortress, a stone castle where nobody could hurt them.

And then, because that was suddenly dangerous territory, she picked up the book she'd been reading yesterday in one hand, and held her gran's fingers in the other, and started to read.

Staff dropped by to check on Violet and to turn her or moisten her dry lips and mouth, but mostly it was just Pip and Gran and the story of the Cornish miners who had travelled so far and risked so much to make a dangerous living in the colony of South Australia, as Violet's own grandparents had done so many years before. And as she read, she was struck with the uncomfortable knowledge that her forebears had worked so hard and in such difficult conditions to carve out an existence in their new home - and she'd all but turned her back on it. She shouldn't feel guilty, she knew. It was a different time and a changed world. Nobody would have expected her to be beholden to the past, her forebears would no doubt be proud of all she'd achieved, and yet still, the hollow feeling in her gut persisted.

For their lives had been filled with work and family and festivals, while her life was filled with numbers and spreadsheets and reports. Somehow it didn't seem enough.

Someone brought Pip a sandwich and a cup of tea around noon, and it was then that she noticed Gran's breathing becoming more laboured.

'It's changed,' she told one of the carers when they looked in and it hadn't improved. 'It's like she needs to cough.'

The carer squeezed her shoulder. 'It's normal for this stage, lovey. We'll get her something to help her breathe.'

And they moved her ever so gently, so Pip tried to once again focus on the words she was reading, but though quieter, her gran's breathing still seemed erratic – racing one minute, stalling for seconds the next – so that she waited, breathless herself, for the next shuddering intake.

Except that when it came, she didn't know whether to be relieved or sorry. 'Oh, Gran,' she said softly, with tears in her eyes, 'I wish there was something I could do.'

'You're doing it, sweetheart.'

She turned to see Molly at the door behind her, a soft smile on her face. 'I'm about to clock on. Is it okay if I come in for a minute first?'

Pip wiped at her cheeks and nodded and she felt Molly come alongside her on her soundless shoes. The older woman leaned over and stroked Violet's hair. 'You know, we're not allowed to have favourites, but it's hard not to. Our Vi is a special woman. How's she doing?'

She shook her head. 'Struggling at times, and then . . . I don't know. I don't know how she keeps going.'

'It can be like that. People can hover on the edge for hours or days, and I sometimes think it's harder for those of us watching on than it is for them. But just know that she's not suffering, Pip. She's just taking the time to sort things out in her mind,' and she looked at the woman in the bed and smoothed her covers and said, 'Aren't you, Vi? You're getting everything in order before you go.'

Pip laughed a little then, remembering being instructed on how to dry up the cutlery and place the knives and the forks in the right compartments just so. 'That would be Gran. She was always dotting the i's and crossing the t's.'

'There you go then. She's still got a little work to finish up, that's all. So don't you go wearing yourself out. There may be a way to go yet.'

She smiled up at Molly. 'Thank you. And I'm glad you're

here because I wanted to ask something. Tracey's asked me to be godmother to her baby, Chloe, but the christening is this Sunday. I'm not sure what to do. I mean, I'm not sure if I should leave Gran.'

Molly looked over at Violet. 'Well, I don't think your gran is the kind of person who'd expect you to miss something as special as a christening of a new baby on her account, especially when you've been asked to be the baby's godmother. Do you?'

Pip thought about it. 'I guess not.'

Molly patted her hand. 'But why worry now. Let's see if we get that far and work it out then. Now, can I get you a cup of tea or coffee?'

Pip looked at her watch, surprised to see how much of the afternoon had slipped by. 'Thanks, but no. I have to go visit a friend before five. I'll be back tomorrow morning. But you'll call me if. . .'

'Of course,' Molly said, giving the younger woman a hug. And she sniffed like she wasn't completely unaffected and picked up the book Pip had left bookmarked on the bedside cabinet. 'In that case, I might just read a few pages of this to Vi myself before I officially clock on.'

THE MAIN STREETS of Kadina were wearing their Christmas best. Bunting had been strung between the light poles, which were also decked with bright Christmas banners, big gold stars and Christmas trees. Pip had been away so long, it seemed almost wrong to have Christmas in summer, with the sun so bright and hot in the sky. It felt strange not to be dressed in a down coat and boots.

She pushed open the door to *Arrangements by Betty*, the florist shop Fi's late mum had established decades ago in the ground floor of a building that had once been one of Kadina's grand hotels before being converted into a row of posh shops. A cafe held pride of place on the corner, right next to Arrangements, and next door to that was the bridal store that had served the Copper Coast's bridal needs for more than a decade. Alongside that was the studio of Kadina's finest wedding photographer.

It was like a one stop shop for brides-to-be, with coffee and cake on tap to recuperate.

Either side of the door to *Arrangements by Betty* sat buckets of brightly coloured flowers and a table of Christmas poinsettias shaded from the summer sun by the verandah above, while the inside of the shop was filled with more flowers and potted lilies and a fridge full of arrangements.

A girl who looked no more than fifteen stood behind the counter, making up a mixed bunch. Pip looked to the door leading out the back, waiting for her friend to appear. 'Can I help you?' the girl said brightly after the door jangled open.

'Yes, I was looking for Fi.'

'She's not here.'

'Oh. Has she gone home already?'

The girl cocked her head. 'Did you want to order flowers? Only I can do that.'

'I really just wanted to see Fi.'

'She's not here.'

Ri-ght. 'So is she at home then? Should I should try her there?'

The girl frowned. 'You're a friend?'

'Yes. My name's Pip. I heard she had to go to Wallaroo for a procedure yesterday, but I was told she'd be back at work today. I was hoping to catch up.'

The girl's heavily lined eyes bugged open. 'You're Pip? That Pip? The one who orders flowers for the nursing home every week? All the way from America?'

'That's me.'

'That's why you sound American.'

'I didn't realise.'

'Oh, you do. You really do. I really love your accent. You sound just like Annasophia Robb in *The Carrie Diaries*.'

Pip blinked. 'Um, about Fi?'

'Oh.' She shook her head, looking conflicted. 'What did you ask again?'

Pip wanted to scream. Any minute now she'd reach over the counter and shake the girl until her brain dropped out. She wondered if Annasophia Robb had ever done that. 'Is Fi okay? It was just a day procedure, wasn't it?'

'I thought that's what she said, but she called me last night and said she needed to have more tests and could I work in the shop all day and maybe tomorrow too.'

'More tests for what?'

'She didn't say. Only that she had to go to Adelaide for them.'

Oh god.

But then she checked herself. Just tests, the girl had said. It didn't have to mean anything. Just because of what had happened to Fi's mum, it didn't have to mean anything.

'Did she say when she'd be back?'

The girl shook her head. 'She wasn't sure. The only thing was –'

'What?'

'She sounded really upset.'

Oh double god!

'Thanks,' Pip said, and turned and was halfway to the door when she remembered. 'Um,' she said, looking at the bunch the girl was still making up. 'Is that bunch meant for anyone?'

She blinked and shook her head. 'No.'

'Then I'll take it.'

*A*s much as she tried to rein in her fears, the questions plagued Pip as she drove the fifteen or so kilometres to Moonta. Why would someone need to have tests in Adelaide unless the hospital here had found something it couldn't deal with? Unless they'd found something entirely more sinister?

Otherwise surely Fi would have been in touch, even just to send a text saying she'd been delayed a while, especially given that she and Tracey had been expecting to catch up tonight.

But maybe she'd texted Trace.

That was it. She was probably worrying about nothing. Fi was probably just upset about the inconvenience of having to go to Adelaide and what to do with the shop and the twins.

She parked the car outside the cemetery under the shade of a scrubby ti-tree and dug in her bag for her phone.

'Hey Pip,' Tracey answered on the third ring. 'Everything okay?'

'Yeah, no news. Just wondering, has Fi been in touch at all?'

'No,' she said, and the fears Pip had been trying to calm bubbled and churned some more. 'Didn't you see her at the shop?'

'She wasn't there. The hospital sent her to Adelaide for more tests apparently.'

There was silence on the end of the line. And then, 'Crap. You don't think it's what her mum had? You don't think it could be ovarian cancer rather than fibroids, do you?'

Pip squeezed her eyes shut. 'I don't know what to think,' she lied, because that's exactly the fear that had been uppermost in her mind. 'But from what the girl in the shop told me, she was pretty upset.'

'Oh god, poor Fi! That would be so unfair. What about the twins? They're still practically babies.'

'I know,' Pip said, feeling helpless. 'What can we do?'

'Tell you what, I'll text her and say we heard she had to rush off down to Adelaide, but we're wishing her all the best and we'll be here whenever she needs. In all the excitement she's probably just forgotten we had a date tonight.'

'And if she doesn't answer?'

'Then I guess we just have to wait. And hope.'

Pip slipped her phone back into her bag before scooping up the flowers from the passenger seat and taking a deep breath, grateful for one thing. At least thinking about Fi had stopped her thinking about what she was doing here.

She stepped from the air-conditioned car, the white painted stone pillars and gates of Moonta's cemetery bright under a late afternoon sun that still packed a powerful punch. Today's maximum was supposed to be around the mid-thirties and the temperature was still hovering somewhere near that mark. Nowhere near the low to mid-forties she knew summer was capable of delivering, but hot enough for someone fresh out of the northern winter, the dry summer air smelling of dust and harvest time.

Just inside the gates, the quaint old curator's office was as pretty as it had always been, looking like a miniature church with its white painted quoins and green roof, and she wandered past the cemetery bell that had long ago stopped mournfully tolling at every funeral, and through the vast section where babies and children who had succumbed to fever and sickness in the nineteenth century were buried.

Far too many babies and children. Far too much heart-break to linger on.

But trees cast shade and muted the sounds of the traffic passing on the nearby highway, and there was a kind of peace here too, along with the tragedy. She felt that peace unexpectedly wrap around her as she followed the path through the old cemetery towards the new, and she figured there must be worst places to spend your final rest. The perfume from the bouquet in her arms coiled sweetly around her and the song of birds in the trees reminded her that this was not a place solely for the dead.

It was a place, also, to remember and reflect.

On a sudden whim she took a detour and found the grave of her grandfather, who had died more than fifty years ago – long before she was born – a grandfather she'd never known other than from photographs and family lore.

She stood there a moment, wondering about this man her gran had married, a man she'd spent only twenty years with before enduring the last half century of her life a widow. She'd talked of him, while she could still remember, with love and with a fondness that transcended the years. Death couldn't be all bad, Pip mused, if it reunited lovers torn apart too soon.

'You've waited a long time, Granddad,' she said softly, tugging a single red rose from her bunch and placing it on the grave where Violet would soon join him. 'Soon you'll be together again.'

And then she turned back to the main path to the new cemetery and found the wide plot beneath which her family lay. She stood there a while, looking at the granite stone with its humble but heartfelt message that they would be forever missed. And she looked at the first two names and ages and dates. Her mother, Deirdre Mavis Martin, and her brother, Trent Gerald Martin. Both dated the twenty-second of December.

Trent, aged eleven, just a boy. Forever a boy.

Her mother. Thirty-five years old. A scant three years older than Pip was now, and by then already a wife, and a mother of two. And Pip shivered, because she'd always thought of Dee as her mother first and foremost, her age irrelevant, and suddenly age *wasn't* irrelevant, as never before had she been so struck with the concept of her own mortality.

Thirty-five was way too young to die.

Her fingers tightened on the bouquet in her hands as her eyes lingered on the third name.

Gerald William Martin, aged forty-six, dated one week later.

Gerald Martin. The man she'd sat beside for seven straight days – holding his hand, willing him strength while he'd teetered between life and death.

The man she'd grown up believing was her father.

A man who'd been a father to her, and yet . . .

She sniffed and raised her face to the sky. Was it any wonder Christmas wasn't her favourite time of year?

A crow cawed loud in the scrubby trees nearby, shattering the peace and reminding her of that day with her old great aunties, shrunken and bent and lining one side of the hall in their black funeral weeds, and an old familiar ache pulsed loud in her bones as she placed the bouquet of flowers by the headstone. She'd been talking to Gran at the wake, the poor woman already confused and struggling even then, already on the long road to nowhere. And she'd overheard the old crows behind her talking in their stage whispers, and the words that were as deeply carved in her psyche as those names and dates on the stone.

'The end of the Martin line then,' one had said with a sigh. 'Such a shame.'

'There's always Pip, of course,' someone else said. 'But then, she was never really a Martin, was she? It's not like Gerald was her father.'

And the old crows had cawed their agreement as Pip's already fragile world had shattered into tiny pieces.

Luke finished the final bit of the paddock he was working on and sat for a moment in the cab, looking out over the pattern of even lines the harvester had left on the stubbled earth, feeling satisfied with what he'd achieved today. He'd started early, with the rising sun, and the day and the harvester had been good to him, the new fuel filter behaving itself and no other running repairs required. And best of all, no unexpected encounters with former girlfriends.

There was something to be said for not leaving the farm. Another few days like this and the bulk of the crop would be in and he could afford to take a couple of hours off on Sunday for Chloe's christening.

He curled his fingers around his dog's ears before turning the header for home. 'Okay, fella. Let's go rustle up some dinner.'

Turbo sat up at attention while Luke told himself what a good job he was doing. Yes, sir, he thought. Another good long day like this and he could probably handle seeing Pip again without missing a beat too.

She'd taken him by surprise yesterday, that was all. But he'd been thinking about it all day, thinking about the sheer dumb luck that had seen him going into the cafe in the very same moment she was coming out, and now he was almost grateful it had happened that way.

Now there would be no need to be surprised come Sunday. Now there was no need to dread that first meeting.

Not that he dreaded it anyway, mind. It wasn't like he even cared. Not really.

It's just he'd have preferred not to run into her if he had the choice. Because Pip was his past. His long forgotten past.

And he was definitely over her.

CHAPTER 11

*V*iolet Eliza May Cooper passed away a few minutes after seven o'clock the next evening. There were no more twitches of her lips that day, no more smiles that morning when Pip had kissed her hello, no warmth in her gnarled fingers and no hint that her gran was still with them, if you could discount the gravelly snore of an occasional, troublesome sounding breath.

Pip sat by her side all day, wondering at the strength of this tiny woman, cursing the cruelty of a disease that had cost Gran her mind and left her body to continue on for so many years without her, while a parade of nursing home staff dropped by to visit, with a quiet word and a touch of fingertips to her papery cheek or a stroke of her snowy white hair. As if they knew.

When it was this close, it seemed, everyone knew.

So Pip stayed right there by her bedside, still reading from the tattered book that Gran had considered her bible, and she was there when the sun slanted, sending red rays through the garden doors to bathe the room in a warm, ruby glow, and Violet took one sudden gasp and then another, and Pip looked up from her reading and held her own breath as her gran left this world on one long, slow exhale.

Pip sat there a while, waiting – suspecting – and this time there was no answering intake of air after an impossibly long wait. No sound in the room but the thump of her own frantic heart beating out of time with Andrea Bocelli singing 'Ave Maria'.

Her gran.

The last link to her family.

Gone.

Finally, she could put off the inevitable no longer. With a heart that was breaking, torn between relief and despair, she squeezed Gran's hand and said, 'I love you,' and kissed her brow, before she went to let them know.

Molly Kernahan came bustling out of a corridor carrying a bundle of towels when Pip was halfway down to the nurses' station. The other woman started to smile at first, until she saw the look on Pip's face and dropped the towels to pull her straight into her embrace instead. Pip dissolved into tears on her shoulder. 'There, there. It doesn't matter how much you expect it,' Molly said, rubbing her back and squeezing her tight. 'It's always a shock.' She rubbed her back some more, before she said unevenly, 'It's always a shock.'

CRAIG CAME TO COLLECT HER, both he and Tracey refusing to let her drive. And Tracey hugged her close when she got back to the farm, and then pulled her dinner from the warming oven.

'It's mad,' Pip said, feeling numb as she forked at the meal in front of her, still trying to make sense of it. 'She hadn't been with us for years. Not really.'

'It's the end of an era,' said Trace. 'There's ninety years of history gone right there.'

And Pip sighed, because what Tracey had said was true, and because whatever secrets her grandmother knew, whatever secrets she might once have known, were gone with her. 'My boss texted today,' she said numbly, because it was easier to concentrate on the here and now and the future rather than that which was gone and lost forever. 'He wants to know when I'm coming back.'

'Oh no, Pip. Surely not already? You only just got here. Surely they can't expect you to turn around and get back on the next plane?'

'No. They know I have a funeral to organise. But they're flying in the London Vice President of the bank for these interviews in a week.'

'But it's almost Christmas. Summer holidays. Haven't they got anything better to do?'

'They had their summer holidays in July and August. Now they want to set up the branch for the coming year, before the end of this one. They were good to give me leave to come and be here. But after the funeral, I have to get back.'

Her friend shook her head. 'You only came home this time because your Gran was dying. How long before we'll see you again?'

'I don't know,' she said, her heart already heavy with the thought of leaving, and then added with a sad laugh, 'Maybe when Chloe decides it's time to visit me.'

'OH, I MEANT TO TELL YOU!' Tracey said the next morning. 'Fi texted me last night.'

It was ten o'clock and because there'd been no need to rush to the nursing home, Pip was sitting in Tracey's kitchen munching on vegemite toast while giving Chloe a cuddle.

But Pip sat up straight now. 'What did she say? Is she okay?'

'She said she was sorry she missed getting together, but they're coming home from Adelaide today and she's hoping we can catch up tonight instead.'

'So everything's all right then?'

'I don't know. If there's anything wrong, she didn't say, and I didn't like to ask. I just suggested a barbie here. I figure the men can cook, my kids can look after the twins, and we girls can open a bottle of wine and talk. And if there is anything wrong –'

'She wouldn't come, would she, if it was seriously bad news? Surely the hospital wouldn't have let her go if it was that bad.'

Tracey nodded. 'That's what I'm hoping.'

'Phew. I think. I'll grab some wine when I'm in town. I have a date at the funeral director's and then with a funeral celebrant –' she looked at her watch '– ooh, in about an hour's time. And then I have to clean out Gran's room.'

Tracey pulled a face. 'A bit bizarre to call someone who does funerals a celebrant.'

'Yeah, my thoughts exactly.' Pip kissed Chloe's forehead one more time before she handed the baby over to her mother. 'I better scoot. Thanks for lending me your car. Let me know if you need anything while I'm there.'

Her mother let Chloe grab hold of the index fingers of both her hands, but she didn't accept the baby, not properly, not yet, leaving her suspended by Pip's hands under her armpits. 'Pip, I know you said you had to go back to New York soon, but what happens next? What happens after you've seen this funeral celebrant person?'

'Then I'll be pretty sure of when the funeral will be, and I'll be able to confirm my flight home.'

Her friend looked up at her. 'Home,' she repeated. 'You

called it home. Is New York home for you now? Is that how you see it?'

Pip got stuck between a shrug and a shake. 'I've lived there for nearly ten years now, Trace. And my job is there, and if I get this promotion . . .'

Tracey nodded, blinking eyes sheened with moisture, as finally she took the baby from Pip's hands. 'I'm sorry,' she said, kissing Chloe's forehead before turning her around to sit upon her lap. 'Of course your life is there. But it's just so good to see you. So good. I miss you so much when you're not around, and New York is just so far away. It's not like we can just pop over for a weekend.'

Pip leant down towards her friend and wrapped an arm around her shoulder. 'I know.' She kissed her friend's cheek. 'I miss you guys too.'

Tracey nodded. 'I just feel like, with your gran gone and now if you get this new job . . . I just feel like we're going to lose you.'

Pip shook her head. 'No! That won't happen.'

'It's already happening though, isn't it? You wouldn't even be back now if it wasn't for her.'

'Hey, I'll still have you guys.' She touched a hand to Chloe's head, a baby who was already well on the way to worming her way into her heart. 'I'll still have this little one to bring me back.'

Tracey sniffed. 'You mean that? You really mean it?'

'Of course, I do.' She smiled at her friend. 'You don't get rid of me that easily.'

But as Pip drove towards Kadina, she bit her lip and wondered if Tracey wasn't right. She hadn't bothered to come back for the best part of eight years. The last time was for Fi's wedding, and she *wouldn't* be here now if it wasn't for Gran.

What would it take to bring her back again?

A FUNERAL for a ninety year old woman shouldn't be such a big deal to arrange, Pip reasoned, and yet still it was an hour of sitting down with a serious looking woman in a seriously grey suit and sorting through a seriously long checklist of music choices and prayers and eulogies. Pip was exhausted by the time every last box was checked, and then the woman apologised profusely and told her that the earliest the funeral could be arranged, given the weekend, would be Wednesday. She dutifully nodded at the news – because by now she'd figured that nodding dutifully was her role – while in fact she was breathing a sigh of relief. Because a Wednesday funeral made a return to work next week unviable. But Monday week was eminently doable, giving her a few precious days here and making sure she'd be back in time for her interview with the London VP.

It was the best possible outcome.

It was so neat she could have written it into her CV. 'Able to arrange family funerals half a world away with minimal impact on visiting VIPs.'

That, in New York's pressure cooker work environment, might even earn her a few brownie points towards this next promotion.

And winning this promotion would be so sweet. So very sweet indeed.

Because the guy who'd dumped her two Thanksgivings ago, Edward J Stanwyck Jnr, was going for the same promotion she was. It had taken months of hard work to claw her way up to his level, but she'd made it and now they were both vying for the same job.

If she scored this promotion, she'd be his boss.

And wouldn't that the sweetest victory of them all?

THE STAFF at the nursing home greeted her with hugs and kind words about Violet, and about what a sweetheart she'd been to care for. The room was quiet now, the CD player gone, and there was only the sound of people talking as they came and went along the corridor outside, and of cupboards opening and closing as she sorted through her gran's small wardrobe and chest of drawers, putting anything worth donating in one bag, anything that had seen better days going into another, and all the while trying not to think too much about the empty bed, now stripped and bare and cold behind her.

After an hour, she was done. Some keepsakes she would take. The copy of *Not Only in Stone*. Gran's brush and mirror set and the lace doilies. Tracey might use the narrow hall table in the B&B. The rest the nursing home could keep, to use where there was a need.

And then Pip was back outside in the fresh air and sighed as a couple of stray tears squeezed their way out. Because it was done. Her gran was gone, the funeral arranged, her room cleaned out. All that remained was to write her eulogy and to get through the funeral.

Thank god she had this evening's dinner to look forward to. It had been so long since she'd enjoyed a simple barbecue with friends. She stopped at a supermarket and bottle shop and bought cheese and crusty bread and wine, and then suddenly found herself at a loose end. She didn't have to rush back to the farm. For one of the first times in years, there were no demands on her time at all.

She wasn't sure why she found herself headed out towards Wallaroo and the coast except it would be a shame not to at least visit while she was here. Besides, she was bothered by the strange feeling that if she didn't see it now, she might never see it again.

Which was crazy, she told herself, because of course she'd be back.

But when?

The doubt gnawed away at her as highway gave way to town streets and the car slowed – even if her racing thoughts didn't. Tracey had put these thoughts into her head. Tracey had put this challenge to her and despite all Pip's assurances, it was sitting uncomfortably in her mind like an ugly fat truth.

Because hadn't she been heading towards this exact point for the last fifteen years? Weaning herself from home and her friends, coming back for wedding or two, until there was nothing but a fragile thread linking her back to this place?

A tenuous thread that had finally snapped yesterday evening when her grandmother had given up her valiant struggle to live.

Wasn't this what she had wanted all along? A final severing of the ties? A reason not to have to come back. A reason to put the secrets and lies and betrayals of the past behind her forever.

And for her friends? Tracey and Fi and their families and now tiny baby Chloe? Well, it wasn't like they couldn't still be friends. She could still visit. She would visit, like she'd told Trace.

She breathed deep, steering the car into the car park at the end of the Wallaroo jetty, her mood like a dark cloud, at odds with bright day.

It was being here that was unsettling her, that was all.

It was being here and losing Gran and finding a connection with Tracey that had only needed to be dusted off to be as shiny and warm as it had ever been.

But that was hardly a surprise.

What had happened was hardly Tracey's fault.

Damn. She shook her head, wishing she could shake away the thoughts that plagued her, and ran her fingers through her hair and found a wave where there shouldn't have been one.

She pulled the offending strands around and examined them with disbelief. And then remembered it was three months since she'd had her hair straightened, and the appointment she'd had to cancel because she'd be away, and how she'd been unable to book another since she didn't know when she'd be back. She'd have to see if she could make an appointment for next weekend with Rikki or she'd look like something the cat dragged in at her interview. She'd grab a coffee and text the salon and make sure he could fit her in.

And while she was at it, now that she knew when the funeral was, she would get her agent to check out flights too.

She tugged on the wayward curl as she stepped from the car into warm air that tasted of salt and seaweed and fish and chips, feeling at less of a loose end now she had a plan.

Her hair stylist was a genius. She'd spent her first five years in New York wasting precious time every morning with straightening tongs, and it had been a godsend when someone had told her about chemical straightening and given her a referral to the salon where Rikki had just started. And the bonus was that he was an expert colourist, so her hair was now cleverly streaked in cinnamon and honey and every bit as sleek and professional as the image she wished to convey.

It was worth what the salon charged. Well worth it.

Bypassing the fish and chop shop close to the car park, she headed for the coffee shop overlooking the beach. It wasn't like she was avoiding the fish and chip shop, even though it was the place she'd spent more than a few Friday nights with Luke a lot of years ago.

It was just that the coffee shop looked new and trendy and had a great view over the beach.

That was all.

She found a small table free and gave her order for coffee and then, on a whim and with a promise to herself to do an extra spin class next week, decided on a sliver of lemon tart to go with it.

To her left, the Wallaroo jetty was as long and crooked as she remembered. A huge ship was berthed out in the dark blue waters that signalled the deep, the massive silos rising on the shore above connected to the ship by a conveyor belt hidden in a long white tunnel that snagged out at right angles to the jetty.

Just like it always had. She loved that some parts of the now meshed with the past she remembered. She'd forgotten how much she had loved these beaches when she was a kid. She loved the colours of the sea – the clear sandy shallows fading into turquoise as the water gradually deepened, before the abrupt dark line that indicated the start of the channel.

Her family had celebrated Christmas at Moonta beach once, just for fun, although the day had ended early when the wind had blown and they'd all ended up eating sand with their Christmas turkey. She and Trent hadn't cared though. They'd spent most of their time playing in the clear aqua waters and laughing with Gran, who'd tucked her floral dress into her long drawers and had cackled her head off as she splashed like a kid through the shallows.

She smiled at the memories.

Dear, dear Gran.

The end of an era indeed.

Her lemon pie was sweet and tart when it arrived, the coffee strong and bitter. The perfect combination, she thought, as she texted Rikki and begged him to fit her in. She was pushing it, she knew, being so close to the holidays, but like the best doctors, Rikki always kept space free for emergencies – and she was one of his longest and most loyal clients and this was definitely an emergency. Nothing, least of all a wayward curl, was going to come between her and this job.

Next she emailed her travel agent and asked her to find a flight home on Thursday or Friday so she'd be back in time for the weekend, and then she sat back and drank in the view. The shaded terrace overlooked the sunlit beach and the only downside was that she could also see the fish and chippery she'd avoided going to because it reminded her of Luke.

She angled her chair away. She refused to let Luke hijack her thoughts. She refused to let memories of their past or concerns about seeing him again rattle her and ruin the peace of this place. She could cope with him being Chloe's godfather, of course she could.

And she'd show him she was over him in the process.

So instead of thinking about Luke, she concentrated on the rhythm of the tiny waves that shooshed in and out, and Pip actually felt her pulse slow with it, relaxing for the first time in days. Weeks. Probably months if she thought about it.

But that last week or so had been the maddest – the rush to get here in the hopes of saying goodbye. She sighed. Even though Gran hadn't known it was her, she'd known someone was there, and Pip was glad she'd come.

And now, in just a few short days, she would be back in New York City.

Mad really.

But soon was good too. Because once she was back there, this feeling of belonging and yet not belonging – this feeling that some piece of the puzzle of her life was missing – would be gone and everything would slide back into its proper perspective.

It would be easier to think once she was back. In New York she'd be so busy with work that she wouldn't have time to fret about secrets and unresolved mysteries in a tiny place half a world away.

Especially once she got this promotion.

Excitement zinged through her at the prospect.

The job was hers, her boss had all but told her. She had the inside running. All she had to do was be confident and show the UK VP that she had the goods.

She could do that.

Damn it to hell, she *would* do that.

She sipped her coffee and toyed with her sliver of tart, still wondering at the choice and trying not to think of the calories – even if she had skipped lunch – because dessert had never been a food choice she'd taken in New York. This place really was messing with her head. She turned to the view instead. There was a tugboat moored out in the blue depths, a tugboat that swayed and danced with the shifting tide, and it was serene and beautiful and a million miles from New York City.

And if she concentrated on the swaying tugboat and the loading ship and the lemon tart that graced her plate, she could almost ignore the shouts and laughter of the young kids hanging out over at the fish and chip shop, the boys in board shorts and bare chests, the girls in bikinis or shorts, the teenagers that reminded her of the girl she'd been, and all the times she'd been here with Luke. Buying a pizza or fish and chips and eating them on the wall overlooking the beach, or sitting on the rocks that lined the shore.

She could almost forget about holding hands and kissing late into the night. Getting hot and heavy before pulling back and going home, still wanting . . .

Oh good grief, what was she thinking?

What was the point of dredging that all up again?

That was her past.

This place might be pretty, but it was her past.

Once upon a time she might have stayed. If things had worked out differently, if she'd grown up like everyone else out here, knowing who you were and confident of your place in the world, she could have. But then, what kind of life would that have been, stuck here in the Yorke Peninsula for life?

Whereas she'd left, and seen what life could offer, and maybe her work life was filled with numbers and spreadsheets and reports, but living somewhere else could offer lots – especially in New York City.

Wanting a distraction, she snapped a photo of the tug atop the turquoise waters and under the clear blue sky and sent it to Carmen with a message:

It's a tough life.

Carmen came back to her a moment later.

I hate you. It's snowing here!

I'm wearing shorts.

I'm wearing everything I own.

And she attached a selfie of herself rugged up on the sofa with a furry hat and mittens and a big blanket wrapped around her, and Pip laughed out loud. Carmen seriously felt the cold. She'd grown up in California and hated New York's winters.

You would so love it out here.

Stop torturing me! Have you seen the cop?

No.

And Pip wondered that she hadn't even spared Adam a thought. Then again, she hadn't exactly been sitting on her hands waiting for his call. And it wasn't like he'd made any attempt to contact her. A throwaway line to make conversation when he'd pulled her over? Probably.

Carmen sent a sad face.

If you do, send me a pic.

Sure. Oh, and I should be home in a week.

Oh. Sorry Pip, I should have asked. Does that mean?

Gran passed away last night.

I'm sorry.

It's ok.

And it was. She looked out at the shifting blue of the sea and knew that it was, that despite the wrench of loss, that her gran was in a better place.

Right now I'm chilling out and soaking up the sun.

Go you good girl!
Just make sure you bring that sunshine back with you.
And the tugboat.
And the cop.

Not sure it'll all fit in my carry on.

You're in business class and I've seen your carry on. It'll fit.

Pip smiled as she settled the bill and headed back to the car. She missed Carmen. It would be good to get home.

But snow? Callan would be thrilled to hear it. She wasn't sure she was. She was just starting to enjoy the feel of the sun on her skin again. Icy pavements and slush filled kerbs weren't exactly her favourite things about the city. But that was the only downside to going home.

That and missing her friends right here.

CHAPTER 12

The potato salad had been made, a green salad tossed and a bottle of Clare Valley riesling opened and tested by both women to ensure it was drinkable when the twin cab ute pulled up outside the house.

'They're here!' Trace said with a squeeze to Pip's arm, and they made it outside in time to see two red headed boys all but explode from the back seat, the three farm dogs barking in pursuit. Richard climbed out and yelled after them, 'And stay away from the machinery shed this time!' and Tracey leaned towards Pip.

'Little monkeys started up one of the tractors last time they were here,' she said, and sent Ben and Callan off to supervise.

And Pip would have laughed, except Fiona had emerged from the passenger side, her eyes red rimmed and puffy, her lips turned up in the corners in a tremulous smile. 'Hello stranger,' she said to Pip, and promptly burst into tears.

'Oh god, Fi,' said Tracey, wrapping her in her arms while the men disappeared to sort out the barbecue and check the beer situation. 'Come inside, we've got a bottle of wine open.'

'Wine!' she wailed between sobs, before hauling Pip into the circle of their arms and giving her friend a squeeze. 'It's so good to see you! I'm so sorry to hear about your gran.'

'Hey Fi,' Pip said, hugging her right back and wishing whatever was worrying her away. 'We've been so concerned about you. Come on inside and we'll pour you a glass.'

'No,' she said, as they led her towards the house. 'No wine. But I sure could use a gun.'

'Come on Fi,' said Pip exchanging glances with Tracey over their friend's head. 'Nothing can be that bad.'

But Fi burst into tears all over again. 'You want to bet?' she wailed. 'I'm pregnant.'

'What?'

'And it's sodding twins again!'

Tracey looked aghast at Pip, and Pip looked askance at Tracey, and they bundled her inside.

THE MEN WERE SLAVING over a hot barbecue, the boys and dogs no doubt up to mischief somewhere, and the women were gathered in the kitchen with Fi talking about what had gone wrong.

'So I go in for fibroids and I'm prepped and ready and they do a scan – again – and this time they find what they think is a bloody heartbeat, so they send me to Adelaide because they're not sure what's going on. And when I get there they do some fancy new scan, only now they find *two* heartbeats. What are the chances? Twins again. Oh my god, I might as well shoot myself now.'

'You are not going to shoot yourself!'

She nodded, already halfway to her feet. 'You're right. I'm going to shoot Richard. He promised me he'd get the snip. He damn well promised me. Where's that gun?'

'Hey,' Tracey said, with a hand on her arm to hold her

down. 'They don't have to be boys this time. You might have girls. You might get a couple just like Chloe that sleep through the night at four weeks.'

Fi hiccupped. 'Two sodding chances of that,' she sulked, looking morose as she sipped on a lemon squash. 'Buckley's and none. Oh, I should have known. I should have known. I'm craving steak every other night. I should have known!'

'Hey, if it's any consolation,' Pip offered, 'we were really worried about you. We thought you must be really sick.'

Fi laughed, if you could call the hysterical noise she made a laugh, and pointed at her belly with both hands. 'You mean there could be something worse than this?' She shook her head. 'Last time I was pregnant I spent six months kneeling in front of the toilet bowl, and I've spent the five years since they were born wishing I could trust the little bastards alone long enough to sit on it. They've just started school and the shop's finally going well and I thought, I really thought, I was going to have a chance at getting my life back. But now . . .'

She looked like she was going to burst into tears again so Pip poured her some more squash and because that hardly seemed any kind of consolation, pushed a bowl of potato chips closer to her.

Fi reached for a chip and held it in front of her face. 'Five years of Weight Watchers to get back into shape after those two ratbags bent me out of it. And for what? Bam!' And with that she stuffed the potato chip into her mouth.

'Sorry,' said Pip, reaching for the bowl.

'No!' Fi said, snaffling it closer as she crunched. 'I'm raw. I'm upset. And I'm damn well pregnant! Do not deny me my chips!'

Pip shook her head. 'Hell no ma'am!' and reached for the wine to fill up glasses instead.

'No more for me,' said Trace, with her hand over her glass. 'I'm still breastfeeding so I'm on the squash from now on. But because I'm breastfeeding – thank you Chloe – I get the chips too.' And she grinned and reached over and plucked a couple from Fi's bowl. 'You have the wine, Pip. You're drinking for three now.'

Pip looked at the half-finished bottle and said, 'Where's the fun in drinking alone? We're all in this together, girls. Someone pass me the squash.'

And across the table Fi laughed, really laughed, for the first time, her brown eyes sparkling like she remembered. 'Oh, Priscilla Martin, where have you been all this time?' Until a second later those eyes clouded over, like she'd remembered exactly where Pip had been and why she was back. 'Oh Pip, how stupid of me. I haven't even said I'm sorry about your gran.'

Pip shook her head. 'It's okay.'

'No, it's not. You must still be raw. Were you with her?'

She nodded, her lips tightly pressed together while she got herself under control. 'She slipped away peacefully. Just took one last breath and was gone.'

Fi leaned over and patted her hand, a soft, sad smile on her face. 'Such a love, she was. It's so good you could be here.' She sniffed and sat up straight, lifting her glass. 'I know, let's have a toast - to Violet Cooper.'

They all raised and clinked glasses. 'To Violet,' and the mood around the table became more sombre for a few seconds.

'She was a treasure, your gran,' said Fi, sounding wistful.

'One of the best,' agreed Trace.

'Remember her butterfly cakes? God, they were so good.'

Tracey laughed a little. 'I remember her at your sixteenth birthday party, running around in her pinny with plate after plate of butterfly cakes and home-made sausage rolls.'

'Oh my god! And the fairy bread!' laughed Fi, 'how long was it since we'd had fairy bread? That was awesome.'

Pip laughed. 'And I remember Mum running around after her, telling her to slow down.'

'She had more fun that day than anyone,' Trace said on a chuckle.

They settled back into silent reflection for a few moments, before Fi suddenly snorted and covered her face with her hand.

'What?'

'I'm sorry, Pip. I was just remembering those bathers she made for you one Christmas.'

'That white bikini!' said Trace, her blue eyes lit with laughter.

Pip dropped her head into her hands. 'Oh no, please don't go there!'

'And you wore them to the pool that day.'

'And when they got wet they turned see through.'

'And that kid yelled out, look at that girl's hairy fanny!'

'Don't!' cried Pip, as her so-called friends snorted with laughter, but she laughed too, shaking her head as she remembered the shock and the humiliation.

'And then,' Trace said, her hand over her heart as she recovered, 'Luke wrapped you in a towel and took you home.'

'Such a hero,' said Fi on a sigh. 'So gallant.'

Pip stopped laughing, a heavy weight lodging in her gut. How on earth had the conversation got around to Luke? She reached for the wine, remembered she was on the squash, and sighed. Soft drink wasn't going to cut it right now. Then she spotted the chips. She shouldn't. She knew she shouldn't - especially not after eating cake earlier - but still she reached for the bowl and took a chip feeling the unfamiliar grease and salt on her fingers, and wondering where her dietary resolve had disappeared. Chad would be horrified if he could see her right now. For some reason, that made her smile. 'Take that, Chad!'

Her friends both frowned. 'Who?'

She looked at Tracey. 'You remember Chad,' and she made quote marks in the air with her fingers. 'That "boyfriend of convenience" I told you about, remember?'

'You've got a boyfriend over there?' asked Fi.

'Not so much boyfriend,' Tracey said with a wink. 'More like a vibrator on legs.'

'Tracey!'

'Well, how else would you describe someone you only bonk when you need it, and not because you actually like them?' She shrugged. 'I rest my case.'

Fi's eyes opened wide. 'You have someone over there who you sleep with when you need a shag? Wow, have I led a sheltered life?'

'Anyway,' said Pip, not wanting to dwell on that any longer. 'Chad is a fitness buff. He runs for miles at a time and he says processed foods are the devil's handiwork and we shouldn't eat anything that isn't made of goji berries or quinoa or raw vegetables. So this baby right here –' she held up a crinkle cut chip '– with its wanton combination of carbohydrate, fat and salt, would be the epitome of evil.' She considered the chip a while. 'God, I hate goji berries,' she said with a grin, before crunching down on the chip, closing her eyes as all those forbidden ingredients combined on her tastebuds in one wicked but delicious pleasure.

'Well?' said Fi.

'Oh my god, that's so bad it's awesome,' she said, and Fi laughed as she reached for another.

'That's the Pip we all know and love. We'll soon knock that New York gloss off you. Not to mention the accent.'

'I don't have an accent!'

'You do sound a little American,' said Fi.

'Though it is getting better than it was when you first got here.'

'Everyone says I sound like an Aussie over there.'

'Maybe to them, you do.'

Pip pouted. 'Anyway, I thought any gloss I had *was* fading. She flicked her hair and found the offending strand. 'You see this curl?'

Fi squinted. 'It's hardly a curl. More like a wave.'

'And that's a problem, because?'

'Because it shouldn't be there.'

Trace frowned as she sipped on her squash. 'But you've always had wavy hair. Apart from that time in year twelve when you got that short blonde bob. God, you looked sexy with that bob.'

'I remember that!' Fi said, pushing her fingers through her own shaggy short hair. 'I wish I could wear my hair like that. That was awesome. But what's the problem?' She shrugged. 'Just give it an extra blast with the tongs.'

Pip shook her head. 'That's just it. I don't use tongs. I get it chemically straightened now.'

'What? You can get your hair straightened permanently?'

'Well, semi-permanently, I guess. It lasts three to six months usually and it saves a lot of time in the morning when I need to be at work early.'

'Because your hair needs to be straight to do your job, you mean.'

'Because I like it straight. I like it to look professional and sleek and under control.'

'Under control,' repeated Trace, frowning disconcertingly.

'So how much does that something like that cost, anyway?' asked Fi.

Pip waved the question away, wanting to change the subject. It was crazy talking NY prices. It was a different world. 'Oh, I don't know. Hey, how good are these chips, eh?' she said, reaching for another. 'Talk about wicked.'

'Of course you know,' said Trace, pulling the bowl away, refusing to be deflected. 'Finance is your job, whatever your fancy title is. You were always a wiz with numbers. You know damn well what your hair costs, Pip Martin, so stop beating about the bush.'

'Well, if you must know,' she conceded with a smile, because she might have been away a lot of years, but her friends knew her better than anyone. She named a price that made Tracey's eyes bulge.

Fi's eyebrows rose. 'And you hair comes out looking like that?'

'Well, the colouring and cut is extra.'

And Tracey and Fi's mouths dropped before Tracey said, 'I knew there had to be a catch.'

'Jeepers,' said Fi. 'I'd need to take out a second mortgage to pay for that.'

'Oh, give me a break, you two. It's New York City. Of course it's going to cost more than here.'

'Sorry, Pip,' said Trace. 'We're just jealous because you look so gorgeous. But then you always did.'

'And you guys don't? You guys look awesome.' And they did, Tracey looking like a blonde madonna with Chloe perched on her shoulder, and Fi looking more relaxed now she'd stopped crying and had a few laughs, looking more like the Fiona she remembered, like a pixie with her auburn hair and big brown eyes in a heart-shaped face.

The years between visits melted away and it was just so good to be here in their company.

'God, but it's good to see you guys. Thank you for making me feel welcome.'

'What did you expect us to do?' said Fi.

'This is your home after all,' added Trace, and Pip got the message, loud and clear.

'Yeah,' Fi said. 'Your home, no matter where you keep your vibrator on legs.'

And Trace looked at Fi and Fi looked at Pip and they all started laughing, and the men came in holding platters of barbecued meat, the kids bowling in like a cloud of locusts behind, and looking at them like they were all mad.

CHAPTER 13

*S*unday saw summer at its picture postcard best. It was a glorious sunny day with just the slightest breeze to keep the flies at bay and not a cloud in sight. They gathered outside the church, family and friends, some more familiar to Pip than others.

But no Luke, she couldn't help but notice.

Tracey's mum squealed when she saw her. 'Pip! Come right here and give me a hug!' Pip smiled and went easily into the other woman's arms. A single parent since she booted her womanising husband out when Trace was barely two years old, Sally Buxton had been like a second mum after Fi's mother had died of ovarian cancer. Then, just a few months later, she'd all but adopted Pip after her own family tragedy.

Sally had told Fi and Pip that they were the daughters she'd never had and that they could come to her for anything. The three girls' already strong bonds had grown stronger as a result, because now they shared a parent in common.

Sally squeezed her tight and then held Pip at arm's length. 'I am so sorry to hear about Violet, but oh my goodness, just look at you!' And Pip was pleased she'd made an effort. She was wearing a fitted royal blue sundress with a modest neckline that would have done the Duchess of Cambridge's wardrobe proud. She'd brought it to wear to the funeral, but now she was here, she saw it was perfect for a christening.

'It's so good to see you,' she told Sally as Tracey came to join them, Chloe in her arms in a gorgeous long christening gown that Tracey had worn at her own christening. Sally looked at them both and shook her head. 'You both look so beautiful,' she said, her eyes flicking from Pip to her friend, and the woman who looked an older version of Tracey smiled, although Pip was sure she didn't imagine the shadows suddenly skating across Sally's eyes and the tiny frown that knitted her brows. But Fi joined them then before she had a chance to ask if she was okay.

'I'm sorry,' Fi said, smiling bravely though her face was ashen. 'I'm not feeling too special today. I may have to leave early.' There were more hugs then, but gentle hugs, before a voice behind them said, 'G'day, everyone. G'day Pip.'

She turned to see Adam wearing dark pants and a slim fitting check shirt unbuttoned casually at the neck, a look that suited him every bit as well as his police uniform had. It wasn't hard to smile. 'Adam, hi.'

'This here's Jake,' he said, his hand on the head of a boy beside him.

'Hi Jake,' she said, and the kid mumbled something back before his father sent him off to find his friends. She looked at Adam. 'I didn't know you were coming today.'

'Craig told me you couldn't make it,' Tracey said.

'Change of plans,' he said, with more than a glance in Pip's direction, and Tracey raised her eyebrows and Pip smiled. She was here for another week. Nothing would happen. Nothing could happen. But that didn't mean it wasn't nice to feel a good-looking man's interest.

'I was sorry to hear about your gran,' he said. 'Mum told me the news. The nursing home staff will probably turn up in force for the funeral.'

She smiled. 'That's nice. They were all so lovely to Gran.'

The minister emerged from the church then, to usher them inside and get the christening service under way.

'Hang on,' said Tracey, looking around. 'Where's Luke?'

And Craig said, 'Typical. He's probably still out on the bloody header.'

As if on cue, Luke's ute sped around the corner and pulled up with a squeak of brakes in the shade of a tree. With an order for his dog to stay, he left the window down and slammed the door behind him, before he looked around and seemed to realise that everyone was staring at him.

Pip sure was. The first time she'd seen Luke in a suit had been at his high school formal, when she'd come up from Adelaide to be his partner. He'd worn a dark suit with a snowy white shirt and she had thought him the most handsome man in the world.

The last time had been at Fi and Richard's wedding eight years ago. But he'd been with Sharon that day and so she hadn't really looked at him then. And if she had glanced in his direction, it was only to earn herself a withering look from Sharon anyway.

But today he was by himself and everyone was staring, and there was no reason why she shouldn't get a good look too. And the more she looked, the more she saw how much he'd changed and how wrong she'd been.

Because he'd been beautiful back then, all those years ago at that high school formal, but he hadn't been a man at all.

But he was a man now.

In a grey suit and white shirt unbuttoned at the collar, he looked urbane and rugged at the same time. There were lines she didn't remember on his face and around his eyes, and his short-cropped dark blonde hair was spiked like stubble after the harvest. She got the impression he'd towelled it dry after his shower and it had stayed that way.

And then his blue eyes found hers among the gathering and her heart lurched and the air stuck in her throat.

Damn.

'Are you waiting for me?' he said, and for one panicked moment, Pip thought he was asking her and her alone. 'I just wanted to finish off the paddock.'

'Nice of you to join us,' said Craig, shaking his head as he gave his mate a slap on the back. 'Come on, let's get this show on the road.'

Pip let Adam guide her into the church, happy for the warm hand under her arm to direct her towards her seat near the front. Because if truth be told, she felt a little blind-sided. Luke had looked good the other day when she'd run into him in that cafe. Really handsome in jeans and Blundstones. But today, freshly showered and all wrapped up in a suit that made the most of his broad shoulders and flat stomach – well, the guy looked hotter than any ex had a right to.

That was all.

Adam sat alongside her, rock solid and real, squeezing her hand when it was time to go up and take her place at the christening bowl.

And it helped that the service was short and sweet and less formal than Pip had anticipated, and that all she had to do was utter a word or two, and that she didn't have to look at Luke.

It helped a lot.

LUKE HAD A ONCE-COLD beer getting warmer by the minute

in one hand and a squeezy bottle of tomato sauce in the other. Beside him, Craig manned the barbie, wearing his 'Where there's smoke, there's Dad' apron the boys had given him last Father's Day, and turning sausages and onions and lamb chops with the skill of a man who'd cooked up a thousand boy scout sausage sizzles. Turbo was crouched low on the ground between them, waiting to clean up anything that might inadvertently drop over the side. Willing anything to drop over the side.

Luke was supposedly giving Craig a hand, but the real reason he'd volunteered to help was that the spot behind the barbie had the best view of everything going on in the church courtyard.

He could see what everyone at the christening party was doing and who they were talking to.

He could see what Pip was doing in that dynamite blue dress, and who *she* was talking to.

And he didn't like it one bit.

He and Adam had been in a few of the same classes at school, and they'd played footy together for Kadina after that, but then they'd both got busy with whatever they were doing. The last time they'd run into each other, Luke had been on the receiving end of a speeding ticket and a lecture. It was hardly the stuff of fond memories.

And not only had Adam marched her into church like she was his prisoner, but now Pip was standing with her back to the church wall while Adam was standing at right angles to her, leaning his shoulder against the old limestone wall. When Pip wasn't taking a photo of someone at the party, it seemed that every time Adam opened his mouth, she laughed. What the hell was that about? Adam Rogers had never cracked a joke in his life.

'She's flirting with him.'

'What?' said Craig, forking a snag onto a slice of bread for one of the kids. 'Hey, do the sauce thing, will you?'

Luke squeezed the bottle without taking his eyes off Pip and that blue dress and whatever Adam thought he was up to.

Someone squawked. The kid. And Craig said, 'Bloody hell, mate. How about you try pointing the sauce at the actual snag this time?'

'Huh?' Luke looked down and saw a jagged red line of sauce across the kid's T-shirt, the boy looking up at him like he was crazy.

Maybe he was.

'Sorry, er, kid,' he said, because though he looked familiar, he couldn't for the life of him place him. And he handed him a serviette to wipe his shirt as he squeezed a perfectly straight line of sauce along his sausage, watching closely what he was doing this time. 'Sauce bottle's got an itchy trigger finger.'

'You've got an itchy trigger finger,' said Craig as the kid ran off. 'What the hell is your problem?'

But Luke had already tuned out. Because she was laughing again, smiling up at Adam like he was the centre of her existence. What was with that? She had her hair up today, tied up in some clip or other thing women stuck in their hair to twist their hair back, and when she laughed up at Adam that way, it showed off the long line of her throat and the smooth angle of her jaw.

'Earth calling Luke.'

He didn't bother looking around. 'What?'

'If you're so worried about her, why don't you go talk to her.'

'Worried about who?'

Craig sighed. 'Lord, give me strength. Pip of course. You haven't taken your eyes off her since you got out here.'

'That's nuts.'

'Sure is. I thought you didn't even like her.'

'I don't. I just don't know what's so goddamned funny about Adam all of a sudden. Have you ever heard him crack a joke?'

'Well, not recently.'

'Exactly. So what's so funny?'

Craig flipped a row of sausages. 'Good to know you're not worried about her or anything.'

His mate's words grated. Luke didn't want anyone to think he was worried about her. He put down his warm beer and the squeezy sauce bottle. 'I better be getting back. You can handle the barbie by yourself?' And Craig just looked at him like was he was from another planet.

'I reckon I might just make a go of it by myself, yeah. You sure you want to leave already though? Party's just warming up.'

'No. I've got some blades to replace on the harvester.' It was a ten minute job, and Craig knew it, and he knew he sounded lame but he wasn't going to stand there and make up more reasons and take himself from lame to completely pathetic. 'C'mon, Turbo.'

Turbo's head swung around and he whimpered, his body still crouched under the barbie on high alert, his expression incredulous, almost as if he was saying, leave now? His human had to be kidding.

'C'mon boy.'

Craig took pity on the waiting dog and flipped a snag over the side. Turbo juggled it in his teeth to cool it off a bit before wolfing it down. 'Just make sure you say goodbye to Tracey before you go,' he said, tongs poised threateningly in his hand.

'Sure', Luke replied, frowning as he saw Adam with his arm around Pip's shoulders. He watched as they brought their heads together and posed for a selfie, thinking he'd rather just get the hell out of there, but he supposed it wouldn't kill him to do the right thing. Tracey was talking to the minister, the baby bundled in her arms, unfussed by all the excitement.

Piece of cake, he thought, as he headed towards the small group. This wouldn't take a second and then they wouldn't see him for dust. And then someone snagged the minister's attention and Tracey peeled away and headed straight for Pip.

Damn.

SHE WASN'T FLIRTING. Not exactly. It was just that Fi had gone home feeling ill and she had to talk to someone. Besides, Adam wasn't hard to look at and some of his work stories were pretty funny. Busting Kadina's Santa for driving his sleigh down the middle of the main street under the influence of alcohol was way funnier than anything that happened in an investment bank back in New York City. And after the week she'd had, Pip was up for all the laughs she could get. What she really wanted, though, was for Adam to tell her something so side-splittingly funny that she would forget all about the pair of eyes watching her every move, the pair of eyes that were all but scorching her with their intensity.

But if they were going to watch her, she might as well give them something to see. And so she laughed at Adam's anecdotes and smiled and encouraged him as she took a few shots of Tracey and Chloe and the boys, and willed herself to ignore those other intense blue eyes.

What was Luke's problem anyway?

How many years ago was it that they'd split up?

Talk about holding a grudge.

'Hey,' she said, suddenly remembering Carmen's request for a photo of Adam. 'My flatmate in New York asked for a photo of you. Would you mind?'

He grinned. 'You've been talking to your flatmate in New York about me?'

'Kind of,' she said. *God, that was awkward.* 'I told her I got pulled over and, you know, she asked, just in case I ran into you again.'

His smile widened. 'Well, we don't want to disappoint her.'

She lifted her phone to snap his photo and he said, 'Nah, better idea,' and held her hand with the phone higher while he put his other arm around her shoulders and pulled her close. 'Smile for the birdie,' he said.

He'd caught her unawares but she smiled and breathed in his aftershave and felt the heat of his body and the arm around her. An arm that lingered as she brought the phone down and checked the photo. 'It's good,' she said, and put her phone away.

'Aren't you going to send it?'

She screwed up her nose and blew what she knew about the difference between here and Eastern Standard Time in the US to the wind. 'She'll probably be asleep right now. I'll wait.' Because the last thing she wanted was her phone beeping every ten seconds with Carmen gushing about the man while he was standing right next to her.

But what she could do . . . She retrieved her phone and found the picture Carmen had sent from the sofa. 'This is Carmen, freezing her ass off in our apartment yesterday.'

Adam's eyebrows tweaked and he smiled. 'Cute!'

'Yeah, she is.'

'Does she work at the investment bank with you?'

'Not anymore. We started out as interns together but the

work didn't suit her. Now she's got an administrative position at Rockefeller University, not far from our apartment on the Upper East Side. Although I think she secretly dreams about going back to California. She seriously does not like the cold.'

He handed the phone back. 'Maybe you should have brought her with you.'

'Hey, Pip. Adam.' Tracey said, as she joined them, Chloe gurgling happily in her arms. 'How's it going?'

'Hey, Trace,' Adam said, straightening up off the wall. 'Nice christening.'

'I'm really glad you could make it.'

Chloe was smiling and cooing like she knew the party was all about her. Pip couldn't resist. She lifted Chloe's tiny hand from her mother's shoulder and grinned at her, earning herself a smile so wide and unconditionally happy in return that it twisted her heartstrings as a long forgotten yearning ached deep inside her. She'd always imagined herself with children. Always assumed it would happen. But the last few years had been filled with career and advancement and babies had slipped off her radar. It wasn't like she was old, exactly, and she loved her job and the pace of life in New York, but now the dull ache of wanting something more awoke and stretched its wings inside her, and it was a battle to fold them back down.

'God,' she said, trying to keep the wistful note from her voice, 'this girl of yours is gorgeous, Trace.'

'She weighs a ton,' her mother said. 'That's what she does. I've had enough of her. Here, you take her for a minute and give me a break.'

This time Pip was only too happy to comply. 'Sure, what else is a godmother for?' She reached for the baby, dressed in the long gorgeous christening gown. Chloe chuckled, bouncing on her arm, reaching for the hair working free from the twist behind her head – that damn curl again. Only this time she didn't really mind as she looked down into Chloe's grinning face. 'Oh my god, you are just adorable.'

Adam reached out a hand and stroked Chloe's short curls. 'Definitely a beauty,' he said, and Pip noticed his eyes were smiling at her and she wondered if she'd been a bit too encouraging.

Tracey didn't seem to notice anything, but then she was busy mopping up drool from her shoulder. 'She's a party girl, all right. I can see I'm going to have my work cut out when she's a teenager. Oh, and, Pip, Craig's going to drop his mum and dad back home after the cake but he says he'll drop you around at the nursing home afterwards to pick up your car, if you can wait that long.'

'Sure,' she nodded. They hadn't bothered to collect the Audi yet. 'No hurry. He looks like he's pretty busy on the arbie.'

She looked over at the barbecue then, surprised to find Craig alone, wondering where Luke had suddenly disappeared to.

'I'll give you a lift, if you like.'

Her head swung back to Adam, wondering again if she had given him the wrong idea or whether he was just a really nice guy.

'Really?' Tracey said, her eyes wide, looking like he'd offered her a lifeline.

'Sure,' he said, shrugging. 'We were going to head off soon anyway. Jake's got homework to finish and I've got an early shift tomorrow.' Pip remembered he had a son here, and so it wasn't like he could pull anything on her. She wouldn't mind slipping away now and skipping cake. The last few days were catching up with her and she wouldn't mind a little downtime.

Tracey beamed at Adam's offer. 'That'd be great. What do you say, Pip?'

'WHAT'D BE GREAT?'

Luke had heard enough. He'd been hovering on the sidelines, exchanging how-are-yous and comments about the weather with a few people, waiting for a chance to catch Tracey alone and make his excuses. But it looked like she wasn't going anywhere in a hurry and he was in no mood to watch what was happening here a moment longer, not when Pip was standing there holding Chloe and looking like she could be the child's mother and with Adam standing alongside looking like he was ready to step in and play happy families whenever she said the word.

'G'day Luke,' Adam said. 'And goodbye. Pip and I are about to head off.'

Like they were a couple. He'd overheard the bit about the nursing home and knew they weren't going far. Still, he attempted a smile.

'I'm just about to leave myself,' he said, not really interested in Adam, but still finding it easier to direct his attention to him and Tracey rather than at the woman holding the baby next to him. He'd always known Pip would make a great mum. He'd known she'd look great holding a child in her arms. A big family, she'd once told him she'd wanted. At least four kids. And back then he'd thought that sounded just fine.

But when he'd seen her holding Chloe, with Adam's hand on the baby's head, somehow the picture was nowhere near as rosy. The fact it even bothered him meant he had to get out of here. Fast. 'Just came to say thanks to Tracey.'

'You're leaving already too?'

'Harvest,' he said, cocking an eye at the sky. Out here a glance at the weather usually explained most things. He was relying on it now. 'You know how it is.'

Tracey nodded and reached up to give him a kiss on the cheek, 'Sure, we know. Thanks for coming, and for being Chloe's godfather. We really appreciate it.'

He let go a breath he hadn't realised he'd been holding. Because he hadn't wanted an inquisition. He'd just wanted to get away and he was just about home free. Except Chloe chose that moment to squeal, and there was no way he could ignore the child, or, more to the point, the woman who was holding her, a moment longer.

Chloe squealed again and pumped her arms and legs and squirmed against Pip's chest and he looked down to see Turbo sitting innocently at Pip's feet. And he'd have sworn his dog was almost grinning.

'She's crazy about animals,' Tracey said, taking the baby back from Pip. 'You guys go if you need to go. We'll see you later.'

Adam called out to his son, 'Jake, you ready? We're leaving,' and a kid came running up. He took one look at the red stain on his son's T-shirt and said, 'Bloody hell, mate, can't you even eat a sausage sanger without making a mess of yourself?'

And Luke realised why the kid had looked so familiar. He was like a mini Adam.

Bloody hell.

'It's not my fault,' said the kid, glaring at Luke and about to earn himself a clip around the ear from his dad for his efforts when a mobile phone beeped and Adam reached for that instead.

He scowled when he looked at the screen. 'Damn.'

'What is it?'

'Crash on the Wallaroo Road. Caravan's flipped. Ambulances are on their way. Jake, get someone to drop you home. Pip, I'm really sorry, but we'll have to take a raincheck. I'll give you a call about having that drink. I've gotta run.'

'You get going,' Tracey said. 'Back to Plan A. Craig'll drive Pip.'

'No,' said Luke. 'No need to bother Craig. I'm going that way. I can drop her off. There's something I have to talk to her about anyway.'

CHAPTER 14

*I*t would have been churlish to refuse. Despite the
sizzling rush of sensation down her spine at his
offer, despite the thunderous voice in her head warning her
that being anywhere near this man who looked far better
than any ex had a right to was the last place she wanted to be,
it would have been out and out ungrateful to turn his offer
down. Let alone protest there was nothing he needed to talk
about that she'd want to hear.

It would have looked like she cared.

Which is why five minutes later she found herself in the
front seat of Luke's ute.

Not that she was sitting next to Luke, by any means.

There was a dog between them, a red kelpie with intelli-
gent eyes and a keen sense of atmospherics, judging by the
way it looked from Luke to her and back again with something approximating a questioning glance. She'd never
realised dogs could cock an eyebrow until now.

In fact, if she didn't know better, she'd have said the dog
was protecting him.

Not that that she was about to throw it any reasons to

have to.

She stared out the window to assure the dog she wasn't interested in its master, and watched the passing parade of houses. Even out here, new suburbs had sprung up in places where there'd been nothing but bare paddocks before.

Evidently Luke noticed her looking. 'Been a while since you've been back then? Place has changed a bit.'

'Eight years. Came over for Fi's wedding, the last time.'

He nodded at the wheel. 'Long time then.'

She shrugged. Eight years had gone quickly enough. 'So what was this thing you needed to talk to me about?' Because she sure as hell wasn't here to make small talk.

'Oh that, yeah. I've got some furniture I've been storing for you.'

'Furniture? How come?'

'From your old place. Just a few pieces that were worth saving. I've been storing them until you decided what you want to do with them. I forgot to mention it the other day when we ran into each other, and today seemed like a good time to ask, with the christening'n'all.'

She stared at his profile, the profile of the face he absolutely refused to turn her way, no matter how intently she watched him. 'That's very good of you,' she said flatly. 'Only, why are they at your place?'

It was his turn to shrug. 'Someone had to look after them.'

'Why? I thought the house was let out furnished. I thought that was the deal when I moved to Sydney for uni.' She sure as hell hadn't been interested in hauling the furniture with her back then, and it had seemed the easiest solution to let the owner of the property deal with it.

This time he did turn and look at her, his brow knotted. 'Didn't you know?'

'Know what?'

'Bloody hell,' he said on an exhalation, looking at the road again.

'Why? What is it?'

'The house is gone, Pip. Didn't anyone tell you?'

'Gone?' She laughed. 'What do you mean, it's gone?' But there was a note to her voice she didn't like, one that sounded more panic than challenge. 'The last time I was here . . .'

'That's eight years ago, Pip.'

'Yeah, I know, but the last time I was here, the house was fine.' Looking shabbier than she remembered, but you'd expect that with tenants rather than share farmers. Even so, it had still been there, all late nineteenth century stone walls and tin roof and a wraparound verandah protecting the windows from everything the weather could throw at them. A big expansive house. A solid house. How could it be gone? 'What happened? Did it burn down or something?'

'It was levelled. Knocked down.'

'Someone knocked down our house?' But it had never been their house. Not really. It had come with the share farming job her father had done for a local named Sam Riordan, and they'd lived there for so many years it had felt like their house. But still she felt sickened to think it might be gone.

Was gone.

The sprawling kitchen with its original wood stove. The big lounge room with Gran's old pedal organ around which they'd gather and sing carols at Christmas. The big bedroom where she'd lain at night looking up the ceiling rose and dreaming of Luke, dreaming of the day they'd spent building castles in the mounds of limestone piled up between their adjoining properties.

Don't go there . . .

'The tenants trashed it,' he said. 'Pulled up the floorboards and planted marijuana crops in the ground beneath. Then they took off and left it with broken windows and a rusting roof letting in the rain along with the possums. It was a mess. It's a wonder there was anything left to salvage.'

'But to knock it down?'

'It would have cost a bomb to fix it and now his sons are old enough to help him out, it's not like Sam needs a share-farmer. He figured he might as well use the land for cropping.'

She nodded, too choked up to talk. But they were nearly at the nursing home. There was no need to speak.

She fumbled with her bag as he pulled into the car park, pulling up alongside the red Audi as the sick to the stomach realisation dawned on her.

Crap.

She'd changed bags today, to a sleek little clutch purse instead of her usual carryall, and she'd forgotten one little thing.

'I don't believe it,' she said, closing her eyes and leaning back on the headrest.

'Problem?'

'Slight problem, yeah. Seems I left the key in my other bag. Shit!'

'So,' he said, drumming his fingers on the steering wheel. 'How do you want to play this? Do you want to go visit your gran, seeing you're here, and worry about getting back to Craig and Trace's later. Or go back to the party for now?'

Pip blinked at him.

Oh, god. He doesn't know.

'Haven't you heard? Gran died two nights ago.'

LUKE WISHED for a hole to swallow him up. 'Aw, damn, I'm sorry, Pip, I didn't know.'

He should have realised, but he'd been so fixated on what she was doing with Adam that every time someone had said to him today that it was such a shame about Violet, he'd nodded and shaken his head and assumed it was because she was fading.

So much for the bloody bush telegraph.

But then he could hardly blame it when he'd been the fool who hadn't bothered to join the dots.

'Craig and Trace wouldn't let me drive home that night.'

He nodded. Well, that would explain why her car was still here. He hadn't thought to ask that either.

'I'm real sorry. She was a good woman.'

PIP NODDED AND SIGHED, not wanting to dwell on Gran or she'd start crying again, and she would not go there while she was sitting next to this man. Least of all when what she needed to do was work out what she was going to do next. She couldn't call Tracey and expect them to come pick her up. She'd call a cab and wait inside, that's what she'd do.

'Well, thanks anyway for the lift,' she said, unbuckling her seatbelt.

'What are you going to do?'

'I'll call for a cab.'

'You're kidding. A taxi all the way out to Craig and Tracey's? You'll have to pay for it to come back too. That'll cost a fortune.'

'It's not that far.'

She heard him draw breath and readied herself to decline his offer to run her all the way back to the farm – she was pretty sure that was coming next.

'Do you want a lift back to the party, then?'

She frowned. She wasn't bothered about going back for

cake. 'Not particularly.'

'In that case, do you want to come out to my place and check out this furniture?'

'Now?'

'Unless you already have plans?'

Turbo sat between them, his head going from side to side like a spectator at the Australian Open tennis final, waiting to see who won the point.

Pip blinked. All the way out to his place? Together? Her teeth found her lip. Even with the dog riding shotgun, it was going to be a big ask. 'And then what?'

'Then I can run you back to the farm, you pick up the key and I'll drop you back here again. Problem solved.'

'That's miles out your way. Don't you have a harvest to bring in?'

'Pretty much done. The weather's holding and I reckon I'll be done by Tuesday. So, how about it?' He paused. 'You have to decide what you want to do with it at some stage.'

'What kind of furniture?' she asked, wondering about the small table she'd found in Gran's room. 'Any of it any good for Tracey's B&B? She's looking for some pieces.'

Any good and it might repay Tracey for her hospitality – and then she wouldn't have to think about it again.

'I dunno. Come and have a look and you tell me.'

She guessed he was right. Might as well get it over with.

'Okay,' she said, and clicked her seatbelt around her again as Turbo snorted and dropped his head on his front legs.

'You know, I never picked up for a sports car kind of girl.'

Her lips pulled tight. They'd left the town limits behind, the ute cruising along the Copper Coast Highway at an easy one hundred kilometres an hour, and she'd been enjoying the quiet. They'd discussed the furniture and her gran. Surely that should have exhausted the things they had to talk about?

'Or is that,' Luke continued, 'the type of car you drive

over there in New York?'

Apparently not quite exhausted. Trust him to zero in on her least favourite topic of conversation.

'I don't have a car in New York. There's no point in the city.'

'So you thought you'd live it up a little when you came home.'

'Not exactly. A friend booked it for me. I had no idea until I picked it up.'

'A friend booked it.' He smiled at that, and she would have hit him if he hadn't been more than an arm's length away and if there hadn't been a dog sitting between them that would probably take her arm off if she tried.

'Yes, a friend. And for the record, I would have been perfectly happy with a Toyota.'

He glanced at her, one eyebrow cocked. 'But that would have been nowhere near as flashy.'

'You think?' She looked out her window and her hand twitched and she thought maybe the dog and his fangs were worth risking.

'So when are you heading back to the big smoke?'

She rolled her eyes. 'Why?'

'No reason. I just figure you won't want to hang around here any longer than you have to. Makes sense you'll leave the first chance you get.'

Her head snapped around, her lips tightly pressed. Was he judging her?

'So when's the funeral?' he continued, seemingly oblivious to her bristling on the other side of his dog.

'Wednesday.'

'So, Thursday or Friday you'll head off then?'

She hated the way he sounded like he knew how her mind worked.

She hated even more that he was right. Her travel agent

had confirmed a Friday afternoon flight out of Adelaide to connect with a late night flight to San Francisco and onward to New York. And the beauty of it was that she'd get home late Friday New York time, make her emergency hair appointment with Rikki on Saturday afternoon and be all bright-eyed and bushy-tailed for her interview on Monday.

It was seamless. Perfect.

It was a sign her life was getting back under control and she liked it.

'So what if I am?'

He shrugged. 'Just making conversation,' he said, but the smug tilt to his lips told her he was doing a hell of a lot more than that. He *was* judging her.

She looked out at the endless stubble covered paddocks, gold on gold, the clouds of dust in the distance signalling another header at work, bringing in the harvest.

It wasn't a bad view. It sure beat looking the other way, with him sitting there in that grey suit and white shirt undone at the neck and with his big sure hands on the steering wheel.

She knew those hands.

She remembered them.

She remembered what they could do.

God, the man was infuriating! If he wasn't baiting her with his comments, his very presence was reminding her of their shared past and all the things they'd once done together. She didn't want to remember.

She stared intently out the window, concentrating instead on the view.

She could see for miles here. So strange when she was used to seeing no further than the next intersection or the next building, and where the only gold was the endless sea of yellow cabs, and when the sky was a tiny patch of blue where the skyscrapers couldn't reach.

'So what do you actually do over there?'

'You mean my work?'

'Yeah.'

'I work for an investment bank. In the finance division.'

'But what does that mean? What do you actually do?'

'You really want to know?' She was wary. Most people's eyes glazed over when you mentioned investment banking.

'Yeah, I really want to know. I've got no idea what you actually do for a crust.'

And because she knew her job and because she couldn't find an angle in his questions that came with some kind of attack, she relaxed a little. 'Okay. Seeing as you asked, I work in market risk management. That means I get to analyse and report on the firm's exposure to risks in various markets. My area of expertise is the US market and I have colleagues looking after the European region and others in Asia, and together we build up a picture of the bank's global market risk.'

'Wow.'

'Sorry you asked?'

He shook his head. 'Very impressive.'

'Yeah,' she said, liking that he was impressed and relaxing into this other world she knew so well on the other side of the globe, a world where she felt in control and valued and somebody. Because her job *was* important and she'd ploughed herself into it one hundred and ten per cent. 'It's a career you have to have a lot of passion for, of course,' she continued, echoing the sentiments she'd heard plenty of times from her superiors in the bank, and liking how it sounded. 'It's intensive at the best of times, with long days and hard work, but there are rewards that come with that too, of course.'

He grunted.

'What?' she said, taking umbrage.

'Sorry,' he said, glancing over at her. 'Only I was thinking that sounds a lot like farming.'

And Pip deflated like a balloon.

She'd tried to impress him with how special her job was; she'd tried to make herself sound special, but all she'd done was sound like a pretentious wanker.

Of course he knew about work that required passion and commitment and sheer bloody hard work. For a girl who'd been raised in a farming family, it was funny how that hadn't occurred to her before. And she'd tried to make out like her job was somehow special.

'Yeah, doesn't it just?' she said, crossing her arms and shifting lower in her seat.

SHE WAS WITHDRAWING AGAIN, looking out that damned window as if her life depended on it. He'd seen the way she'd caved in on herself when he'd made the crack about farming. He hadn't meant anything by it, it's just that he'd been struck by the similarities and opened his mouth and seen whatever bubble she'd been blowing had pricked into nothingness right there.

And sure, she'd been blowing that bubble up, making it sound like her job was something so goddamned special it should come with an inferiority warning for all other mere mortals, but at least she'd sounded like a woman and not a shell.

He liked it when she sounded like a woman with a bit of passion and spunk. And he liked it that the twang that flavoured her voice now and again wasn't half as noticeable as it had been when they'd bumped into each other in town.

Because now she was sounding more like the Pip he once knew – able to string an entire sentence or more together in his presence – and less like somebody who was here in his car under sufferance.

'My job's better though,' he said at length, because he'd been trying to find a topic that wouldn't immediately either have her on the defensive or the attack.

She looked across at him, and when he glanced at her, he could see the wariness in her eyes. 'How do you figure that?'

'Because I get to take my dog to work.' He ruffled the fur on Turbo's head. 'Don't I, mate?'

And Turbo put his head up.

'Yeah,' she said. 'There is that.' She pushed herself a bit higher in her seat and held out a tentative back of her hand to the dog.

Turbo sniffed it and then nudged her fingers, letting her know it was okay to pat him. He looked at Luke then, tongue lolling out his mouth, his expression saying, *I don't know what your problem is. I can be friends.*

Luke's eyes narrowed. He'd bought the dog a year into his marriage, thinking a puppy would cheer Sharon up because god knew, nothing he did could. But bringing Turbo home had only proved to be one more crime in a long line of them, and by then he was so far up shit creek without a paddle, he'd figured he might as well keep him.

But Turbo was supposed to be *his* dog. He wasn't sure he wanted him fraternising with the enemy.

He noticed as Pip ran her fingers over his collar and scratched behind his head and his disloyal dog lapped it up. 'So, how long have you two been together?'

'Six years now, haven't we, fella?' He laughed, because it almost sounded like they were an old married couple. And the temperature in the cabin warmed up a few degrees, melting the ice as they talked about dogs for a while. Luke slowed the car and grinned as they approached a town. 'Speaking of hounds, remember this place?'

'Paskeville? Sure.'

'Remember that kid on the school bus, the one that used to howl every time we went past that sign?'

She smiled. 'Yeah. We called him The Hound of the Paskevilles.'

'He tried to get us all to do it and the bus driver always threatened to stop and throw him off the bus.'

Pip laughed. 'And one day we all did! Oh my god, I can still see his face as the driver told him to get out and drove away. I'd forgotten that. What was that kid's name?'

Luke shook his head. 'Neville . . . Neville something?'

'Schroeder!' she said. 'Neville Schroeder!'

Luke howled and Turbo cocked an ear and howled a duet with his master, and Luke and Pip laughed as they headed through the almost deserted town, the softly fluttering teardrop flags advertising the church-turned-gallery the only sign of life.

Pip recovered first, wondering what the hell she was doing. She didn't even like the guy and he was making her laugh.

But then he'd always been able to make her laugh.

'Whatever happened to Neville Schroeder, do you know?' she asked, because it was easier to talk about the buffoon on the bus than about how it was before.

'I don't know. Didn't his parents split up when we were in high school?'

She shook her head. She didn't know. She'd spent most of her high school years in college in Adelaide. And she didn't want to think about those years because sooner or later she'd think of that final year, and what happened afterwards, and . . .

No. She wouldn't think about it. She wouldn't let herself.

So she changed the subject. 'Are your parents still on the farm?'

'Nope. They're retired down to a place on the coast near Stansbury. Dad decided the day I got married that he was moving on and making way for the next generation.'

And she buried the flash of concern that his parents wouldn't be there to play chaperone at the farm – it would just be her and Luke – because there it was, lying fat and pregnant right there in the open between them, and all she had to do was ask.

'I heard you and Sharon broke up.'

'Yup.' A muscle twitched in his neck.

'I didn't know it ended until Trace told me the other day.' She saw the way his fingers tightened around the steering wheel. This was not comfortable territory for Luke Trenorden. 'I was sorry to hear the news.'

He sighed, raising his eyebrows. 'Ah well, shit happens.'

She could feel his hurt and taste his bitterness. And suddenly she was his friend once again, and not the woman estranged from him because of what had happened in the past.

'How long were you married?'

'Two years, seven months and three days – which strangely enough was exactly two years, seven months and three days too long.'

'What happened?'

'She left me,' he said with a hollow laugh. 'Just like you did.'

'Ouch,' she said, and turned her gaze out the window again.

'Hell, Pip,' he said a moment later. 'I didn't mean it to sound that way.'

'I think you did. You probably think it's fair too.'

'Isn't it?'

And the fragile camaraderie that they'd found amongst the bones of the past crumbled into ash.

CHAPTER 15

*H*e turned off the highway onto Melton Road, and the car rattled and bounced along the gravel road. Pip grabbed the handle above her window and held on tight for the few kilometres until what was left of the old town emerged, a few tin roofed houses and sheds and the spaces where other houses had once been.

And then her stomach rattled and bounced, not only because she and Luke had sparred, but because she knew the house she'd grown up in was no longer there. But knowing it was one thing. Seeing it – that would make it real.

They met up with the main road, asphalt again, the going smooth and she looked left down the highway as the car turned right, thinking it wasn't only the house that was gone. She'd have to go there sometime, to visit that place where the crash had happened. And an old familiar guilt knotted itself tight inside. They'd been on their way home from a Christmas party, her mum driving because Gerald was a stickler not to drink and drive, when the car had collided head on with the grain truck.

A Christmas party she'd wheedled her way out of, pretending to be sick, because she'd had plans to meet Luke.

She shut her eyes against the pain, but the guilt was still there.

It was always there.

They were almost through the town when she opened them. The train had once travelled through Melton, ferrying passengers and freight from Adelaide to Kadina and on to Moonta, but the service had stopped long ago, most of the tracks ripped up, and pine trees sprouting in the space the lines once were, so now all that remained were the rails buried under the Upper Yorke Road, the bitumen wearing over the metal like the old lines refused to be forgotten.

Another bend and they were out of the town. One more and they would be heading down the long straight where her old house was.

Where her old house had been.

She frowned as the car travelled down the road, searching for the telltale trees that once marked the approach to the house. 'I can't see anything.'

'Pip. It's gone.'

'But where are the trees? There were trees you could see coming around that bend. Slow down!'

Luke sighed and slowed the car, and they reached the bottom of the long dip and she saw a gap in the roadside bushes and what looked like a patched up fence and an old tank on the other side of the road. 'Here,' she said. 'Stop here!'

Luke pulled off the bitumen and she clambered out of the car. 'Pip,' he said, following her to the fence line where she stood blinking disbelievingly across the paddock.

'It's gone,' she said. 'All of it, gone.' Even though he'd told her, she'd expected to find something. Anything. A house didn't just disappear without a trace. But the house was gone, and with it the windmill and the huge sheds and the wall around the garden. Even the trees were gone, and all she could see was a paddock filled with a crop of ripening barley, their heads dancing in the breeze.

Mocking her.

'I told you,' he said, behind her.

And she wheeled on him and said, 'But you didn't tell me there was nothing left! Not a tree or a wall or a windmill or anything. You didn't tell me someone had planted a crop.' She shook her head in disbelief. 'It's like we were never even here!'

'Pip, what would have been the point of leaving anything?'

'It would have said that once upon a time someone lived here. People who had lives and dreams and hopes. People who'd laughed and cried and worked the land and raised a family.' She sniffed. 'They could have left a sodding tree.'

He put a hand to her shoulder. 'Pip.'

'Don't touch me!'

She sniffed again, swiping at her cheeks with the back of her hand. 'Where did it go? After they levelled it. What did they do with it all?'

'Some went to salvage, the tin and windows and any bits worth saving. And the rest they pushed into a pile in a corner of the paddock, where the old stone mounds already were.'

She nodded. That would be right. She'd had dreams once, dreams that were formed amongst those very mounds when she'd played with Luke and her kid brother and they'd built their castle strongholds amongst the stones. And later, when she'd snuck out late at night with a torch and a blanket for clandestine meetings with the boy she'd planned to spend the rest of her life with.

And look what had happened to those dreams.

Why not pile what was left of her shattered family home

on top and crush the first eighteen years of her life completely?

'Take me there.'

'Pip –'

'Or I'll walk myself.'

'In those heels?'

'They're wedges, and they're not that high.'

She turned and started walking along the gravel edge of the road and he rubbed the back of his neck with his hand and said, 'Okay, hop in.'

It was only a few hundred metres further on, but she felt a weight pressing on her chest as they approached and she wondered if she'd been hasty in wanting to come out here now, with this man, who'd spent so many long hot days out here with her in the past.

The long ago past, she insisted, even if that past still seemed too raw, well drawn and less blurry edged with the passage of time than she'd have liked.

Why was it so easy to remember these stone mounds?

Why was it so hard to forget?

She breathed in deeply, finding resolve as the car pulled up nearby. Because it was almost inevitable that she'd end up here, where it had all started.

She undid her seatbelt and opened her door and took in the view.

Mounds of stone were piled up in a corner of the paddock where they'd be in nobody's way, stone mounds that were nowhere near as large or as romantic as she remembered, with random ears of grain springing up between the scattered rocks around the edge, mottled shade from the scrubby trees and the smell of summer on the dry dusty air.

THERE WAS a makeshift gate structure so the fence could be pulled aside when needed and he pulled it aside now so she didn't have to clamber through the wires. Not that he wasn't sure she would if it came to that.

She might be all New York gloss in that dynamite blue dress that skimmed her perfect body in a way that said class act, but he had no doubt she could switch to bulldozer mode and head straight on through if she needed.

'After you,' he said, and she didn't spare him a glance. Her eyes were on those low stone mounds, searching for a trace of her past, a hint of the life she'd lived in a house long gone. 'And whatever you call those things on your feet, just be careful where you put them.'

He smiled as she suddenly paused, looking down at the ground in front of her. Message received, loud and clear. Good.

He watched as she clambered up over the stones in that thoroughly inappropriate footwear, pausing every now and then to pick something up and examine it, more often than not only to discard it. He watched her, choosing not to accompany her on this pointless task, not really fussed about being back here amongst these remnants of their adolescence.

Not with this woman. Not when there was so much history here, so much shared past. Who could forget those long hot days? Those long hot nights? Jeez, he'd taken fifteen years to get this woman out from under his skin and here she was again.

Nope, no way was he getting up there with her.

Turbo was happy to follow her though, skipping over the stones alongside her and sniffing at gaps in the rocks as if it was playtime, looking back at him every now and then as if to wonder why his master wasn't joining in the game.

But this was no game. This was Pip and it had never been a game. It was serious.

Damn.

He still had to get her home to show her the furniture and then take her back to Craig and Tracey's before dropping her at her car. What the hell was she doing wasting time here?

'Pip, we should go.'

'In a minute.' She stooped down to pick something up and Turbo went from playful sniffing to ballistic barking, his hackles raised, and Luke knew what that meant and was already striding towards her as a big brown snake near her took off across the stones with the dog in hot pursuit.

She was shaking when he reached her. 'Jesus' she said, one hand over her mouth. 'That was a big one. I haven't seen one of those in a long time.'

'I guess there aren't too many snakes in New York City.'

She looked up at him then, still white as a sheet, 'Not the reptile kind anyway.'

And he had to hand it to her, she could still make him smile. There were smudges of dust on her blue dress and on her stone coloured shoes, and bits of her hair had worked their way out of their twisted knot so they hung around her face, and suddenly she looked more like the Pip of old than New York Pip and he had to check himself.

This was the woman who had dumped him and walked away. The old Pip wasn't someone he necessarily wanted back.

Turbo came bounding back then, looking like he was grinning, pink tongue lolling out his mouth, eyes bright, his work done. 'Good dog,' said Luke. 'Now let's get the hell out of here.'

A rock shifted under her foot and she wobbled. Instinctively he reached for her free hand and this time she didn't pull away but let him steady her down from the stone mound. Smooth skin. She'd always had smooth skin. His must feel like sandpaper to her.

Not that he felt bad enough about it to let go. She was the one who'd insisted on clambering up here. By rights, he should let her go and let her find her own way down. But he didn't. He liked the feel of her hand in his. Even if it was the hand of a woman who had as good as hung him out to dry.

Besides, it was only polite.

'What have you got there?' he said, noticing the other hand at her waist, cupping whatever she'd found amongst the stones as they clambered down.

She raised her hand and opened her palm for him to see. 'Pottery. Pieces of Gran's old dinner service.' She held up a few a shards of china and the curved handle of a tea cup decorated in the unmistakeable blue on white of the willow pattern.

He nodded and tried to understand why these fragments were so important. Maybe if someone had levelled his place and his gran and all his family were gone, he'd be desperate to find something that reminded him of the past too. 'What are you going to do with them?'

'I don't know, but Gran loved her willow pattern. I'm thinking they belong with her.'

And because she looked so determined and he was totally unprepared for that answer and whatever it might entail, he said lamely, 'That sounds nice.'

SHE DIDN'T SPEAK during the short ride to his place, a couple of hundred metres as the crow flies, but more than double that by road. The rock had wobbled under her foot and he hadn't hesitated. He'd reached a hand out and taken hers to steady her and he hadn't taken it away.

And she'd left it there.

What was happening to her?

When had holding hands with Luke Trenorden featured on her list of things she must do while she was here?

Never, that's when.

She needed to get back to New York. She was unravelling back here. Forgetting. And she couldn't afford to forget.

Or forgive.

HE DIDN'T PULL up near the house as she'd been expecting – perhaps naively. He pulled up behind it, near the shed.

It was a place they'd spent hours as children, as young adults.

A place she remembered in excruciating detail.

Images from the past flashed through her mind, crowding out the present in a flood of memories. They'd danced together out here, to old records they'd bought in second hand shops. They'd kissed and ended up on one of the old sofas. They'd given each other their virginity and afterwards, he'd kissed the tears of wonder from her eyes and told her he loved her. Right there. In that shed.

Crap. Today was fast becoming an exercise in revisiting all the haunts of their shared past.

Maybe she should have asked him where he'd stored the furniture all this time. Maybe she wouldn't have come if she'd known. She'd just assumed it was in the house.

She'd never once imagined he'd leave it out here.

But then, why would he want her stuff in his house? If the old place had been in such dreadful condition, maybe what was left of the furniture was only fit for a shed, but in that case, why had they bothered keeping it?

Maybe they should have just trashed it. Then she

wouldn't have to be here at all, deciding whether or not it would be fit for use in the B&B.

She cursed the fates that had brought her to this place. The fates that had mocked her plans to avoid Luke, and just kept right on mocking them.

And then he opened the big sliding shed door and she held her breath as the dust motes danced in the slanting sun and that familiar scent hit her. Hay and dust and engine oil.

It was like being in a time capsule.

It was like snatching a memory of her past from the air and breathing it in. The sheds at their house, the ones she'd played around when she was a kid growing up – the sheds that were long gone – had smelled the same way.

It was comforting and welcoming and warm but at the same time it was unsettling too, threatening to throw her off balance more than any wobbly rock on a mound of stones had done.

Because she didn't want to feel comfortable here.

Not here, in Luke's world, where so many ghosts of the past still resided.

He snapped on a light and the sun's rays and dust motes disappeared under the all encompassing, shadow banishing fluoro lighting.

And Pip sent up a silent prayer of thanks because it helped wipe the shadows from her mind too. She didn't need pesky shadows or ghosts getting in the way of what she needed to do right now. Which was to look at furniture. Make decisions.

She made decisions all the time. She analysed markets and trends and made recommendations to increase or reduce the bank's exposure, decisions with implications in the multi-millions – if not billions – of dollars.

She could make a simple decision or two now without coming over all weak-kneed about the past.

And then she'd get the hell out.

It was that easy.

She stepped inside, avoiding looking at the old leather lounges with the wide arms where she'd rested her head too many times to count, and the old gramophone where they'd played the seventy-eights and thirty-threes they'd found, and concentrated on the tarpaulin wrapped bundles she could see lined up against the other wall.

'Is this them?' she asked, venturing closer.

'This is them.' He pulled off the ropes and peeled one of the covers away.

Pip's hand went to her mouth as their old Singer treadle sewing machine was revealed. 'Oh my god. Gran taught me how to sew on this.' She checked it over, front and back, lifted the cover over the machine hanging upside down below. It had survived. That was so cool. Because she'd more than learned to sew on this machine. She'd won first prize with the dress she'd made on this machine during her school holidays, all the while cursing it and complaining because they didn't have a decent electric sewing machine like all her friends.

And she'd still won.

'Hello, old friend,' she said, tracing her fingers along the bevelled edges. 'I'd forgotten about you.'

She snapped a couple of photos on her phone to show Trace and looked up to see Luke already peeling the tarp off the second item. She smiled when she realised what it was. Gran's big old writing bureau. She remembered it sitting in pride of place in her gran's room, next to the dressing table that they'd later taken to the nursing home. How hard it must have been to leave this. Next to the old pedal organ in the lounge, it was one of Gran's favourite things.

'The organ?' she asked, suddenly worried, because whatever was under the third looked as big as a wardrobe. 'What happened to the organ in the lounge room?'

He pressed his lips together and shook his head and she sighed. But given the extent of the damage done to the house through its neglect, it was a wonder there was anything worth saving. How these pieces had survived was a miracle.

She snapped a couple more quick photos and then slid the wooden cover up on the bureau, fingered a couple of envelopes that were still filed in one of the little compartments like they were just waiting for someone to finally deal with them, before putting them back. Gran's old papers.

'Treasure,' she said, misting up as she pictured Gran sitting at the bureau, writing long letters in spidery script that always seemed to Pip more loops than handwriting. 'It's like finding treasure.'

'And there's this,' he said, his voice thick, as if the dust lying over the tarps was getting to him. 'It's got a bit of water damage to the back, and a couple of the hinges could do with a bit of work, but it's otherwise sound.' He flicked back the tarp and her misty eyes grew damper.

'Oh my.' The kitchen dresser. It had three glass doors etched with gold arches like church windows, behind which the willow pattern crockery had been displayed. Below the glass doors were several hinged compartments where they'd kept the bread, the vegemite and jars of homemade plum and apricot jam, and the drawers for the cutlery.

She remembered exactly where it had stood, tucked up against the thick stone chimney surrounding the old wood stove.

She remembered fetching the bread and the vegemite and jam when she set the table for breakfast.

She remembered like it had been yesterday, not fifteen years ago – a whole lifetime ago.

She took a few photos to give Tracey an idea of its size

and condition before pocketing the phone and just standing there, gazing at this familiar old piece of furniture that had been so much a part of her life back then.

And then she opened one of the glass doors and the smell reached out long scented fingers and carried her back there, into their big kitchen with the sprawling table and her mum cutting slabs of fruitcake for Trent and their dad, who'd just come in thirsty and hungry from a stint in the paddocks to a feast of freshly baked scones and jam and cream and cake and with Gran serving up big cups of tea to everyone with milk straight from the cow.

She closed her eyes and breathed it in and she was back there in that kitchen with them all. And the tears rolled unchecked down her face as she stood there, silently sobbing.

'Pip?'

'It's a gift,' she said turning to the man behind her, the man with the troubled blue eyes who had made this possible. 'It's the most unexpected, wonderful, magical gift. Thank you.'

HE HADN'T MEANT to be standing so close, but she'd started to cry and instinctively he'd moved forward, but then she'd turned and he was right there and she was looking up at him that way, her gorgeous blue eyes brimming with tears and he knew they were in dangerous waters and that if he took a dip in their depths he'd be lost forever, but she was so close and so beautiful and her lips were right there, and all he wanted was one tiny taste.

She almost breathed those words – 'thank you' – and he couldn't help but watch her lips, slide a hand around her slim smooth neck, dip his mouth and brush his lips over hers. And he groaned, because she tasted of summer and sunshine and easy smiles, just the way he remembered.

Just the way he liked it.

His lips lingered on hers, and she sighed into his kiss and for a moment he thought he had her. For a moment he thought she was coming with him, wherever he was going because he didn't know, only that it felt so good and it had been so long and he wanted to be back in that place.

Until he felt her hands press hard up against his chest and she was pulling back her head and pushing him away.

'No. Don't. Let me go.'

He didn't want to let her go. 'Pip –'

'Let me go!' She wheeled away, her eyes burning cold, her chest heaving, her voice like a rasping file. 'That should not have happened.'

'Why not?'

'You know damned well why.'

'Because of what happened in the past? Are you still mad about something that happened fifteen years ago, because you already dumped me for that.' He clawed fingers through his hair. 'Boy, you sure can hold a grudge.'

'You know it's more than that. It's always been about more than that.'

'Like what?' His hand slashed through the air. 'Lay it on the line, Pip, because frankly I've never quite understood what the hell happened back then. Let's clear the air, once and for all.'

'Okay, because it would be wrong, that's why.'

'No. It's perfectly right. I'm a man and you're a woman and all we were doing was sharing a kiss. What is your problem?'

'My problem, as you so *eloquently* put it, is that you might be my brother.'

CHAPTER 16

*L*uke's guffaw echoed around the lofty heights of the shed, unsettling pigeons and sending them flapping.

'What! Tell me you don't really believe that claptrap?'

'Is it claptrap though? Because you don't know, and I sure as hell don't know. So it's possible, isn't it, that we could be brother and sister.'

'My dad and your mum? Come on, Pip. That's mad.'

'But that's the thing. I don't know! Nobody knows who my father really was and if they do, they're not telling.'

He reached for her. Somehow he had to make her see sense, but she held up her hands to stop him coming closer and he had to deliver his argument from where he stood, eight feet and a million miles separating them. 'If our parents *had* had an affair, if my dad *was* your father, don't you think your mum would have said something about us being friends if she thought there was any chance of us hooking up? Don't you think they would have warned us off each other? Moved house or something? Moved states?'

'That's just it. She did warn me.'

'About me? Specifically?'

'She told me to be careful about who I –' *fell in love with* '– paired up with.' There were some things he didn't need to hear. 'So that's what I'm doing.'

His voice, when it came, was flat as a tack. 'Being careful.'

She didn't care if it sounded ridiculous. If she sounded ridiculous.

She remembered the day her mother had told her. She'd been helping her do the dishes and they'd been planning the menu for her parents' wedding anniversary dinner that weekend. And still in the haze of discovering she loved Luke, she'd asked her mother whether it had been love at first sight when she'd met Gerald or something else. And it had seemed a funny thing for her mum to say when she and Dad were so in love, and when she'd asked her why, her mother had said, 'Because it's all too easy to fall in love with the wrong man.' And for a moment she'd thought her mum was going to say something else, but then her kid brother Trent had bowled into the room and the moment was gone. The next day she'd been back at college in Adelaide and whatever her mum had been going to say was forgotten.

'Why would she have told me that if she wasn't trying to warn me about you?'

'No, Pip. I don't believe that. It could mean anything.'

'Exactly my point!'

'But not my dad! Not my dad and your mum. No way in the world!'

She raised her chin. She didn't want to believe anything could have happened between them either but they'd been friends a long time and how could she rule anything or anyone out, however unlikely or distasteful? 'How do I know that? You've got blue eyes, haven't you?'

'What? And that makes us siblings? Lots of people have blue eyes, Pip. Tracey's got blue eyes. The lady in the fish and chip shop's got blue eyes. Half the bloody world's got blue eyes. It doesn't mean we all share the same biological father.'

She shook her head. 'That doesn't change anything. Until I know who my real father was, I don't know who's a friend, who's a relation. And how am I ever going to find out?' She cocked her head, angry, remembering back to when the bottom had dropped out of her world twice in the same day, the first time overwhelmed with grief, the second with betrayal. 'Although apparently plenty of people knew that it wasn't Gerald, didn't they? Plenty of people, including People. Who. I. Thought. Were. My. Friends.' She spat the last words out like bullets.

Luke raised his eyes to the roof and ran a hand through his hair. 'Jesus, so we're back to dredging that all up?'

'The truth doesn't go away, just because you want it to.'

'So you're still mad at me. You've never forgiven me. Because I walked into the laundry and overheard some poisoned whisper from the town busy body to my mum that you weren't really Gerald's daughter and I didn't share it with you.'

'Of course I'm still mad at you. I thought you were my friend – my best friend! How could you keep something like that from me?'

'Would it have helped you to know what I'd heard was a *rumour*, and that I didn't believe it myself? That I wasn't even sure I'd heard it right? And how exactly would that have helped if I'd told you?'

'At least then I wouldn't have found out from a bitter and twisted line-up of old crows who couldn't keep their mouths shut or their stage whispers to themselves. Don't you under-stand? I sat with Gerald for seven days after that crash. Seven days of holding his hand and willing him to pull through only to lose him as well. And when I heard them talking I felt like I'd just buried my entire family only to find out I wasn't who I thought I'd been. I didn't know who I was. Because the man I'd sat beside for seven days while he clung to life wasn't even my father.'

'He was always your father, Pip,' he said gruffly. 'You couldn't have had a better father.'

'No. He was my dad. And you're right. He was a good dad. The best. But I have a right to know who my biological father was. I need to know. Otherwise I don't know who I am. Not really. All I know is I'm not a Martin.'

'Gerald would be disappointed to hear you say that. He was proud as punch of you. Proud you'd won a scholarship to that fancy college in the city. Prouder still when you won that scholarship to Sydney Uni.'

'Don't you think I know that? Why are you so angry with me? I loved him. But the fact remains, Gerald was not my biological father. And because you decided – by whatever twisted reasoning your mind came up with – to justify it, and because you decided not to share with me knowledge about my identity that was fundamental as to who I actually am, I lost any chance of finding out.'

'For god's sake, it was only a rumour! Why the hell would I want to upset you with something like that?'

'It was something! And had I known, I could have asked questions. I could have got someone to explain what happened, how it happened. I could at least have had a name to go by. If I'd been given the chance while people were still around to ask. But by the time I knew, they were all gone and Gran was halfway there.'

His lips were set in a thin, grim line. 'Maybe they just wanted to protect you.'

'Lucky me! And so now I'm protecting myself. Take me back to the farm. You can drop me there.'

'What about your car?'

'I'll get it some other time.'

THE MOOD WAS SULLEN on the way to the farm and Luke didn't feel inclined to brighten it up any. His passenger was busy staring out her window and he was content to let her have at it. He had other stuff on his mind.

Like that night fifteen years ago when he'd met her at the stone mounds and spread a rug on the ground and opened a cheap bottle of fizz and they'd made love under a blanket of stars. That night when he'd asked her to marry him and she'd told him yes, and that she'd turn down the scholarship to Sydney University and go to Adelaide Uni instead so they would still have every weekend and every holiday together.

The stars had twinkled in the night sky above and the leaves had rustled on the trees and her skin had glowed silver under the light of the moon and stars, and the world had been a perfect place for a short time, until she'd called him in the early hours and told him that the police were at the house and begged him to come over.

But she'd still been his then.

He'd been her rock, she'd told him, dropping her off and picking her up from the hospital. He'd been her anchor in a world gone mad. She'd held on to her ailing Gran and he'd held onto her, and he'd got her through the worst week of her life.

He was going to be her anchor forever. That's what he'd thought. Despite all the changes in her life, despite the losses, he'd still be there, holding her hand.

Until that dark day she'd confronted him after the wake. Luke hadn't wanted to leave early but his dad had wanted to get some work done before dark because there was rain coming and he'd promised he'd go around after they were done. But the skies had opened up before they'd finished and his dad was cursing up a storm and Pip had turned up in the middle of it after walking across the sodden paddocks with her T-shirt and shorts clinging to her and mascara streaming down her face. At first he'd blamed himself for leaving her, until he'd wrapped her in towels and sat her down on the old leather sofa in the shed and she'd told him what she'd heard.

And then he'd cradled her in his arms and listened as she'd shivered and poured out her shock and her despair and her helplessness and her tears. He remembered nodding as he'd held her, before he'd uttered those two stupid words.

'I know.'

'What do you mean, you *know?*'

'Not a lot. I just overheard someone talking once.'

'Who?'

'Does it matter? It was a long time ago and I wasn't even sure I'd heard right.'

'And you didn't think, in all the years we've known each other, to tell me? You didn't think that the woman you professed to love might be interested to hear that snippet?'

Before he knew what hit him, she'd turned from a sobbing mess of grief to a blonde ball of rage, and all he knew was that he was the bad guy.

And the engagement that had never been announced was off and the scholarship to Sydney Uni was back on the agenda and she was leaving.

He'd never understood what had happened. Not really. Only that it was all suddenly his fault – the accident, Gerald, the mystery of her real father, everything – and she couldn't get away from him fast enough.

And now she was still saying that. What the hell had she expected him to say? What if what he'd heard had been wrong? Why the hell would he throw a grenade into his best friend's life like that? He glanced over at her, sitting silent and sullen and unrepentant.

Well, so was he - unrepentant - and if she couldn't understand that, it was her problem.

PIP'S PHONE beeped and she looked at it, hoping it was something from Carmen that might cheer her up.

She rolled her eyes. Chad. But of course it would be him. It was still early bird time in New York and Chad, of course, would be up catching worms in the just opened London market.

How're the wheels?

Nice. Thanks for asking how she was.
Not moving.
Let him make of that what he would. Then she found the photo of her and Adam from the christening and pinged it off to Carmen, who would no doubt check her phone before her early pump class. She smiled. Carmen would get a kick out of this one.

By the time she'd done that, Chad was texting again, wondering what was wrong with the car and his question was like a mosquito buzzing and she wondered what the hell she was even doing with him. They'd been 'together' – if you could call it that – for twelve months now. But maybe their convenient relationship had just about reached its use-by date.

She turned her phone off as Luke slowed the car, the indicator ticking, and looked up as he took the turn onto the gravel road that led across the peninsula towards Tracey and Craig's farm. The sun was dipping lower, the white glare of summer giving way to a ruby glow. There were still some crops to be harvested here in the centre of the peninsula, and the grain swayed and shifted in formation like flocks of birds in the sky, turning the crop into a lake of gold.

God it was beautiful.

She'd forgotten this kind of summer, where the air was clear and dry and tasted of harvest and not of exhaust fumes and steam from the subway and bags of garbage piled up in the street.

Nearly there. She breathed out, wishing that harvest and summer didn't come with the scent of the man beside her. Warm and masculine and musky.

She looked at Turbo, stretched longwise on the seat between them with his head on his paws, and found a wry smile.

Then again, she kidded herself, maybe it was just the dog that smelled so good.

Across the paddocks she could just make out the windmill standing tall over the farm. And she had a sudden panicked thought. From what she'd heard, men weren't supposed to talk a lot to other men, but still . . .

She licked her lips. 'You won't tell anyone what happened out there?' She'd die if he told anyone.

'You mean about you suggesting that my dad and your mum had a fling, you mean? No, I'm hardly likely to share that with anyone anytime soon. Personally I'd rather just blot it out, myself.'

God, did she have to spell it out? 'No. I meant what happened in the shed. When . . .'

'Hell Pip, what do you think I'm going to do? Slap it up on Facebook or something? It was just a bloody kiss. If you could even call it that.'

'It was a mistake.'

He grunted. 'I think we're both agreed on that.'

'Besides,' she said, licking her lips and thinking that maybe she should set some boundaries. Maybe a little late, but . . . 'There's someone back in New York. A friend. A *man* friend.'

'Is that some longwinded New Yorkified way of telling me you've got a boyfriend?'

'Yeah. His name's Chad and he's a stockbroker and he's really successful.'

'He sounds like quite a catch. I'd snap him up, if I were you.'

'Thanks for the advice. I'll give it some thought.'

LUKE MULLED over what she'd said for a few moments, rolling her words this way and that in his mind, testing them.

'Did you tell Adam Rogers about your successful stock-broking man friend?'

'What?'

'You remember Adam, Pip. He was the guy you were all over at the christening, getting all chummy and taking selfies together. Was that to send home to Chad then?'

Pip pushed back in her seat. 'No. That was for . . . another friend.'

'Another . . . man friend?'

'What is your point?'

'Just curious. Only I didn't see you warning Adam off about your special friend back in New York City. Could it be that Chad is just an imaginary friend, Pip?'

'Sorry to disappoint you, but Chad's real, Luke. Very real.'

'Just not real enough to warn Adam about.'

'Adam didn't kiss me.'

'Well he sure looked like he wouldn't say no.'

'Don't be ridiculous.'

'What colour are Adam's eyes, Pip?'

'Why?'

He shrugged. 'Just curious. I mean, small towns 'n' all. What did his dad do? Oh, that's right,' he continued, not waiting for an answer. 'He was a copper too, wasn't he? Must have known just about everyone in town. And you know how things can happen, between consenting adults and all. Ah, here we go.'

He pulled the car into the driveway that led to the big turnaround area beside the house. The dogs came running and Turbo stood to attention, ears pricked, ready for action.

Craig was kneeling out front by the white house fence, pumping up a tyre on one of the kids' bikes and Pip saw him he look up at the ute's approach, a frown knitting his brow.

'Luke Trenorden,' she said, holding her crockery chips in one hand as she swung the door open and climbed out with Turbo in close pursuit, 'I do believe you're jealous.'

'Ha,' he called after her. 'You wish.' But curse the woman to hell and back, she had a point.

CRAIG NODDED as Pip walked by, and then wandered over to the ute, leaning his butt against the front fender and wiping his hands. 'Trace said you'd offered Pip a lift. I told her she must have been dreaming.'

'Not dreaming.' More like a nightmare.

'So where's the Audi?'

'Someone forgot her car key.'

Craig smiled and looked over at the house where Pip had disappeared. 'Get out of here. So, er, where you guys been all this time then?'

Luke scowled and scooted imaginary dust from his pants. 'I showed her that furniture I've been storing. Thought it was about time someone worked out what to do with it.'

'Yeah? Any good?'

'Pip seems to think it might be useful for Trace in the

B&B. I don't think she plans on carting it all the way back to New York.'

'Nah. Guess not.' He looked up at the sky. 'Hey, it's getting late. You want to stay for dinner? Got a leg of lamb in the Weber. Pip can't get enough of it apparently. Trace won't mind one more.'

'Nope. I don't think Pip would appreciate that. I've just been on the receiving end of the boyfriend-back-in-New York lecture. I wouldn't want her to think I was stalking her or something.'

Craig's eyebrow arched. 'What did you try to deserve that then?'

'Beats me,' he lied.

'Well, from what Trace says, this Brad bloke –'

'Chad.'

'What?'

'His name is Chad. Not Brad.'

'Oh, right, anyway, he's not really a boyfriend so much as a sleepover friend.'

'What?'

'You know. What do they call it? Friends with benefits?'

'You mean like a fuck buddy?'

Craig's eyes opened wide. 'Is that what they call it these days? Boy, am I out of the loop.'

'Anyway,' Luke said, having heard enough, 'I better get going.' He whistled for his dog and Turbo came barrelling around the back of the house with the other the dogs barking madly behind him, looking like he was having the time of his life and surely his master must be joking.

'A fuck buddy, huh,' he said, as he pulled out of the driveway and onto the dirt road to the highway. 'Maybe that's our problem.' Turbo whimpered and looked up at him as if he was on the same wavelength, as he tried not to think about how long it had been. 'Maybe that's what we both need.'

PIP WAS DIGGING in the fridge for that half empty bottle of wine she knew was there somewhere when Tracey came in and found her.

'Hey,' she said, as Pip straightened, pulling out the bottle and grabbing a glass from the cupboard. And then her eyes widened. 'Bloody hell,' she said, taking in the dog haired dress, messy hair and scuffed shoes. 'What happened to you?'

'Luke happened to me.' And then she put a finger to her lips raised and shook her head and said, 'No. Don't ask.' She waved the bottle. 'You want one of these?'

'No, but then I've got a feeling there might not be enough for the both of us in that bottle.'

Pip shook it to gauge how much was left inside. 'We got any more of this?'

'Is the Pope a Catholic?'

'I don't know. I don't care. So long as he doesn't want any of my wine.'

Tracey frowned. 'Oh boy. We are so going to have a good lunch tomorrow.'

'What lunch?'

'Fi called and suggested lunch at the pub if she's up to it, seeing she had to leave early today and the funeral's on Wednesday. She wants to see you as much as she can before you go, and we thought maybe lunch. Possible?'

She nodded. 'Lunch with the girls is a very good idea.' She needed to talk to women. Women who knew her and her past and wouldn't judge her. Or maybe just wouldn't judge her too harshly. 'And while we're there, if it's not too much trouble, maybe you can drop me off at the nursing home to pick up the Audi.'

Tracey glanced out the window. 'But I thought Luke was dropping you there this afternoon.'

She shook her head sadly. 'That was the plan, wasn't it?' Even if it had never been a good one.

'What happened?'

Pip gulped down some wine before topping up her glass on a long sigh. 'Someone who shall remain nameless changed purses and forgot the sodding car key, didn't she?'

'Ah,' and Tracey suppressed a grin and looked her over again, taking in her dust scuffed dress and shoes and her wayward hair. 'So, you've been with Luke this whole time, huh?'

'Yup.'

'Doing what?'

Pip glared at her friend over her glass. 'He took me out to his place. Turns out he's been storing some furniture for me.' She paused. 'I hadn't expected . . . Trace, I didn't know about the house being bulldozed.'

'Oh god. You didn't know? I'm so sorry, we only learned about it one day when we drove by a couple of years back and it was already gone. But I didn't think . . . I didn't realise –'

'It's okay,' she said, shaking her head. 'Why should anyone have told me? We hadn't lived there for years and it never really was ours. I just wasn't expecting . . .'

Tracey frowned and put a hand to Pip's shoulder, rubbing it. 'So how was it?'

'Rough,' she answered honestly, shaking her head. 'It felt like the first eighteen years of my life had been wiped from the face of the earth.'

'I'm so sorry you weren't warned.'

She shrugged. 'Luke took me to the old stone mounds

where they'd piled up the rubble and I found a few bits of Gran's old crockery.' She waved her glass in the direction of the few bits she'd put on a corner of the big table when she'd come inside. Her friend frowned. 'Mad, I know, but I couldn't leave them there. Anyhow, somehow a few bits of furniture survived with Luke and they look okay. I thought they might do for the B&B if you can use them.' She pulled out her phone and found the photos she'd snapped. 'Our old kitchen sideboard would look so good on that blank wall, and there's our old Singer treadle sewing machine and Gran's old writing bureau. They'd be brilliant, Trace, if you could fit them in, and I'd be so happy if they could find a home.'

Tracey's eyes opened wide as she flicked through the photos. 'I remember that kitchen dresser.' She looked at the slivers and curves of crockery on the table. Wow. 'It was so pretty with all that blue and white crockery on display. But are you sure you don't want to take them with you? So you have a piece of your history over there?'

'No. There's no room where I live and they wouldn't fit the decor anyway. It would be pointless.'

'Okay. Then how about I agree to look after them for you, until you come back.'

'Trace, really?'

'Yeah, really,' her friend said with a grin. 'Until you come back. Never say never.'

CHAPTER 17

The spa was deep and delicious and bubbly. The riesling was smooth and fruity and still. The scented candles were lit and delicately perfuming the air. The perfect combination. Pip rested her head back on a rolled up towel on the edge of the spa and closed her eyes and let the jets massage her weary body. It had been a long day. She so deserved this.

Her phone pinged and she glanced at it. Carmen. She was smiling even before she opened the message.

OMG! He's gorgeous!

He's okay. Yeah.

So?

So what?

!!!

Pip giggled.

???

Are you seeing him again?

I don't know. Maybe.

Holiday fling?

Pip's thumb hesitated.

When he'd supported her arm going into church he'd smelled good, and when he'd wrapped his arm around her to take the selfie he'd felt warm and strong. It had been nice to have a little male attention when Luke's arrival had sent her senses into a tailspin.

But he hadn't made her heart race, like Luke had, when his eyes had been on her mouth and his lips mere centimetres away. He hadn't made her blood fizz and her senses tingle. He hadn't made her have to fight to keep control.

But then she and Luke had history. He was bound to set her senses to red alert.

Nah. Saving him for you.

A souvenir? For me?

He thinks you're cute.

Huh?

I showed him your selfie on the sofa.

Oh no! I looked like a dork!

I think he likes dorks.

You just ruined a beautiful romance. Hey, gotta run. xx

Pip sent kisses back and then put her phone down on the side table and rested her head back on the towel, wanting to wipe her memory clean of everything after the christening.

Well, maybe not the furniture and that feeling of being back in their big old kitchen when she'd opened the door of the dresser. Strange how she'd filed away that memory without even registering it. Strange that it had the power to transport her back to the past in a moment.

To when times were good.

To when she'd had her family around her.

To before.

But as for the arguments and the handholding and that damned kiss that should never have happened. What was that about? What was she thinking?

That was the problem right there.

Because she hadn't been thinking at all.

She'd been sideswiped by that damned emotion and there hadn't been room for thinking.

Fool.

If only she could wipe it all clean.

Wipe away the mistakes and the blunders as thoroughly as they'd wiped away any trace of her old home.

On a whim she picked up her phone again and flicked to the photos she'd taken, scrolling through them, the sewing machine table, the writing bureau and the dresser, smiling until she reached the one where she'd captured Luke's reflection in the glass. He'd moved away so she could take her photos but she'd caught him standing behind her, his white shirt undone at the collar, his shoulders broad and the tilt of his head telling her he'd been watching her. A tremor, warm and tingling, rolled through her.

What had he been thinking? A minute later they'd been kissing.

And if she hadn't stopped him?

Thank god she'd stopped him.

Five minutes more and there'd have been no doubt what he'd be thinking.

She hauled herself out of the spa, remembering Luke's face set like stone in his outrage. In his deadset rejection of the possibility that his dad and her mum could have had an affair.

Well, she didn't really believe it either.

But she had to believe something.

CHAPTER 18

'So who's minding the shop?' Tracey asked.

Pip, Tracey and Fi were reading the menu at a table on the verandah outside the Moonta Hotel. Baby Chloe was fast asleep in her pram alongside, still recovering from the big day before.

'Amber.' Fi was still looking a bit seedy, but nowhere near as grey she'd been the day before, something she swore was down to the discovery of ginger tea. 'She's the girl you met when you bought that bunch of flowers the other day. That's something else I have to sort out too...'

'Why?'

'Well, she's a nice girl, but a bit slow in the uptake department, if you know what I mean. I don't mind leaving her for short periods, but . . . I just don't know what's going to happen there.' She shook her head as she looked up from her menu. 'Anyway, what are you guys having?'

'Fish and chips,' said Tracey, nodding.

Pip put her menu down. 'Salt and pepper squid for me.'

'I'm having the steak.'

'I don't know why you bother looking at the menu,' said Trace, with a smile.

'I can't help it,' Fi said. 'I'm craving red meat.'

'Gotta feed your inner vampire,' said Pip. She went inside to order, insisting it was her treat, and came back laden with plates and cutlery and bread rolls. And then did another run for some sparkling water.

'Okay,' said Fi, helping herself to a roll, 'so what did I miss yesterday? I hear you and Luke patched things up.'

Pip looked disbelievingly at Fi. 'What?'

'Well, Trace said you'd gone off with him. I figured something major must have happened for you to get in the same car.'

Pip scoffed. 'You must be kidding. I didn't 'go off' with him. He gave me a lift home, that's all.'

'That's not all,' said Tracey, buttering her own roll. 'There's heaps more.'

'Hey, whose side are you on?'

Tracey leaned towards Fi. 'Luke took Pip out to his place.'

'Tracey!'

'What?' she said innocently.

'Do you mind?'

'Well, if you're not going to tell her, I will.'

'All right.' Pip sighed. 'It's all perfectly innocent. Luke's been storing some of the furniture from the old place in his shed and he wanted to find out what I wanted to do with it. So I took a look and then he dropped me back at the farm. End of story.'

Fi looked from one friend to the other. 'That's it?'

Pip shrugged. She wasn't going to get into the emotion of learning her old place had been bulldozed and everything that had come after. 'That's it.'

Across the table Fi sighed. 'Oh, well, that's a shame.'

'How do you figure that?'

'Because if you two got back together then you'd have to come home from New York and we'd get to see you more often.'

Pip smiled. 'That's really sweet of you, Fi, but that's not going to happen. There's way too much water under the fridge.'

'Luke kept your fridge?' asked a grinning Fi and Pip laughed.

'Besides,' said Trace, 'she still hasn't forgiven him yet.'

'Really? That's a bit rough,' Fi said, munching on her bread. 'It was such a long time ago, and besides, it was hardly his fault.'

'Hey, you guys, I just paid for your lunch,' she said, only half joking, 'The least you could do is be a bit more supportive.'

'We do support you,' Fi said.

'We love you,' Trace added, 'It's just, well, Luke did kind of get the rough end of the stick.'

Pip almost choked on a piece of bread roll. 'What?'

'Look, it's understandable. You were eighteen and you'd just lost your family and your gran was going downhill fast. You were hurting. You were looking for answers. Of course you were going to lash out. It just happened to be Luke who copped it. But he's a good man, however you think he might have wronged you in the past.'

Pip sniffed. Any minute now they'd be trying to make her feel sorry for the man. Why couldn't they see? 'Luke got everything he had coming to him. If he hadn't kept his damned secret to himself, I might have had a chance to find out who my real father was – I might have had a chance to ask. Have you guys got any idea what it's like to turn up for medical appointments and be questioned about the medical history of my family, and I can't answer half the questions because I don't even know who my biological father was? And that's only a fraction of it. Because this is about me. It's about who I am. How can I know who I really am without knowing something so fundamental?' She held up her hands, appealing to her friends to understand. 'Surely I have a right to know who my biological father was? If Luke had filled me in, I might have had a chance to by now.'

'Hey Pip,' said Fi, 'I know it's been tough, but isn't it time you stopped blaming Luke? So he overheard someone talking and he didn't tell you. So what? How was he supposed to know it might be true? I sure never heard a whisper. Not until you told me afterwards.'

Trace nodded. 'Nor me. And our mums were so close. If there was some shady secret around, surely I would have heard something?'

Pip searched for words that would give her traction, in an argument that was rapidly turning to loose sand. 'If he'd only told me . . .'

Tracey threw her hands up into the air. 'Oh come on, Pip, and what would you have done if he had? How could it have fixed things?'

Chloe stirred then, snuffling and whinging, and Trace reached over and took the pram's handle, rocking it gently. 'You know, Pip,' she said, more measuredly this time, 'I'm sure it's rough, not knowing, always having that question going unanswered in your mind, but you're not the only one with father issues. Sometimes it's not all that great knowing who your father was – especially when you know he was a lying, cheating scumbag. I was just a baby and *my* fabulous biological father was dropping his pants and spreading his biology far and wide for any passing bit of skirt. I'm so proud that my mum had enough guts to get rid of him, even if it meant she'd be a single mum and I'd grow up without a dad. At least you had Gerald when you were a kid. Even if he wasn't your biological father, he loved you, and your mother and brother.'

Tracey's words left her stunned and reeling, but hadn't she deserved every bit of it? She blinked and excused herself and headed for the bathroom, where she sat in a stall and let the words of the last ten minutes wash over her. And where she realised that it was about her, all right. And only about her.

Tracey had been so right. *Pip had been* lucky enough to have a great dad in Gerald. He was the best. A memory flashed in her mind of them all going to the Kadina Show, and how he'd picked her up over his head and she'd sat on his broad shoulders as he strode past the stalls and rides, laughing with the thrill of being so high off the ground, but feeling safe because she knew he would never let her fall.

He'd never let her fall.

Had she ever told him how much she'd loved him?

Did he know?

And now she was so focused on the father who had never been part of her life that she was as good as dishonouring the memory of the man who had taken that role and had been that person.

She put her shaking head in her hands and then lifted it on a sigh. It was time she was getting back. She washed her hands and dried them on paper towel, all the while looking at her reflection and at her troubled eyes. She'd known it wasn't going to be easy coming back, but she'd never for a moment realised how hard it would be.

Tracey and Fi looked relieved when she finally reappeared and sat down.

'Hey,' said Trace, putting a hand to her arm. 'I'm sorry, that was bitchy.'

Pip held up a hand. 'No, I deserved that. And you're absolutely right. You must be so sick of me banging on about everything You'll be so happy when I go back to New York.'

'I won't,' said Fi.

'Me neither.'

Pip smiled, feeling humbled by friends who'd known her forever, known her warts and all, and yet were still her friends. 'You guys are the best. I promise, no more whining about secrets and missing fathers. It's time I accepted how things are and put it behind me.' She took a deep breath, determined to be brighter company. 'So that's that, then. How about we change the subject?' And then their meals arrived. 'Brilliant, saved by the squid!'

Fi laughed. 'Oh, it is so good to have you back in town. We are going to miss you.'

Tracey's fish and chips landed on the table next, looking golden and gorgeous and giving Pip serious food envy.

Fi's plate went down last, the steak almost as big as the plate, a pile of chips balanced precariously alongside. Fi unwrapped her steak knife and fork and grinned down at the plate like she'd just won the jackpot.

Pip looked at her size ten friend and said, 'There is no way you are going to eat all that.'

'Ha,' said Fi, grinning, already slicing the first chunk of steak. 'Watch me. So, tell me about this furniture.'

So they chatted and ate and Pip told her about the sewing machine and the writing bureau and the dresser that had taken her back to their old kitchen, and showed her the photos, making sure nobody saw the one with Luke's reflection. Her squid was divine, the plump white spiced coils of squid deliciously melt-in-the-mouth tender, the salad fresh and crisp and dressed with a balsamic dressing, and the chips

. . .

Oh boy, the chips. She intended trying just one. One

wouldn't kill her. But that one was so packed with crunchy golden sinfulness that before she knew it her plate was empty and she was thinking about how many more spin and body pump classes she'd need to work this little lot off.

But she dismissed the calculation in the next thought.

Why worry about it now?

The spin and body pump classes were half a world away.

And it was so nice for a change to simply sit and enjoy a meal with friends she hardly ever saw. A pang of remorse hit deep. She was going to miss them more than ever when she left this time.

Across the table, Fi battled valiantly with the steak and looked like she was winning. 'So,' she said, with a forkful of red meat primed and ready just centimetres from her mouth, 'when do you pick up the furniture.'

Pip looked at Tracey and shook her head. 'We haven't worked that out yet.'

'I could send Craig to collect them if being around Luke is going to upset you,' Tracey said. 'You looked a bit shattered when you got back to the farm yesterday.'

'I was,' Pip said because being with Luke had awakened all kinds of emotions that she'd thought long buried and probably should remain long buried. But at the same time, she felt strangely disappointed at the thought of not seeing Luke again. 'Although I really should go through the drawers and clean out all Gran's old stuff.'

Fi put down her knife and fork and sat back in her chair with a long sigh.

Pip laughed. 'You finished it!'

'Told you.'

Tracey shook her head. 'No bovine is safe when Fi is pregnant.' She turned to Pip. 'What kind of stuff are you talking about?'

'Just old letters and papers mostly. I should go through them.'

'Your gran's papers?' Fi asked.

'Yeah.'

And Fi frowned at Tracey and then both of them frowned at her and a sizzle went down her spine right there.

'You've never looked through them before?'

'No,' she said, her mind suddenly going a million miles an hour. 'Because they were Gran's. I wouldn't look through her private papers.'

'Maybe it's time you did.'

The cogs of Pip's mind whirred and meshed as she remembered the papers still sitting in the bureau. Old letters. Old documents. Anything could be in the old bureau. And a coiling buzz of excitement built in her stomach.

Could it be possible? Could there be some hint about her biological father hidden away amongst them all?

And did she really want to know?

Maybe Tracey was right. Maybe it was better to let sleeping dogs lie.

But the possibility there might be an answer tucked away in Gran's old things was too ripe to resist.

'Oh god, didn't I just say I was going to put this behind me?'

'You have to look,' said Fi. 'If there's a chance.'

Tracey nodded. 'It's important to you. You've been carrying this around a long time. If there's an answer some-where in those papers . . .'

She nodded.

Fifteen years ago she'd left in a white-hot rage. She hadn't bothered to look for anything then because she'd already affixed blame to the person she held responsible.

Luke.

She'd blamed him all along for her not knowing.

She'd been his judge, jury and executioner.

And she'd never thought to look . . .

She gazed at the faces of her friends, at their eyes filled with compassion and concern. 'I better go look then.' And it would have to be soon because she left Friday and Gran's funeral was Wednesday. Which left tomorrow and Thursday – and Thursday was probably leaving it too late. She looked over at Trace. 'How about tomorrow? Could you come with me?'

And Trace shook her head. 'No can do. Tomorrow is Chloe's pre-natal class Christmas party and I'm taking the cake.'

Fi just held up her hands without being asked. 'I really have to spend some time in the shop. Someone has to make up for a bit of lost time. But if Luke's still working on the harvest it shouldn't be a problem. He won't even be there during the day. You'll have the place to yourself.'

That made sense, she told herself. She could be in and out while he was out there, doing his thing in the paddocks.

It could work.

And maybe she'd find something to change that lingering question mark in her mind into a full stop. And then she really could put it all behind her and move on with her life.

She looked at the faces of Trace and Fi, who had remained friends even though she'd left them to live half a world away with only an occasional visit. The friends she was already booked to leave when she was just getting used to being back with them. The friends who had still stayed loyal to her even if they sometimes sympathised with Luke a little too much for her liking – even if she was starting to see she might have been a little heavy-handed with him.

'I'll do it,' she said. 'I'll text him and see if it's okay to go out tomorrow.'

And Tracey and Fi both raised their glasses of sparkling water to her and said, 'Attagirl!'

LUKE FROWNED down at his phone. After the way they'd parted the other day, the last person he'd expected a text from was Pip. Warily he opened it and scanned its contents before texting back.

Sure. Shed's open. I'll get the tarps off. Help yourself.

He wasn't sure whether to be relieved or disappointed that it was about the furniture. He settled on relieved as he turned the header for home after a long day. Because he had no place being disappointed.

Even if her being back was playing all sorts of tricks on his mind. Like the other day, when he'd had her in his arms and his lips had been on hers and he'd almost felt like he was coming home. Which was crazy, because he was already here, and she was the one who didn't belong.

She'd made her home halfway around the globe in the biggest and brightest of cities, and she was already planning on leaving again.

But he had plenty enough to be happy about. This year's harvest for one. The sun hadn't burned too brightly to burn the crops and the rain had held off.

It was a good season. A bumper crop. One more day in the paddocks and another harvest would be in.

'What do you reckon, mate?' he said, as he looked at the dog curled up on the seat alongside him. 'What say we celebrate tomorrow night with dinner at the pub? We'll have to sit on the verandah mind, no going inside.'

Turbo pricked up his ears and wagged his tail, looking keen in spite of the onerous conditions.

'That's what I like about you, fella,' he said with a grin.

'What you see is what you get. There's not enough of that going around these days.'

But as he jumped down from the header he was still thinking about that kiss with Pip in the shed, and of the warmth and pleasure and the sheer wonder of it.

And, he thought, maybe there's not enough of that going around either.

CHAPTER 19

$\mathcal{T}$he shed door rumbled open with a squawk of metal on metal and then there was just silence and Pip and the dust motes dancing in the cracks of light.

She stood there on the cusp of entry, armed with a box for anything worth keeping and a bag for rubbish, and a firm resolution, even if her stomach felt anything but settled.

Because forget about what she might or might not find, this was Luke's world.

Once upon a time, it could have been hers.

Something twisted inside her like barbed wire pulled tight around her gut, and she gasped at both its suddenness and severity.

It was a bit late to start thinking about what could have been.

Too late for regrets.

She stepped over the threshold and snapped on the lights to banish memories that flitted like shadows in the gloom, but not even the harsh fluoro lighting could banish the what-ifs. They crowded thickly around her mind, jostling for attention as she put her box and bag down next to the bureau.

What if she found something?

What if she didn't?

And what if she'd given Luke the benefit of the doubt all those years ago, instead of taking it all out on him?

Tracey's words from lunch came back to her.

You were hurting. You were looking for answers. Of course you were going to lash out.

Strange to see your actions from another's point of view.

Strange how those words wormed their way into her mind, digging holes in the absolute truths she'd constructed to justify her actions.

She'd spent last night tossing and turning as the worms had set to work, burrowing away at her cleverly constructed justifications until they were riddled with holes and the light and the fresh air had streamed through.

And the walls and her truth had become so fragile, like the lace doilies her Gran had crafted on tiny crochet needles before her mind had drifted shut, that she could deny it no longer.

She had never given him a chance.

Tracey was right. Luke had copped it all. Her pain. Her despair. Her anger.

Her rage.

And now?

Now it was too late.

A good man, Tracey had called him, and Pip looked at the neat pile of folded tarpaulins. He'd said he'd remove them in preparation, which meant that sometime after he'd dropped her back at the farm on Sunday, he'd put them back over to protect them.

A good man indeed.

She'd joked with Tracey and Fi about too much water under the bridge.

But the problem wasn't the water at all.

The problem was the bridge.

But she hadn't just burned her bridges. She'd well and truly blown them into smithereens.

She sighed wistfully. So be it. She couldn't change the past.

Nor did she necessarily want to.

She had a good life back in New York City. A great job. And the chance of a big fat promotion the other side of this weekend.

She wouldn't change her life for quids.

Mind you, if she got the chance, she might tell Luke she was sorry before she left. He deserved that much at least.

And then she thought about the way he'd been there for her in that week before her family's funeral service - how he'd supported her and kept her half way to upright in a world that had been turned upside down, only to unceremoniously cut him off - and she knew he deserved even more. It was going to have to be one hell of an apology.

But that would have to wait. Right now she had a job to do. She took a deep breath and rolled up the sliding lid as a swarm of butterflies took flight in her stomach.

It was time to get to work.

'THAT'S IT, FELLA,' said Luke on a sigh. 'Another harvest in the can.' And it literally was, the row of augers spaced out across the paddock behind him all now full to the brim.

Plenty of grain producers worked in teams, using trucks to offload the grain direct from the harvester when it was full before starting the next run. But Luke had grown up with his dad doing it this way and he liked working by himself and not relying on others. Besides, it wasn't as if he was alone. He had Turbo to keep him company, even if his faithful companion spent more time asleep on the seat alongside him than on the job.

With a weary sigh, and a pat on the head for the dog, he turned the machine for home.

TOO MANY HOURS TO count after she'd started, Pip rocked back on her heels, feeling deflated. She'd opened every envelope, read every handwritten letter and note, and flipped through the pages of every book in case anything had been tucked away, and yet found not one clue. Halfway through the bureau she'd tackled the dresser, to give her knees and ankles a break, but it had been a quick job, the cupboards and drawers long ago emptied of their contents.

Not that the box she'd brought for keepsakes was empty. She'd found a few old photographs of Gran and Gramps, one with them standing outside the farmhouse holding her mum as a baby that had brought a sad smile to her face.

And there was the payment book for the treadle sewing machine that she didn't have the heart to consign to rubbish. It had cost twenty pounds back in nineteen twenty-six and her great grandmother – Gran's mum – had paid it off at sixpence a week for years. She hadn't seen any reason to keep the old bankbooks with their meticulous entries of deposits and withdrawals of amounts that seemed ridiculously tiny now, nor the old timetables from when the train still ran through town.

But she'd found a couple of old seventy-eights buried under the piles of old papers, and they had made her smile,

Bing Crosby singing 'White Christmas', and 'Chattanooga Choo Choo' by Glenn Miller and His Orchestra.

But nothing that might give her any clue as to her identity.

And although it had been such a long shot, she still felt a pang of disappointment that her search had uncovered nothing.

She picked up the old recordings and looked over at the gramophone. Luke had that collection he used to play sometimes. Maybe he still did.

He might as well have this couple to add to it.

Her ankles protested as she crossed the room, stiff with being bent underneath her for so long, and little wonder. She'd been here for hours. But now she could go back to the farm with her box and her bag for the rubbish and have a long cool glass of wine and finish up the words she was preparing to say at tomorrow's funeral.

The wooden storage box where Luke kept his record collection was still right there, next to the table holding the gramophone. She swung up the heavy hinged lid to add the ones she'd found, only to feel the air sucked from her lungs.

CHAPTER 20

*I*t sat there in pride of place. Right in front. The Ella Fitzgerald and Louis Armstrong album she'd found in a second-hand store years ago when she'd been trawling for a gift for Luke's eighteenth birthday. The album that still bore her inscription written in texta on the cover:

To Luke,
Forget the song, you know what excites me,
It's you.
All my love, forever.
Pip xox

Her head spun and she had to remember to breathe.

The first time she had heard 'The Nearness of You' it had been Sheena Easton singing in the movie *Indecent Proposal*. The video was already years old when she'd watched it with Luke one night out in the shed, and she'd heard that song and it had said everything she felt, everything she wanted to tell him better than she ever could, and that night it had become their song.

She hadn't realised the song was much, much older, until

she'd found this album. This was the version she'd fallen in love with.

She couldn't have found a more perfect gift. Luke had loved it, and made love to her with Louis Armstrong's evocative trumpet playing in the background.

She bit her lip and glanced at her watch. Yeah, it was early. She'd have time to play it just once.

What could it hurt?

It took a while to remember how the old gramophone worked, and she had a couple of false starts, but finally the machine was spinning and the record in place and she slowly lowered the heavy needle and heard the scratch of metal on vinyl and then the tinkling piano riff before Ella Fitzgerald's heavenly rich tones sounded out in the big shed. Pip found herself smiling at the lush sound and the memories that went with them, and then Armstrong's trumpet joined in after the first verse like another voice.

How could one song say so much?

And yet this one did. It had been their story.

The story of then.

The story of them.

She closed her eyes and stretched out her arms and let herself drift and sway with the music.

BLOODY HELL! He pulled the header up short. She was still here.

What the hell was that about? After their run-in on Sunday, he'd expected her to have flashed in and out as quickly as she could. What was she playing at?

Approaching the door to the shed he stopped short, because he heard the music – that music – and it was enough to raise the hair on the back of his neck. But he didn't turn away because he caught sight of her and he couldn't.

She had her back to him and she was moving to the music, her arms outstretched, her body swaying to the beat of Louis Armstrong's gravelly voice and a strumming bass and god, she was gorgeous. Dressed in shorts and a tank top with her hair tied back into a ponytail, she looked like she'd just stepped out of his past, and the way those hips moved . . .

Against his will, he felt himself harden. He'd always loved the way she danced, like her body was an extension of the music, another instrument adding to its richness.

And that, he realised, was what had been missing on Sunday night. He'd dug the record out after he'd dropped her back at the farm. He'd come out to the shed to put the tarps back over the furniture and it had been too damned quiet in there, especially with the air still scented with her perfume, so he'd thought he might as well put on one of his old records and brighten the place up.

He'd been flipping through and that one had stopped his searching fingers, and lingered, and he'd thought, *it's not about her*. It was just such a classic. And it wouldn't kill him to hear it one more time.

Yet it hadn't moved him then, as it did now. Then, it had left him feeling hollow and empty. Now, he realised what had been missing.

Pip.

He should have left then, before she turned and caught him watching, knowing he was intruding. He would have, except that Turbo, crouching otherwise patiently at his feet, chose that exact moment to bark. So Pip, with her arms still outstretched and a dreamy look in her eyes, did turn then and saw him standing there, her lips half open in surprise.

He was still halfway to making an apology and going. He knew when he wasn't wanted and she'd made it more than clear that she didn't want anything to do with him. He wasn't about to give her the chance to push him away again.

He had one hand raised, ready to wave in acknowledgment and leave her to it, when she angled her head, smiled a soft, sad half smile and whispered the words, 'Luke. I'm so sorry.'

And even though he knew he should put distance between them, his mouth refused to work and his feet refused to move.

'So very sorry.'

Her eyes were wide and soft enough to melt into and Louis' trumpet was singing and pleading with him in the background and he knew he should get the hell out of there while the going was good.

She smiled, a smile of apology and regret and she sure didn't look like she wanted to push him away, and he wanted to believe her, wanted to believe those outstretched arms might once again be wrapped around him.

And he knew he was going to regret it. He knew he was headed for disaster. He damned well knew it.

But still there was not a thing he could do to stop himself.

'Aw hell, Pip,' he groaned, and breached the distance between them in the space of one pounding heartbeat. He swept her into his arms to Ella singing about dreams coming true, and she offered up her mouth and he thought, *Oh yes.*

HE'D BEEN A BOY BEFORE. A boy with broadening shoulders and whiskers on his face and well on the way to manhood, sure, but he'd still been a boy. Whereas the Luke of now was a man.

All man.

He tasted of a long day worked in summer, musky and

masculine and spiced with desire, and a man had never tasted better.

His chest was hard, his arms were bunched and corded with muscles and tendons, and his mouth was hot and hard and damn near magnetic, the way it was so impossible to leave it. And when his big hands cupped her behind and pressed her close to his hardness, she nearly came apart right there.

It was madness, she knew it, as his lips moved over hers, their mouths meshed and tongues duelled. A kind of madness and desperation and a sudden aching, pulsing need that refused to be shut down.

There was no shutting this down.

There was only one way to go from here.

Her hands were on his shirt, fumbling with his buttons, needing to feel his skin. He was one step ahead and reefed his shirt open, shrugging it from his shoulders even as his mouth never left hers.

And then it was her turn as he found the hem of her cotton tank and tugged it up and peeled it away. This time they had no choice but to separate, and as he pulled it from her head and arms she looked up at him and saw him gazing down at her breasts, his own chest heaving, his eyes wild. He lifted those eyes and she saw the hesitation and the questions flicker across their surface and said, 'Don't you dare stop now, Luke Trenorden.'

And he gave a half smile as he let go the tank top bundled in one hand, and gathered her head between his hands to pull her into his kiss. 'No ma'am.'

Skin against skin. Was there any better feeling?

While his mouth made magic on hers, her hands drank him in, both remembering and learning anew. He'd filled out in the intervening years, her fingers discovered, filled out with hard, lean muscle, and he groaned as she raked her nails down his back, toned flesh shifting under the skin. His hands trailed to her shoulders and lower, cupping her breasts and it was her turn to mewl. And then the scrap of cotton and lace that was her bra was gone and his hot hands fairly sizzled against her flesh.

His hips were narrow and lean, his butt cheeks hard, growing harder when she squeezed, his hips pressing into her.

She liked.

She slid her hand down between his legs while his thumbs worked her nipples into bullets and his mouth trailed hot kisses down her throat, and felt the hard length of him under her hand and squeezed, feeling him buck.

She liked that even more.

But it was nowhere near enough. He was still wearing too many damned clothes. She tugged at his waistband, wanting in, wanting him naked, frustrated when it didn't happen. 'Nnh,' she growled as she fought with the unfamiliar fastening.

'Boots,' he said, pushing her hand aside as he kicked them off, wrenched off socks and unbuttoned his pants in the same frantic moments.

For a moment she couldn't speak. Couldn't think. He was the most beautiful thing she'd ever seen. She'd forgotten just how beautiful. How big. Forgotten, or maybe she'd just buried the memory? Either way, it was a happy awakening. The perfect boy had become the perfect man. Broad shoulders, lean hips, his chest covered in a smattering of dark blonde hair that whorled in circles before arrowing down to the dark nest and that jutting erection below.

Even under the unforgiving fluoro lights, his body was flawless.

Her hands went to the button on her shorts and his eyes followed the movement. He stood there immobile as she popped the button. He swallowed and she saw his throat kick as she peeled the zipper down.

His blue eyes grew dark and heavy with longing as she put her fingers on her hips and wiggled her shorts and lace thong down, flicking them away with one foot until she stood naked before him.

She wasn't nervous about how she looked or worried what he'd think. This was no time for false modesty. She was in the best shape she'd ever been in her life and she knew it. All those spin and pump classes had to have some kind of pay-off.

The heated look in his eyes was the pay-off.

The hungry look in his eyes that told her that all those classes, all those planks, all those spins of the pedals had been worth every drop of sweat and every last cent.

'My God,' he said, those hot, hungry eyes devouring every inch of her, leaving scorching trails in their wake that flared along secret lines and pooled into a burning lake deep in her belly. He reached out a hand, cupped her chin in his big hand and growled, low in his throat, like he was claiming her, and it was simultaneously the sweetest and sexiest sound she'd ever heard.

She reached for him but he took her hand instead, and led her to the couch that had borne witness to so many of their encounters before. He pulled a coverlet out of a chest nearby and threw it over the leather sofa.

'What do you want?' he asked, his voice gravelly tight.

'I want you. Now.'

His lips twitched as he drew her towards the couch. 'That's the right answer.'

CHAPTER 21

The music had stopped. Strange how he hadn't noticed before. But then he had been slightly distracted by the naked woman now slumped on his lap.

God. Pip, of all women. He didn't know what the aftermath of this was going to be. There was bound to be one. All he knew was that he'd just experienced the best sex he'd had in a whole lot of years.

He lay back on the sofa, nestling her limp body close to his. The air was warm around them, musky with sex and sweet with woman.

She gave a loud exhale and pushed her long hair from her face. 'God, I needed that.'

He smiled, and kissed her brow, figuring he'd needed it more. 'I wouldn't tell Chad that, if I were you.'

She peeked up at him from beneath her lashes. 'He's not really my boyfriend. Well, not really a friend at all. We, um, have an arrangement.'

'Yeah,' he said, with more gravel in his voice than he'd meant to put there. 'Craig told me.'

'Craig?' she squeaked, and buried her face in his armpit. 'Oh, good grief.'

And he chuckled in spite of himself. Without even meeting the guy, he didn't like him – let alone their cosy little arrangement. But it did something to his ego that he'd been the one to turn her knees to water. And it definitely said something that she'd trusted him enough to go there without a raincoat.

Take that, Chad.

He knew there was a place for protection but he'd always preferred skin on skin, and it hadn't improved marital relations any that Sharon had insisted on condoms from day one, even though she was on the pill. It was like she thought he was unclean, or that she couldn't bear to have him naked inside her, or that she wanted absolutely no chance that she might get pregnant.

Looking back he was grateful that she hadn't wanted his kids or skin on skin. God knows how long she'd been fucking around behind his back before she'd taken off with her new best friend.

He sighed, stretching his neck, for the first time noticing the box and bulging bag near the bureau. 'Sort out all your gran's stuff?'

'Yeah, but I didn't find anything.'

He stilled. He'd assumed she'd just wanted to clean it out before it went to the B&B. 'You mean anything that might tell you who your father was?'

She nodded. 'I was hoping,' she said, and turned her head up to him. 'I'm sorry, Luke, I know it wasn't your dad. I don't think I ever believed that. Not really.'

He dipped his head and kissed her hair. 'I know.'

'It's strange. I didn't come back with any thought of finding out who he might be. But I guess every time I'm here, I'm reminded that I don't know.'

He nodded, stroking her hair. 'If there was a chance, it was probably going to be in that bureau with all your gran's things.'

She sighed. 'That's what I figured. I just have to accept that I'm never going to find out, although I did find some extra photos I can display at the funeral.'

'How are you going with all that?'

'Okay. I've written the eulogy, or mostly written it. I change it every time I look at it.'

'I'll be there,' he said, pressing his lips to her head and he felt her lips smile against his shoulder.

'Thank you.' And then she groaned. 'I really need to pee.'

If there was one downside to the shed, Luke thought, it was the lack of bathroom facilities. But there was an upside too, at a time like this. 'Come over to the house. You can take a shower.'

She blinked up at him, her eyes cloudy like she was disappointed. 'Oh, yeah, I suppose I better get going.'

'That wasn't what I meant.'

'What do you mean?'

He grinned. 'You haven't seen the shower.'

'YOU'RE KIDDING,' she said five minutes later, after they'd put on enough clothes to be decent in case anyone suddenly turned up, and strolled to the house. She'd already oohed and aahed over the new loo he'd had put in, only too happy to give it a test drive. Now her eyes were as wide as her smile as she took in the sparkling bathroom. 'When did you have all this done?'

He shrugged. 'A few years back. The pipes were going and needed to be dug out of the wall and I thought it was about time. You like?'

'It's gorgeous!' She remembered it being pink and green

the last time she'd been here, with vinyl peeling off the floor and a cracked mirrored cabinet above the tiny sink and the old loo holding pride of place on the back wall. Now it was decorated in traditional black and white, the glossy white wall tiles were at least two feet by one, the big square black and white floor tiles laid in a diamond pattern. On one side was a double vanity, while on the other sat a vast white bathtub that looked like it had been carved from a slab of rock. At the end of the room was a wall of glass with a silver handle.

She smiled, 'That's your shower?'

He nodded. 'But there's a catch.'

'You don't say. What is it?'

'I'm trying to save water.'

She quirked an eyebrow. 'Would it help if we showered together, do you think?'

He grinned. 'You catch on fast.'

Which is how she found herself ten minutes later trying to get her breath back, and with her arms around his neck, not willing to let go until she was sure her knees would hold her, 'how much water do you think we saved?'

'Come to dinner,' he said, his hands curving around her behind.

'What?'

'I'm taking Turbo to the pub for dinner tonight, seeing I've finished the harvesting. I'm asking if you'd like to come too.'

'Wow.' Boy, this was unexpected. 'I don't want to play gooseberry or anything, if you two were planning a date night.'

'Turbo's good with it.'

'You haven't even asked him yet.'

'It's not that kind of relationship.'

'Well, that's a relief!'

'So will you?'

'I'm not exactly dressed for dinner.'

He looked down at her slick body, beaded with moisture. 'I don't know, you might create a bit of a buzz. But no, shorts will be fine.'

'Just dinner, then?'

'Yeah. Just dinner. Well, and sex. Dinner and sex.'

'Luke . . .' She shook her head. 'I don't want you getting the wrong idea.'

'You'd rather have sex and dinner? We can do it your way. I'm easy.'

She smiled. 'I don't want you thinking there's anything happening here. It is just sex. Great sex admittedly. Mind-blowing sex if you must know. But I'm going home in three days. It can only be sex.'

'I know. The way I figure it, we can either forget today ever happened, or we can make the most of those three days and nights. So, is that a yes?'

It was all kinds of madness, she knew. Nothing could come of it. And yet, her skin already tingled at the thought of having sex with this man again. She smiled up at him. 'That's a yes.'

'DID YOU DISCOVER ANYTHING?' Tracey asked, as soon as she picked up the phone.

'Nothing.' Other than that Luke was as good a lover as she remembered, but Tracey didn't need to know that. 'Hey Trace, is it okay if I skip dinner tonight?'

'You mean, miss my famous apricot chicken?' She laughed. 'Of course. What are you doing?'

'Oh, just going out for dinner.'

'Yeah, who with?'

Well, Tracey was bound to ask that. 'Just, um, Luke.'

'Just, um, Luke, hey? That sounds cosy.'

Pip winced. 'Well, and Turbo.'

'Oh, the whole family's going. That'll be fun.' There was a moment's hesitation before, 'Pip, is something going on between you two?'

'No! What could possibly be going on? It's just a . . . a thank you for looking after the furniture. Only I thought I should make an effort after that conversation we had at lunch yesterday. We don't even like each other really.'

'Yeah, that's what you keep saying. Makes perfect sense you'd want to go to dinner with him. I guess we'll see you later, then.'

'Yeah,' Pip said, biting her lip.

Much later.

SHE WAS PICKING up the last of her stuff from the shed before they went to dinner.

'You looked through this?' he said, pulling out one of the small drawers of the sewing machine.

'Yeah. It's all bobbins and wooden cotton reels from what I could see. I thought I might as well leave them for a bit of atmosphere for the B&B.'

He nodded. 'Fair enough,' he said, as he pulled out the second one for a quick look and then the third. The bottom drawer stuck and he pulled and it still stuck so he squatted down.

'I know. That's one's stuck. But it's empty.'

Luke crouched down lower and looked underneath. 'Oh.'

A shiver went down her spine. 'What is it?' she asked, coming closer.

He pressed his fingers up under the drawer and pulled and the little drawer slid out. He flipped it over, and this time the shiver became a bloom of warm tingles that worked their way from her insides out.

An envelope was stuck to the bottom of the drawer, the paper now yellow with age, the strips of sellotape around the edges cracking and split so that the envelope was peeling off and falling down and blocking the drawer's slide.

Luke looked up at her. 'You might want to take a look at this.'

She ventured closer, her mouth dry, fear and excitement warring for supremacy in her gut.

He prised the buckled envelope away from the base of the drawer and handed it to her. She turned it over in her hands. There was nothing written on the outside. Over a thumping heart, she told herself not to get too excited – it could still turn out to be nothing.

But the fact that it had been there, stuck so far out of the way that nobody might inadvertently find it . . .

Her hands were shaking, all her senses on alert. Could it contain the key to finding out who her father was?

Nervously she pulled back the flap and pulled out the contents. There was a letter. Or at least a folded up note. And another bankbook, this one much more recent, from when entries were made by a printer.

Quickly she rifled through the pages of the book. It was made out in her mother's maiden name – Dierdre Cooper – and there was an opening deposit made thirty-three years ago – the year before Pip was born. There were subsequent withdrawals, but none of it offered any clue.

And so she opened the letter that had been folded into four, a handwritten note addressed to her grandmother that read,

DEAR MRS COOPER,

Please find enclosed a cheque in the amount of five thousand dollars in full settlement for the unfortunate incident.
Your utmost discretion in this matter is appreciated.
Yours sincerely,
Colin Armistead.

SHE FROWNED and flipped the paper over. What 'unfortunate incident'?

And she looked at the date, one month before her parents' marriage, but perhaps more significantly, six months before she was born, and certainty zinged down her spine.

She dropped to her knees. 'Oh god.'

Luke was down on his knees with his arm around her shoulders in an instant. 'What is it?'

'It was me,' she said, holding up the paper. 'This man paid money to my gran because of me. Because I was coming.' And she looked up at him. 'Do you think this Colin Armistead could be my father?'

CHAPTER 22

'Show me,' he said, and she handed him the note that had rocked her world. 'Wow,' he said, 'I imagine that was quite a bit of money back then.'

'Hush money.'

'Yeah. The "appreciate your discretion" kind of gives that away.'

'You know, Luke, I might take a raincheck on that dinner.'

'You think you're going find this guy tonight?'

'I have to look.'

He frowned and shook his head 'I've never heard of him. Or anyone around here with that name for that matter.'

'He must be out there somewhere. I have to find him.'

'Yeah, but, where Pip? This was more than thirty years ago. Where are you going to start?'

She turned to him then, the blue in her eyes swirling with uncertainty, and he had a glimpse of her as that tortured teen, fleeing to him across the paddocks, dripping wet and bereft, her beautiful eyes filled with nightmares, her lips fraught. 'I don't know.'

'Tell you what, come back over to the house. You can

check the phone book for Armisteads and I'll fire up the computer and start searching.'

She blinked up at him. 'Why? Why would you do that?'

He gave her shoulders a squeeze. 'Because it's important.'

He'd hauled her to her feet when she turned to him and said, 'I really am sorry. For everything.'

And he kissed the tip of her nose. 'Come on. Let's see if we can't track down our Mr Armistead of the big pockets.'

Pip sniffed. 'Sounds like that wasn't his only claim to fame.'

She picked up the receiver and dialled the first number she'd found in the phone book, took a deep breath when it answered on the third ring and said, 'Hi, I'm hoping you can help me. I'm looking for a Colin Armistead...'

AN HOUR later Luke pulled a tray of golden potato gems from the oven. He tipped them into a waiting bowl without losing one overboard, like he'd accomplished the feat plenty of times before. The kitchen had been done up since she'd last been here too. It was now all clean lines and dark grey marble benchtops with stainless steel appliances, with Luke in fresh jeans and a white T-shirt and an oven mitt at the centre of it all.

It was a good look.

'Not exactly haute cuisine,' he said, as he put the bowl in the middle of the wide kitchen bench and pulled a couple of fresh beers from the fridge, screwing off the tops and passing her one as he sat down next to his laptop. 'But it is hot. Now, what have we got?'

Pip tried to ignore temptation sitting less than an arm's length away. She looked at the bowl. And then there were the potato gems.

She gritted her teeth against an ill-timed pang of lust.

Luke had awakened something in her today, a desire she associated with her past. A desire she'd always attributed to youth and an excess of hormones. But she was a grown woman now. Things should be different. Things usually were different. Back in New York she might have sex as little once a month, and that was enough to keep any untoward urges at bay, but she'd made love to this man twice today and was already thinking about ripping off that T-shirt and jeans and getting tangled up on the floor. Or the table.

Both ideas appealed.

She squirmed on her chair and reached for a potato gem instead. What the hell was wrong with her?

She nibbled at the gem and hauled her mind back into line as she looked down at her list.

Focus!

Deep breath. 'I don't have that much to report. According to the phone book, there are no Armisteads on the Yorke Peninsula at all,' she said, 'although they could have private numbers or mobiles, of course. And a check of the White Pages reveals ten C Armisteads spread around the rest of the country, only two in South Australia, but when I called them – those that did answer – well, not one of them is called Colin or knows anyone called Colin.'

She took a breath and finished off the gem, brushing her hands and reaching for her beer to wash it down. 'And before I called every other Armistead in the phone book, I checked Facebook and didn't get much further than a bunch of American teens with biceps and tatts. So, after a lot of dead ends, I'm wondering if this Colin has a social media presence at all. Maybe I'd be better just getting back on the phone.' She looked across at Luke, all freshly washed with a two-day growth of stubble on his jaw and a white T-shirt that hugged his biceps, and figured the bowl of gems in the centre of table was the lesser of two evils. She helped herself to another one.

'Yeah, well, we're talking someone who's thirty years older than when he wrote that note, and we don't know how old he was then.'

'He couldn't be that old. Surely Mum wouldn't have done it with someone . . .' She shivered and stuck out her tongue. 'Ugh.'

'Well, that's assuming our Colin Armistead is the one. What young bloke would have a handy five grand hanging around back then? Besides, look at the language he used. He picked up the note from the table. "Appreciate your discretion." It doesn't sound like a kid who's just got someone's daughter banged up.' He looked up. 'Sorry, that sounded a bit rough.'

But Pip nodded, daunted by the size of the task and the sheer number of unknowns. Having a name had seemed like an answer but all it did was raise more questions. 'No, you're right. Maybe Colin was his father?'

'Yeah, I've been wondering the same thing.' He looked down at his laptop. 'Anyway, so here's what I've got. Google tells me there's a Colin A Armistead JP in Newcastle, a foot-baller aged twenty-eight in the UK who I think we can safely rule out, and I found a death notice for a Colin Armistead from 1997 somewhere in Perth.'

Pip blinked. 'That could be him. He could be dead by now, right?'

Luke shrugged, but the frown tugging his brows together told her he wasn't half as casual about the prospect. 'Yeah, he could,' he said, reaching for a couple of gems, flicking one to the waiting Turbo at his feet. 'I think the JP in Newcastle might be worth following up on.'

Pip glanced at her watch. It would be after seven in New South Wales by now but tomorrow afternoon was the funeral and she was running out of time. 'I might try calling tomorrow morning'

'Do you really want to be doing that on the day of the funeral?'

'I can't leave it any later - not when I'm leaving in two days.'

She reached over and picked up another potato gem, crisp and golden in her fingers. 'I'll be up for excess baggage if I keep eating my way through these babies.'

She crunched into it. Oh god, she was going to pay for this. 'I never realised how much I missed these.'

He shrugged. 'Nobody's making you go back.'

She stopped crunching and looked at him, her eyes narrowing. Maybe this sex thing had been a mistake after all. Maybe he was getting the wrong idea. 'My job is making me go back. My life is in New York now. I like it that way.'

He held up one hand. 'Hey, don't be so sensitive. It was a throwaway line. I'm not on some kind of mission to bring you back. Believe it or not, we all get by perfectly well when you're not around.'

She blinked and took a deep breath. So okay, maybe she'd overreacted. 'Good to know,' she said, even though his words had stung. Had she really needed to hear they coped so brilliantly without her? Of course, she knew they did. Nobody called or emailed and begged her to come back because their lives were falling apart. She just hadn't needed to hear it.

But she'd get on fine too, just as soon as she was back in New York.

'I should go,' she said. 'There's probably not a whole lot more we can do tonight, and I've still got to finish off my words for the service tomorrow.'

'Already? I thought we had a deal.'

'What?'

'Dinner and sex.' He glanced at the bowl. 'Admittedly the dinner's been a bit of a let-down, but I'm hoping to make up for that in the sex department.'

She smiled warily, her overreaction having taken the edge off her earlier surge of lust. 'You know, this is probably a mistake.'

'Yeah,' he said, with his own smile that warmed her all the way to her toes. 'But they reckon you learn from your mistakes, so I'm figuring it can't be all bad.' He cocked an eyebrow as he leaned over, snaking an arm around her neck and drawing her closer. 'Want to teach me a lesson or two?'

'Well, if you put it like that.'

'I'll put it any way you want.'

'Now you're just bragging.'

And he smiled and pulled her mouth against his. 'Yep.'

CHAPTER 23

'You were back late last night.'

Pip had let herself into the house the next morning and was sitting in the kitchen drinking a cup of coffee and working a list of phone numbers, crossing off those she'd already called when Tracey walked in, still wearing her dressing gown.

'Was I?' she answered innocently, and then frowned when she noticed how bleary-eyed her friend looked. 'What happened to you?'

Tracey stood by the sink with the kettle in one hand and a tap in the other, her head on her chest, rolling it to left and right. 'Chloe's teething. We had a rough night. Which is why I was up at two o'clock and noticed your car still wasn't back.' She put some water in the kettle and snapped it on.

'How's Chloe now?'

'Sleeping like a baby, of course. Not a care in the world.' She turned around and arched an eyebrow. 'So, how was dinner?'

'I've had better.'

'Shame. So I guess you had to talk about how disappointing it was until two in the morning, huh? That makes sense.'

Pip smiled. 'Trace, after we spoke, Luke found something hidden under the Singer. Stuck to the bottom of a drawer.'

'Really? Show me.'

She pushed the note across the table and Trace picked it up, her eyes opening wide as she read.

'There was a bankbook too, in Mum's name, where the money got deposited. Looks like she used it for expenses over the next few years.'

Tracey looked up. 'Oh my god. Do you think this Colin Armistead could be your real father?'

Pip frowned. 'I don't know. Luke think he sounds too old. Maybe it was his son.'

Her friend shook her head and pushed her hair back from her face. 'I've never heard of anyone from around these parts with that name.'

'That's what Luke said. I couldn't find any in the local phonebook, and so far I've checked every C Armistead in Australia apart from one I was about to call. I'm going to work my way through the rest of the Armisteads this morning.'

'How many are there?'

She grimaced. 'Only about ninety.'

'You want a hand?'

'You mean it?'

'Hey girlfriend, in case you've forgotten, you're heading back to the States the day after tomorrow. If you want to track this guy down before you get on that plane, we'd better get started.'

'You are the best.'

'Yeah, that's why I was imagining you doing the dirty with Luke all night.' She looked over, clearly expecting Pip to share the joke, but she was keeping her lips shut and her face blank. 'You DID do the dirty with Luke! Priscilla Martin, I am shocked!'

'Hey, I never admitted anything.'

'You didn't have to. It was written all over your face.' She shook her head. 'I should have known by that glimmer in your eyes! So are you two back together again? How is that going to work? Oh my god,' she said, looking around for the portable. 'Where's the phone? I've got to tell Fi. She'll be so excited.'

'Tracey,' she said, reaching her hand across the table to latch onto her friend's arm. 'For god's sake, don't tell Fi! We are not "back together" or anything, and if there is *any* glimmer in my eyes it's about finding a clue about who I am.'

'But you and Luke made love, right?'

'We had sex,' Pip said with a shrug. 'It's a bit different'

'How do you do that?' said Tracey throwing her hands into the air. 'Call it sex, like it's nothing more than taking an aspirin? I don't get that.'

She shrugged. 'It's just a physical urge. So you fix it. Exactly like taking an aspirin.'

'But this is *Luke* and he is not just some random guy.'

'It's lust, Trace. It's just a *physical* urge. We all need to get off somehow.'

'But Luke? You have history with him.'

'Trace, you yourself said I was leaving in two days. Nothing's going to change that.'

'But –'

'Nothing is going to change that. Now, do you want to help me make some calls?'

CHAPTER 24

*P*ip had promised herself that she was done with tears, that she wouldn't cry again, and that Gran was in a better place, but it was hard.

It seemed like half the population of the Yorke Peninsula had turned out to farewell Violet Cooper. The funeral parlour chapel was standing room only, and there were still ten minutes to go before the service started. Shelving running around the walls heaved with flowers, bright and beautiful, and the coffin at the front was piled with more. There were so many flowers that the air was sweetly scented with them. Pip gave a wistful smile. Gran would have loved it.

Everyone there, it seemed, wanted the chance to pass on an anecdote or to tell her how much Violet had meant to them. So many people with so many beautiful stories to share. So many people whose lives Gran had touched in one way or another.

With the backdrop of 'Abide With Me' playing softly on a loop, it was almost overwhelming.

Molly Kernahan was there with a number of staff from

the nursing home, and even some of the residents, those who could manage with their walkers or in wheelchairs. She wrapped Pip up in one of her signature hugs and Pip felt the love the woman had for her gran right there.

There were a group of women who'd served alongside Gran in the local Country Women's Association for many long years, creating magic out of toilet rolls and kewpie dolls and raffia, or baking trays and trays of scones and fairy cakes to raise funds for worthy causes.

Even Luke's old English teacher from high school was there. 'I'm so sorry about your gran, dear,' said Jean Cutting, holding her hand in between her bony and surprisingly strong fingers. 'But we're all so proud of you. Have you seen much of Luke at all since you've been back?'

'I do believe he's coming today,' she said, evading the question, and Jean Cutting looked pleased with herself until Adam arrived and wrapped an arm around Pip's shoulders and gave her a kiss on the cheek like they were best friends.

I really did give him the wrong idea, Pip thought with a stab of guilt as he introduced her to his mother, who worked at the nursing home too. She listened while Betty Rogers told her about Violet's favourite dessert of crushed up shortbread in custard – how she'd made it specially for her towards the end, when she'd lost interest in just about everything else.

So much love. It was humbling to know how well loved her gran had been, even though she'd been gone, for all intents and purposes, for years.

And yet despite all the love in the room, Pip still felt nervy and on edge. Not because she had to deliver the eulogy. But because the one person she'd been looking for wasn't here.

Surely Luke wouldn't let her down today?

Sally Buxton rushed in and gave Pip a hug. 'Oh my god, I'm so sorry I'm late. How are you, sweetie?'

'Okay,' she said. 'Thanks for coming.' She would have let the other woman get seated but then she remembered. 'Did Tracey tell you I had a lead about my father?'

Sally blinked. 'Er, no. No, she didn't. Did you get a name?'

'Yes. No. Well, we're not sure. But it looks like someone paid Mum off before she married my dad.'

Her eyes opened wide and then kind of vagued out, looking into the middle distance. 'Really.'

'And we found a bank book - it looks like someone paid Mum and Gran off to keep quiet about me. So it's exciting. I might even find out while I'm here.'

And Sally smiled thinly as Sam Riordan joined them then to pay his respects, the farmer her father had share-farmed with and who she hadn't seen for years. A widower now, apparently, he was a big burly man with a deep voice and a steel-like grip, and he pumped her arm like he was hoping to draw water. 'Good to see you again, Pipsqueak,' he said, calling her by the childhood nickname Gerald used to call her – a name she'd long forgotten.

She smiled widely, warmed at the memory. 'Thanks for coming, Sam.'

'G'day Sally,' he said to the woman standing next to Pip, like he'd only just noticed her.

Sally nodded and blinked.

'I actually thought I might see you at the CFS Christmas do the other night.'

And Pip felt slightly superfluous when the older woman shook her head and Sam and Sally continued as if she wasn't there. 'I was too busy.'

'Ah well, always next time. How about we grab a seat while there's still a couple left?'

And then the funeral director indicated it was time, and Sally sat in the seat Tracey had saved next to Chloe's pram, and Sam squeezed into the seat she'd half planned would go to Luke. Pip took a seat between Tracey and Fi in the front row.

And then the music stopped and the funeral service began.

A few minutes later it was her turn at the lectern. Pip was about to begin the eulogy when a movement caught her eye and she glanced up to see Luke threading his way through the people crowded along the back wall. Their eyes connected and he smiled and her heart gave a little flip. With relief, she told herself, because he had made it.

Nothing more than relief.

And she took a deep breath and began. 'Violet Eliza May Cooper. Aged ninety years and seven months, four days. Today is truly the end of an era.'

She took them through Gran's life; daughter of a miner who'd married a farmer when the economy of the Yorke Peninsula was moving so rapidly from copper to grain, a woman who'd suffered six miscarriages before bearing her husband their one child, only to lose her husband way too early and then her only daughter, her son-in-law and her grandson.

Her voice broke on the word grandson.

Because it hadn't only been Gran's daughter and son-in-law and grandson.

It had been Pip's mum and dad and little brother.

Damn. She paused and looked up at the ceiling and reminded herself to take a sip of water. Across the rim of her glass, across the room, she saw Luke's creased brow, his lips hitched to one side, but she saw also his nod, willing her on and she felt his encouragement infuse her as she breathed in and found the strength to carry on.

It had been a hard life for Violet, she continued. A tough life filled with more grief than any one person should bear. But Gran had stoically taken it in her stride as people did in those days because that's the type of person she was raised to be and that's how people were made out here.

But it had been a rich life too. A life filled with love, despite the tragedies that had befallen her.

Because of the friends she had in the community and the activities she'd undertaken.

Pip talked about how blessed she was to be her grand-daughter – how Gran had taught her to cook fairy cakes on a wood stove and how, as a young child, she'd watched her make butter from cream she'd separated from milk straight from the cow she'd milked herself, the way she'd always done.

And how her gran had taught her to sew first a straight line and then create something beautiful on a treadle sewing machine that her mum before her – her great grandmother – had bought in the nineteen-twenties when Gran was just a baby herself.

Finally she talked about her gran's disease, and how unfair it was that Gran had spent the last years of her life never recognising a familiar face. After the life she'd led, she had deserved better, but thankfully she'd been surrounded by love and caring support for as long as she'd needed.

She misted up about then, but somehow managed to finish by saying how lucky they had all been to know Violet. Then she retook her place between Fi and Tracey and they squeezed her hands and Trace whispered, 'not a dry eye in the house.' And Pip had to take her friend's word for it, because she'd been too blinded with tears for the last few minutes to see anything further than her notes.

THERE WAS tea and biscuits after the service and another hour flashed by in a whirl of conversation and condolences before the cortege moved off to the cemetery.

The sun shone down hot and harsh, the air was still and the flies sticky. The crowd had thinned only a little for the interment but Luke somehow found the space to get near enough that his hand brushed hers as they walked to the graveside. It was the fleetest of touches – anyone watching would think it so brief as to be accidental – but it made her skin tingle and sent warmth blooming inside. She ached for him to touch her again. 'How're you doing?' he asked.

She smiled up at him. 'Getting there. Can we talk later?'

'Sure. Sorry I was late. Truck broke down.'

'Okay. Later.'

He smiled and gave her shoulders a squeeze and she felt her insides light up. It was good having him here. He was solid. Real. And she needed both those attributes today, as she said a final farewell to Gran, and where the possibility of learning the identity of her real father shimmered in the air like the heat haze in the distance.

It was a big day with the potential to get even bigger.

That was why her heart was hammering so loudly in her chest.

No other reason.

FINALLY THE SHORT graveside ceremony was over, the last floral tribute thrown, the last song played, and everyone repaired to the hotel for a drink in celebration of Violet's life. Adam Rogers worked his way through the crowd towards her.

'Great eulogy,' he said. 'And you're looking good, as usual, Pip.'

She smiled. She was wearing the same blue dress she'd worn to the christening, figuring it hardly mattered if she wore it again, though after Sunday it and her shoes had needed a decent clean. 'Thank you.' He looked pretty good too, but she wasn't about to tell him that. No more flirting. It wasn't fair. She'd been using him as a human shield to protect herself from Luke, telling herself the attention was nice, but enough was enough.

'So,' he continued, 'when are we going to get together for that drink?'

'What's that in your hand?' she said looking at his glass. 'A rabbit?'

He quirked up one side of his mouth, revealing a dimple. 'No, I meant with just the two of us. You and me.'

'Look, Adam, I'm sorry. It would only be wasting your time.'

'You're not interested.'

She gave a shake of her head. 'I'm sorry.'

'Is it Luke?'

Yes and no. *Concentrate on the no.*

'Like I said, I'm going home in two days.'

Adam sighed. 'So it is Luke. Thought as much.'

'What?' She replayed the conversation over in her head. What part of "I'm going home in two days" sounded like 'it's Luke'?

'I saw the way you looked at him over at the cemetery.' He shrugged. 'Actually thought I had a chance with you this time too. I guess Prince Charming missed his chance with Cinderella on Sunday, eh, getting called out like that?'

She laughed uncomfortably and shook her head. Surely he was reading too much into a few stray glances. 'That's really not how it is. It's just I'm going back to New York Friday, that's all.'

'Well, give my regards to your cute flatmate when you get home. The one in the blanket and the hat.'

'Carmen,' Pip asked, having a hard time keeping up. 'I'll give her your number if you like. You can pass on your regards yourself.'

'Yeah?' he said, already putting his beer down and reaching for a pen to write it down on a coaster. 'I'll do that.'

FROM THE OTHER side of the bar, Luke watched Pip and Adam. He was in a group of three or four guys he knew from his footy days – he wasn't paying attention – and every now and then they'd say something and he'd nod or grunt but most of the time he'd say nothing and he was pretty sure they'd forgotten he was even here. Which was good, because now he could concentrate on Pip.

Adam was still standing too close for his liking, but at least he wasn't draping his arm around her like he had on Sunday. And she wasn't smiling up at him like he was the best thing since sliced bread either.

Interesting.

Mind you, if Adam did slip his arm around her shoulders, what the hell could he do about it anyway? It wasn't like he could march over and tell him to get his hands off. It wasn't like they were together.

It was sex. *Just sex.* Maybe if he kept telling himself that he'd believe it.

Yeah, right. He downed the rest of his beer. How the hell was that supposed to work?

'You're here, then,' said Jean Cutting, shouldering into the circle so that she was next to him, a glass of moscato in one hand, a bite-sized sausage roll wearing a dollop of tomato sauce in the other.

'I'm here,' he agreed, dragging his eyes away from the scene on the other side of the bar where Adam was busy writing something down. Pip's phone number? Her address in New York? What else could he be writing down? 'Wouldn't be right not to pay my respects.'

'Oh yes. Dear old Vi.' Jean took a sip of her wine and looked in the direction he'd been staring. 'Still, must be nice to catch up with Pip. You two must have a lot of things to discuss. Old times. Good times.' Luke looked around, expecting any minute to see Sheila Ferguson with her shopping trolley, preparing to block his way out and make it a tag team match.

'We've chatted some, sure.' That was all she was getting.

'You think there's any chance Pip will stay home for good this time?'

Finally a question where he didn't have to beat about the bush. 'Nope. Not a one.'

'Oh, such a shame. You two used to be such good friends. We used to think –'

'Where did you find that sausage roll, Mrs Cutting? I'm starving.'

'Just over on the buffet, Luke,' she said, her sausage roll pointing the way. 'And do call me Jean.'

IT WAS after seven by the time everyone filtered away and they made it back to the farm, Chloe cranky and fretful after another long day out, and Tracey and Pip tired after sharing so many memories.

Craig was wearing his apron and was busy turning fish fingers under the smoking grill for his and the boys' dinner. He looked up with a smile when the women came in. He blinked, the smile getting tangled up in a frown when Luke followed them. He eyed them suspiciously. 'What gives?'

'The funeral was just beautiful, as it happens' said Tracey, rolling her eyes. 'Thanks for asking. I'll just change Chloe and give you a hand.'

Craig looked remorsefully at Pip. 'Aw, sorry Pip, I should have asked that first. How'd it go?'

'Beautifully,' she said, letting him off the hook. 'I'm glad to have it behind us. Luke's just helping me out with something. Did Trace tell you? I've got a lead who my father might be.'

He straightened. 'Oh, maybe that's why Trace called earlier. I was entertaining the head honcho from Adelaide and couldn't take the call. What kind of lead?'

'Ever hear of a bloke called Colin Armistead?' Luke said. 'I figure the Ag store must have accounts with just about everyone in the district.'

Craig screwed up his mouth as he frowned. He gave his head a decisive shake. 'Can't say as I have. Why?'

'All we've got is a note from this guy called Colin Armistead. It looks like he paid off Pip's mum before she married Gerald. This is going back more than thirty years mind, so it could be a stretch.'

Craig shook his head, slower this time. 'You sure he's from around here?'

'No idea where he's from. Pip's been checking phone numbers this morning and I did some searching online. We're about to go over to the B&B and compare notes.'

'Oh, well,' Craig said, as pulled the fish fingers out a second time, gave them an assessing glance before pulling the tray free. 'You can do that here if you like.' He looked over to see Pip and Luke exchanging glances and hastily back-tracked. 'Then again, you might want to avoid feeding time at the zoo and compare notes over there.' He cleared his throat. 'Good thinking.'

Trace reappeared a few minutes later. 'Chloe's exhausted, poor love.' She looked around the smoky kitchen. 'Where did Pip and Luke disappear to?'

'Apparently they're "comparing notes" over at the B&B.'

'Oh,' Trace said, with a glance out the window. 'Is that what they call it these days?' And then she sighed wistfully as the boys bowled into the kitchen and were told to go wash up by their dad. 'Lucky them.'

'Hey,' said Craig, sounding miffed as he divided the fish fingers between three plates. 'Just say the word. I'm always good for a bit of note comparing.'

'What are you comparing?' asked Callan, all washed up, taking his place at the table, looking eager.

Ben swung all gangly limbed into the room behind him, looking mistrustfully from his mum to his dad. 'Seriously guys, forget he asked. You don't have to answer that.'

'You're not the boss of me!' protested his little brother, pouting. 'I asked a question!'

'Here,' said Ben, spearing a fish finger with his fork and flicking it onto his brother's plate. 'Have a fish finger.'

'Ooh,' said Callan, promptly forgetting all about his question as he dug in.

CHAPTER 25

*T*he walk across the yard seemed to last forever and Pip had to check herself from breaking into a run, knowing someone might happen to glance out a window or one of the kids might wander by on the way to dinner. All day she'd been aching to be alone with Luke again, but she'd done the right thing when they left the wake. She'd come home with Tracey while Luke had followed in his ute.

So right now she was desperate for alone time.

That's what Adam had seen in her eyes at the cemetery, she rationalised. Lust. Pure out-and-out lust. After the session she and Luke had enjoyed yesterday, that was hardly a surprise. And after the week she'd had, who could blame her for wanting a little escape?

'Did you learn anything new today?' she asked, her breath catching as he did that thing with his swinging hand again so it brushed against hers as he walked, his fingers almost catching hers before swinging right on by. A tantalising promise of things to come. An unmistakeable hint that he was feeling this same desperate urge to rush.

'I learned you deliver a mean eulogy.'

'Thanks, but that wasn't what I meant.'

'And I learned how much I like that dress.'

She blinked. 'Really?'

'Well, maybe how much I want to peel it off you.'

She gasped, all the muscles between her thighs clenching down. Hard. 'What about Colin Armistead?'

'Nope,' he said, catching her hand this time and raising it to his mouth to kiss. 'He can leave his frock on.'

'I'm serious,' she said, as she unlocked the door.

'Yeah,' he said, as he slammed the door behind them and pushed her up hard against it. 'So am I.'

And she forgot all about Colin Armistead with or without a dress as Luke's hot mouth crashed down on hers and his seeking hands rendered every inch of her body an erogenous zone.

'Do you know what it's like,' he gasped, lifting his mouth from hers for just one second, 'to watch you for hours and not be allowed to touch? Do you know how hard that is?'

She knew. She felt it too, this desperate need to touch this man who had been not merely unavailable, but forbidden to her. And whoever said that forbidden fruit tastes sweeter was right. She couldn't get enough of him.

They never made it to the bed. He made love to her hard up against the door, and she

was breathless by the time he let her down, breathless and boneless and utterly spent.

Utterly satisfied.

And it occurred to her that it was almost a shame she was leaving so soon. Two days before she got on that plane back to New York City, and suddenly it didn't seem anywhere near long enough.

THEY WERE SITTING NAKED TOGETHER in the big old iron bed, Luke with his arm around her shoulders and nothing new to report after a morning spent collecting grain and fixing broken down trucks, while Pip went through the list of calls she'd made with Trace.

The room was lit by two scented candles, softly flickering, and a solitary lamp, a lace shade throwing patterns of light and shadow around the walls. There was just enough light to read.

'This is the most positive lead to date,' she said, after recounting the endless calls and the dead ends and left messages. 'Although I don't know if it's actually going to help. Marlene Armistead in Fremantle, who sounds like she's in her eighties. Her husband's name was Colin. He died a few years back. I've got a feeling he might be that same Colin you found the death notice for.'

'Oh.' His voice was flat.

'She couldn't talk because her carer had just arrived to take her out for the day, but she's asked me to call her tomorrow, around twelve, her time. And I'm not sure if it's anything, or if she's just lonely and wants to talk to somebody, but she mentioned they'd lived in Adelaide for a few years before Colin retired.'

He nodded, eyebrows raised. 'Okay.'

'And that,' she said, tapping her pen on her notepad, 'is the best lead I've got so far.'

'Okay. So you'll give her a call?'

'Sure. I mean, it might be nothing, but I have to try.'

He looked like he was about to say something but stopped. 'What?' she asked.

He shook his head. 'Don't go getting your hopes up too high, Pip. There are no guarantees. There's a chance you're never going to find an answer.'

'I know.' She sighed against his shoulder. It was so

comfortable leaning against Luke, the steady beat of his heart solid and sure - like Luke himself.

One more night, that's all they had left. It would have to be enough.

And then she remembered ...

'Oh, and Luke?'

'Yeah?'

'Trace is planning a picnic lunch on Moonta beach for my last day tomorrow.' Her teeth found her lip. 'Would you be able to come?'

Warning sirens went off in his head. 'A picnic.'

'Sure, it'll be fun.'

'What? Like a date or something?'

'No! Like old friends getting together for a goodbye lunch. It's not like we'd be there as a couple.'

'Oh I get it. It'll be like here, where we're in bed together, only not as a couple.' He couldn't help it. There was no stopping the hint of bitterness from creeping into his voice.

'It's only a picnic, Luke.'

'Yeah, like this is only sex.'

'Exactly. So will you come?'

Of course she was going to ignore the irony. He ran a hand through his hair and over a whiskery jaw. He'd once imagined spending the rest of his life with Pip, and here they were in a romantic little B&B with its pink walls and lace cushions with candles flickering like it was some kind of tryst.

She was the woman who had dumped him, who'd walked away and cut him off completely, left him for a new life on the other side of the world. What the hell was he even doing here?

Having sex, the answer came back. *Great sex.* That's what he was doing.

He sighed, long and hard. 'Why not?' he said, because if he

could manage *just sex*, he sure as hell could manage *only a picnic*. Not that he understood any of it.

Except that she was leaving again. Just when he was getting to like having her around again. When he'd just started feeling like she might belong in his world again. *Don't go there.*

'Of course, I'll come.'

For all the pain he knew was coming, he wasn't about to bring it on any earlier. Friday would come soon enough. But he'd cope. The same way he always had. And he'd have a little storehouse of Pip memories to play back if he got lonely. Might as well add a few more to the playlist.

Pip set her notebook and pen down on the side table, and snuggled in close. He kind of wished she wouldn't that, because it made it harder to remember this was *just sex*. But he liked it too much to object. 'Fancy saving some more water?' she said, and he looked down at her. 'There's a spa in the bathroom. A big one.'

'Yeah?'

'Interested?'

'I haven't had a bath for ages.'

She crinkled her nose. 'I didn't like to say.' And she laughed when he flipped her over his lap to smack her bare bottom.

She squealed a protest. 'And there was me going to offer to wash you. If you wanted, I mean.'

'Maybe I'll let you off with a warning this time, then,' he said, and she scooted off to run the bath.

When the bath was half full, he grabbed her wrist and caught her with the bath gel in her hand ready to pour under the stream of steaming water. 'No bubbles,' he said. 'I don't want you hidden under the foam. I want to see you.'

I want to be able to remember every single little thing about you.

She washed him, like she'd promised, and when it was his turn to soap her skin he slid his hands over every curve, every indentation, committing every sweet part of her to memory. And only when they were mad with the touch and taste of each other, only when they were at fever pitch and she was whimpering with need, did he seat her over him and slowly, achingly, draw her down.

IT WAS DARK, the water cooling, by the time they emerged from the big spa, and they wrapped themselves in white fluffy robes from the wardrobe and turned off the lights and lay on the small patch of grass between the rose bushes, and watched the night-time display of the endlessly shifting cosmos.

'We don't have stars in New York City,' she said softly in the darkness, her head on his shoulder, gazing upwards. An owl hooted somewhere close by and the old windmill squeaked as a lick of wind coaxed it into motion. 'We have stars on the ceilings of stretch limousines and we have stars above the beds in posh hotels to remind us that they're up there somewhere, but we don't have stars. At least, nothing you can see. Nothing like this.'

'Maybe it's true what they say,' he said, drawing her closer.

'What do they say?'

She felt his lips kiss her hair. 'You can't have everything.'

She said nothing for a while, just lay there thinking. She didn't want everything, if that's what he was suggesting.

She just wanted to be back in her apartment with Carmen and for things to settle down and be normal again.

She wanted to get that promotion.

And she wanted this tangled heavy feeling in her chest to unravel itself and go away.

And as she lay beside him feeling the steady drumbeat of his heart beneath her ear, she thought, what was so wrong with a girl wanting a few stars?

CHAPTER 26

The sapphire waters of Moonta Bay sparkled under
the December sun. Pip breathed in the fresh salt
air and drank in the view, the wide white expanse of sand,
the belt of ruddy shore dotted with rock pools, and the long
crooked jetty. It was the perfect day, the temperature in the
high twenties, with not a cloud in the sky, and there were
ripples rather than waves at the water's edge, so the foam
looked like rows of lace edging along a pale blue border to
the deep blue coverlet of the sea.

Tracey's boys were busy trying to herd the twins around
the rock pools, and there were shrieks and whoops and
laughter as Turbo barked happily in pursuit, while Tracey
and Sally packed what was left of the picnic back into plastic
containers. They'd dined on sandwiches and cold chicken
and cake and washed it down with lemon cordial and soft
drinks under the big beach shade and now there was little
more left than crumbs and chicken bones. Even the
squawking seagulls had finally given up fighting for scraps
and flown off in search of new horizons.

Fi was sitting in a corner, sipping on a flask of ginger tea and setting Chloe's rocker gently rocking with her toes, giving wan smiles and generally doing her best to look more cheerful than she felt, while Luke was doing a run to the rubbish bin.

Pip sat on the rug, feeling the peace of the ocean and the warm air wrap around her as she took it all in. Tomorrow she would get back on that plane, and this place would once again be relegated to her past. Strange how once she couldn't wait to get back on that plane, while now . . .

She felt a pang inside her chest. She'd miss it more than she'd realised. She'd miss the dry air and the endless sky and the wide open spaces. Miss the awe-inspiring night-time display of stars. Miss Tracey and Fi and the gorgeous bundle that was Chloe.

And then Luke returned and bent down to pop the lid on the esky and pull out a cool drink and she got a glorious view of his tight butt and the play of muscles in his arms and back.

'Pip?' he said, catching her staring, and adding a smile. 'Anything you'd like.'

She blinked and shook her head. She looked at her watch, realised it would be twelve in Perth and sprang to her feet. 'I have to make a phone call. Excuse me a minute, guys. I'll be right back.'

'Who're you calling?' asked Trace, as Chloe started fussing for a feed.

'That woman in Perth – Marlene Armistead. The one who asked me to call her back.'

Sally looked over, a crease in her brow. 'Who?'

Tracey explained the note Luke and Pip had found as she picked Chloe up from the bouncer and sat down in a chair to feed her. Sally's troubled eyes swung to Pip. 'And you think this person paid your mother off because she was expecting you.'

'It looks that way. Trouble is, this Colin died a few years

back, so I'm not sure what she's going to be able to tell me. Anyway . . .'

Sally nodded, her features pinched. 'Yeah, you better go make that call. I think I'll take a walk,' she said, and headed towards the water's edge, her long maxi skirt floating around her legs in the gentle breeze.

LUKE WATCHED Pip strolling across the sands, holding the mobile to her ear, coming to a stop when someone at the other end picked up.

'What's going on?' Fi asked, coming to stand next to him.

'She's just making that call.'

'No. Not that. Between you and Pip. Are you guys back together?'

His head swung around. 'What gives you that idea?'

She rolled her eyes. 'Oh, come on, Luke. I might be pregnant, but I'm not brain dead. The fact you're even here suggests something is going on. Not to mention the way you guys can't keep your eyes off each other.'

Or our hands.

He looked at Trace, who knew, and who was listening as she fed Chloe, and he figured Fi was going to find out one way or another, so what would it hurt to tell the truth now? 'You ever hear that expression, "making hay while the sun shines"?'

'Is that what you're doing, then? Making hay?'

He smiled, though his gut ran cold at the thought of Pip leaving. 'More or less.'

'But she's still going tomorrow?'

'Oh, yeah.'

Fi flung the rest of her ginger tea on the sands. 'Well, that just sucks.'

Doesn't it just?

'You should talk to her, Luke,' Fi said, sounding determined. 'Make her see that she belongs here.'

He huffed. 'You think that'd work?'

'You have to try.'

He was about to shake his head and tell her it was pointless and that she'd never listen to him anyway, when suddenly he thought about the emptiness of tomorrow after she'd gone, and all the empty tomorrows to come, and thought, dammit, he didn't want them empty.

He wanted Pip in each and every one of them. Because damn it to hell and back, he still loved her. God!

Pip was still on her call when Sally wandered back from her walk, looking troubled. 'You okay, Mum?' said Trace. 'You should have brought a hat.'

Sally smiled. 'I'll be fine.'

'I think we're all a bit down,' offered Trace. 'Not knowing when we'll see Pip again. Especially if she gets this new hotshot promotion of hers.'

'Yes,' said Sally, as she sat down on the blanket. 'That's it.'

Luke straightened. 'She's coming,' he whispered, and every face turned to Pip's, searching for any hint in her expression. 'Well?' Luke said, when she got close.

PIP FLUNG her phone down on the blanket and herself after it, running her fingers through her hair. 'That was twenty minutes of my life I'll never get back.'

'You talked for ages and you got nothing?' said Fi.

'What did she say?' asked Trace.

'Everything. Nothing. I heard about her bridge club every Wednesday, and what Meals on Wheels serves from Monday to Friday, and what her neighbour thinks of the new skirt she bought yesterday at Millers. She's lovely really, but she's lonely. She had the chance to tell someone her life story and she took it.'

'But what did she say about her husband? What did he do in Adelaide all those years?'

'That was useless too. He was with some church. Pretty high up by the sounds. Moderator or something. Not that it matters.'

'What church?' asked Sally softly.

'It's pointless. I just have to accept that I'm never going to find out who my father was.'

'What church?'

And everyone looked at Sally, sitting on the blanket with her elbows on her knees and her face a tightly drawn mask.

Pip shook her head, thrown. 'Um, the United Christian Church or the Christian Unity Church. At least I think it was something like that, but my folks were never religious. We never went to church.'

'Hey,' piped up Fi quietly. 'Wasn't the old church in Paskeville a Christian Unity Church? The one that's now a gallery?'

'Yeah,' said Trace. 'Yeah, it was. Wasn't that the one where Dad's father was the minister? Mum?'

But Sally had slumped her shaking head into her hands. 'Oh my god, I am such a fool. Such a damned fool!'

'Mum!' said Trace, thrusting baby Chloe in Fi's direction before dropping down on her knees and putting her arm around Sally's quaking shoulders. 'What is it?'

'A happy coincidence,' she said through lips stretched tight, 'when you two girls were born three weeks apart. A happy coincidence.'

And Pip felt her blood run cold. 'What? Tell me.'

'Only it wasn't a coincidence. I always wondered, you

know, always there were questions in my mind, but if I ever broached the subject, if I so much as *hinted* that our girls could almost be sisters, Deidre insisted the baby was Gerald's. It was like she'd been sworn to secrecy or something.'

What?

Pip and Luke exchanged glances. He came and stood next to where she kneeled on the rug and put his hand to the back of her head, and she leant her head back against the welcoming warmth and the strength of his touch, grateful he was there, because right now the sands beneath her were shifting and she need something solid and safe to lean against.

'I knew he and Dee were going out and that she was crazy about him,' Sally continued on a hiccup, 'I knew it and so when he told me that she'd turned him down, that if she really loved him, she'd sleep with him, I thought . . . I was so stupid and naive and foolish . . . I thought it was my chance to show him that I loved him too. That I loved him better. And he was so charismatic and so handsome. He was the minister's son and he was in charge of the church youth group. All the girls wanted him, but I *had* him. I really thought he was mine.'

'Mum,' Trace soothed.

Sally put her head up then, staring blindly out towards the sea.

'I guess he must have told her, because she didn't speak to me for a month, by which time I'd found out I was pregnant and my parents had demanded he marry me.' She sobbed. 'It was all arranged and the next thing I knew, Dee and Gerald were getting married too – though he was ten years older than us all and we thought she was mad. Until she started to show not long after the wedding, just about the same time I did. That was when I started to suspect.' She turned her distraught face to Pip. 'Oh Pip, my darling, can you ever forgive me?'

And Pip couldn't answer. She was too busy remembering the warning her mother had given her – a warning that had come from her own broken heart, 'Be careful who you fall in love with,' and suddenly she understood what her mother had meant. She hadn't been warning her off Luke. She'd been warning her daughter not to fall in love with a charmer – a man with no substance, a man with no conscience.

Pip nodded at Sally and then looked across at Trace and Trace looked at her and a throwaway line of Luke's zapped through her mind – *Tracey's got blue eyes* – as numbly she got to her feet and staggered to where her friend was similarly rising. 'We share the same father,' she said, in awe and wonder, and even the knowledge that their birth father had been a useless womanising bastard didn't matter right now, because . . . 'You're my sister.'

'Half-sister? We're half-sisters?'

Pip burst into tears as they fell into each other's arms. 'I have a sister!' They hugged and laughed and cried until Pip looked up with a start, her hands over her mouth as she realised. 'Oh, my god, I have a niece! And two nephews! And a brother-in-law!'

She dropped down to where Sally was still hunched over, and threw her arms around the woman. 'Thank you, Sally,' she said, and squeezed her tight.

Sally blinked up at her, all puffy eyed and tear streaked. 'You don't –' she licked her lips, '– hate me?'

She laughed. 'How could I? I thought I was alone, but now I have family. How could I possibly hate you?'

Sally wrapped her arm around Pip's forearm and squeezed. 'I always said you were the daughter I never had.'

She had too. Pip looked back over the times they'd been together, the times she'd seen her watching the two girls, almost as if she'd been studying them. And who could blame her if she'd wondered all these years?

'You've always been there for me,' she said, giving her another squeeze. 'Always.'

The boys ran up in a spray of sand and squeals. They took one look at the hugging women and the stunned faces in the group, and stopped dead. 'What's wrong?'

'Come on, boys,' said Luke. 'Let's go get an ice-cream.'

CHAPTER 27

*B*ack at the house the mood around Tracey and Craig's big dining table was reflective, everybody still shell-shocked, still trying to absorb the news and come to terms with this new paradigm.

Pip cuddled Chloe, wondering why it should feel so different holding her now that she knew she was her aunt – a blood relative – and not just her godmother. 'All this time I thought my family had never had anything to do with church.'

Luke was leaning against the sink, his hands on the bench at his sides. 'This might explain why.'

She blinked, because it did make a kind of sense. 'It might. Gran loved her hymns. She watched *Songs of Praise* every Sunday. She must have missed going to church terribly.'

'The church closed not long after that,' said Sally, staring blindly at a mug of coffee she was clutching in front of her like a lifeline. 'Jacob and I were married faster than you can say shotgun wedding and then they shipped Reverend Everett back to Adelaide. They said the congregation was shrinking, which was true, but it all seemed very hasty.

Maybe they were worried that something else would wriggle out of the woodwork. Maybe they wanted to cut and run before a scandal hit.'

'Wow.' Fi drained her tea and put her cup down on the table with a thunk. 'I don't know how you did it, Sally. How did you ever manage to keep this to yourself all these years?'

Sally shook her head. 'What could I say? I didn't know, not for sure. Dee always maintained that Gerald was Pip's father.' She sighed glumly, 'Besides, I was too ashamed. I'd betrayed a friend's trust. I'd tried to steal my best friend's boyfriend away from her and for one selfish, blinkered moment, I thought I'd succeeded.' She gave an ironic laugh. 'What an awful, bitchy thing to do. What a fool.'

She shifted her gaze from her mug to Pip. 'My actions nearly ruined our friendship. It wasn't just that first month Dee didn't talk to me, it soured things between us for a long time. I think it was only when she saw how unhappy I was with Jacob, what a jerk he was being, that she extended the olive branch. She didn't have to say anything, but I could see she felt sorry for me. That she forgave me.'

She sighed. 'And later, after he was gone, we slowly got back to a place like where we'd been before. Not that things were ever the same. How could they be, after what I'd done?'

Pip nodded, the pieces of the puzzle that had mystified her for so long slowly fitting together. Her earliest memories of Tracey were at playgroup, and there'd been no hint of friction between their mothers that a toddler might notice. They'd always been the best of friends. Or so she'd assumed.

'And my dad? I mean Gerald. How did he get roped into all this?'

'He was a widower. A friend of the family. I guess it was convenient for all concerned. At the time I was horrified – he seemed so old to me back then – but as time went by, and especially after your brother, Trent, was born, I could see how good he was for her. She deserved a good marriage. She deserved to be happy. And he loved her.'

Around the table there was silence.

'You shouldn't be so hard on yourself,' said Luke gruffly, though he was looking right at Pip and there was something churning in the depths of his blue eyes.

'You deserve to be happy too,' agreed Tracey, with a sniff.

'Yeah,' Luke said. 'You do.' But he was still staring at Pip, and she didn't like the way his turbulent eyes made her feel. Like *she* was the one who'd done something wrong way back then.

Sally shook her head. 'Reap what you sow,' she quoted. 'I think we get what we deserve.'

Ben wandered into the kitchen from the lounge room where the boys were all playing video games. He glanced over the empty stove and opened the oven door. 'What's for dinner?'

'Spaghetti bolognese.'

'Yeah?' said Ben, frowning. 'When?'

And Trace looked at the clock on the wall, and said, 'Oh god, is that the time?' and headed for the fridge.

THE PARTY BROKE up after that, Fi taking the twins and giving a drained-looking Sally a ride home. Tracey and Luke stood by the gate as Pip hugged both women for a long time. 'Will we see you tomorrow?' asked Fi.

She shook her head. 'My flight leaves at nine-thirty in the morning. I'm going to be leaving pretty early to get to the airport in time as it is.'

Fi's face pulled tight. 'So this really is goodbye, then.' And Pip pulled her close and hugged her again. 'It's been so good having you back with us,' Fi said, 'I wish you weren't going. I wish you could stay. I wish . . . Oh, I just wish . . .'

'I know. You take care of yourself.' She looked down in the direction of Fi's still flat tummy, 'All of you in there, okay!'

'You will come back? And not stay away so long next time?'

'Of course I will.'

Fi threw a look over to Luke and said, 'Luke?' And he nodded but before Pip could ask what that little exchange was all about, Sally reached out and put a hand to her arm. 'Take care, Pip. I'm really sorry – about everything.'

Pip pulled her close for another hug. 'Don't be. It's a relief to know the truth at last.' She nodded. 'I hope you feel better about it now.'

Sally shrugged and gave a weak smile. 'Right now, I'm just relieved it's finally out in the open. And that you can forgive me.'

'Please, there is absolutely nothing to forgive.' And the older woman nodded and gave her a final squeeze before climbing into the front seat.

The twins piled rowdily into the back as Tracey gave her mum a hug goodbye with a promise to call later, and then they waved Fi's Subaru off down the driveway.

Pip felt something tug tight inside her, and an all too familiar prick of tears as the car disappeared in a cloud of dust. 'Do you think Sally will be okay?' she asked over her shoulder, to give herself a chance to get her leaky eyes under control.

'I don't know,' Trace said, walking up to her to watch the dust rise behind the car. 'She's bottled all that up for so many years, it's bound to rock her foundations a bit. I'll give her a call after dinner. Speaking of which, I better get back to my bolognese. What you are you and Luke going to do now?

You're more than welcome to stay for dinner, but I'm not naive enough to think you might not want to disappear somewhere together.'

'Up to you, Pip,' Luke said, in a voice that sounded almost like a threat. 'Eat here or we can catch a bite somewhere else.'

A sliver of premonition skittered down her spine. Something wasn't right. The words sounded normal but there was a quality to his voice that hinted of things unspoken.

He'd been weird in the kitchen too, when he'd been talking to Sally but looking right at her.

The hairs on the back of her neck shivered and stood to attention.

'So, what's it to be, Pip?' Trace asked, missing the sudden crackle in the atmosphere. 'Dinner for two or feeding time at the zoo?' She raised her eyebrows. 'I know what I'd choose, although we'd love for you to stay, being your last night and all.'

It was the easiest decision she'd ever made. She'd just today learned her oldest friend was also her half-sister. Just discovered she had a family, where she'd thought she had none. When every next of kin question on every form for the last fifteen years had been answered with a bold stroke of her pen. Not applicable.

Besides, it wasn't dinner she wanted from Luke. It was the after dinner she'd been imagining. The replay of last night's passion. Not conversation. Not when he looked like he wanted to talk . . .

'I'd like to have dinner with my family on my last night here, if that's all right? Maybe I could help feed the animals.'

'Yay!' Tracey said, answering with her own wide grin and an arm around her waist to pull her in tight. 'That is more than all right. And then, I suppose, Luke will be wanting to give you a hand over in the B&B. To pack, I mean.'

Pip cast a sideways look at Luke. 'Well there is –' *just one tiny case* '– so much to pack.'

He shrugged, with his hands in his jean pockets and the slightest curl to his lips 'Sure.'

'Big surprise,' Trace said with a grin, hooking her arm in Pip's and leading her towards the house.

But Pip knew she hadn't misread him. Something was wrong. Where was the man who'd taken her to heaven in the spa last night, and then cradled her in his arms as they'd lain down on the lawn and watched the stars parade across the sky? Where was the man who'd stood next to her at lunch today to support her when her world was teetering off balance?

He almost seemed like a stranger.

Offhand and brusque.

Like he'd been when she'd first arrived.

At that moment, Craig's car turned in to the driveway and Luke peeled off to wait for his mate. Pip put thoughts of him aside for a moment and took a deep breath, steeling herself for something that right now was much more pressing, something that had been hovering at the back of her mind ever since lunch at the beach and the big revelation. 'Before dinner, Trace, there's something I need to do.'

'What is it?' she asked, as they entered the kitchen filled with the hum of the exhaust fan and the scent of tomatoes and basil and garlic, as Tracey picked up a wooden spoon to stir the simmering sauce.

'I want to call my father.'

CHAPTER 28

Tracey stopped dead, wooden spoon in her hand. 'You want to call Jacob? You have got to be kidding.' Her voice was cold, her words smoking like they'd been squeezed through dry ice. 'Why would you want to talk to that bastard? You know what he was like. You heard what kind of low life he is. I hadn't even been born and he was sleeping with every woman he could.'

'I know. But now that I know who my father actually is, I can't just leave it there. I have to follow through. I have to finish this thing.'

'Do you? Really?' Tracey's blue eyes appealed, beseeching her to put an end to this madness. 'Why?'

Pip held up her hands. 'I don't know that I understand it either. I guess I just want to talk to him. To let him know that *I* know he's my father. Maybe just to let him know that his sordid little secret is out and he didn't get away with it. Does that make any sense?'

'No. It makes no sense at all. But you go right ahead and call. I'm over him. The scumbag couldn't be bothered coming over for my wedding to walk me down the aisle, even though I'd gone to the trouble of tracking him down. I gave Mum a nervous breakdown and nearly got myself disinherited in the process. I thought he might care that his daughter was getting married, but he soon burst that little bubble, I can tell you. But why should I be the only one disappointed?'

'Oh, Trace . . .'

'No.' Tracey shook her head emphatically as she held up a hand, the wooden spoon in the other stirring the simmering sauce purposefully. 'Don't take my word for it. You do what you need to do and I'll fix dinner. And because I really don't want you wasting too much time on this, I've actually got his number written down in the address book on the hall table. If he's still got the same one, that is.'

'Why would you keep his number if you hate him so much?'

She sniffed, screwing up her nose. 'It's like you were saying the first night you were here; like it or not, he is my father. Just in case there was some medical emergency with the kids and I needed to find out some medical history in a hurry. Kind of an insurance policy. I'm hoping that because I've got it, I'll never need to use it.'

She threw Pip an apologetic smile. 'I'm sorry, Pip, I should never have discounted you wanting the same thing. And I should have figured that you'd want to try to contact him yourself. He is your biological father. Our father.' She gave an apologetic smile. 'You know, this sister thing might take me a little getting used to.'

Pip came over and hugged the woman who was now her sister but who would always, first and foremost, be her friend. 'I know. And thanks for understanding.'

'If you want some privacy, use my bedroom. I think the boys are still in the lounge.'

Pip gave her a final squeeze and was heading for the hall

when Trace called behind her, 'Oh, but don't look for him under E. His number's filed under A.'

'A?'

'For arsehole.' She gave a wan smile. 'What else?'

THE AFTERNOON SUN lit Tracey's bedroom through lace curtains that wafted on the light breeze. The room was more a blend of the masculine and feminine than the B&B's bedroom, the walls painted in a moss green, the furniture a deep mahogany and the coverlet on the bed snowy white, a lace trimmed cushion resting between the pillows the only real feminine touch.

The effect was restful. Should have been restful. But somewhere on the end of the line a phone was ringing and Pip clung on tight to her mobile, her heart tripping, feeling more nervous than she'd been on her seventh round inter-view with the investment bank all those years ago, when she'd been so desperate to prove herself and win her first job. She'd been so determined to distance herself from the past that she would have taken a job on Mars if it had been offered.

And no wonder her palms were damp. She was about to talk to her biological father for the first time. The man who'd lain with her mother and made love – and Pip – with her. For all his faults, maybe he had once loved Deirdre. Maybe he still remembered her with some degree of fondness?

Suddenly the phone was picked up. She heard the sound of people talking and the clink of glass and laughter, like he was in a bar somewhere. She held her breath.

'Hello?' said a deep voice. A good voice, rich and deep and smooth. In spite of her doubts, she liked it.

'Is this, um, Jacob Everett?'

'Yes. Who is this?'

For a second she froze. 'My name is Pip,' she said, her heart pumping. 'I hope you don't mind me calling out of the blue like this –'

'Now why on earth would I mind you calling?'

She blinked. He sounded charming. He sounded like nothing she said would be too much trouble. More than that. His voice had gone down an octave and he sounded like he was interested.

'Who is it, Jake?' said a woman in the background, and he shooshed her and said, 'Tell me, honey, what can I do for you?'

Honey?

'I'm sorry, but you've got the wrong idea.'

'Who is it?' the woman insisted.

She heard a muffled 'Shut up!' like he'd turned his phone away, but nowhere near enough to miss the snarl in his voice. 'Sorry sweetie,' he said, all velvet over chocolate again. 'You were saying?'

And suddenly she wasn't nervous anymore.

'I heard you were a charmer,' she said, feeling emboldened.

She could swear she could hear him smile down the phone line. 'Did you now?'

'I also heard you're an arsehole. I didn't want to believe it, but I can see it's true.'

'Hey, who the hell is this?'

'Remember Paskeville, Jacob? Remember Sally Buxton and Tracey? Remember Deirdre Cooper? Well, I'm Deidre's daughter. Your daughter.'

The line went dead and Pip felt a part of her die with it.

And she sat there on the bed a while waiting for a frantic heart-rate to slow and for warmth to return to her flesh, and remembered how Tracey had said it was better not to know your father was a scumbag, and thought that maybe she was right.

Because Gerald had been a great dad. She'd never needed to know about her real father, her scumbag father, the one who had left two women pregnant in short order and disgraced a church and who still hadn't managed to keep his dick in his pants, even when he was married to one of those women.

Who was still out whoring by the sounds of it.

Arsehole.

WHEN SHE RETURNED to the kitchen, Tracey turned from juggling pots of simmering sauce and bubbling pasta on the stove, took one look at Pip's crestfallen face and said, 'Oh, Pip.'

'I actually thought he'd be different,' she said. 'I really thought that if he ever loved Mum, he might have been happy to hear from me, just a little bit.' She shook her head. 'I was hoping . . .' She looked up at her friend. 'I'm an idiot aren't I?'

'Oh, come here, you.' Tracey pulled her into her arms, squeezing her tight. 'He was never good enough for any of us. But bugger him, because I love you, you crazy woman. I wish you didn't have to go and live so damned far away.'

And Pip smiled against her sister's shoulder, even as she felt that thing happening inside her, like she had when Fi had driven off, like something inside her was crumbling a little.

'You know, for what it's worth, Trace,' she said, touched by her display of affection, 'I think you've got this sister thing all worked out.'

'You reckon?'

She pulled back and looked at her beautiful blue eyed, blonde haired sister. 'And discovering I have you for a sister is just about the coolest thing that could have happened to me.' They hugged again and Pip laughed because what she'd said was true and a million times more important than some dropkick father who'd walked away from them both. And then she sniffed and swiped at her eyes and said, 'Now, how about I do something really useful and fix us a salad to go with that bolognese?'

It was only when she turned that she noticed Craig and Luke standing just inside the kitchen door. Craig was smiling and said, 'Well, some people sure are happy with themselves.'

Pip looked at Luke, at the grim set of his mouth and the damnation in his eyes, and knew for a fact that Craig wasn't talking about him.

CHAPTER 29

*L*ast night they'd barely made it inside the B&B before he'd taken her against the back of the door. Tonight he stood uncomfortably in the B&B, sucking up all the space with his broad shoulders and bad attitude.

Trace had chased her out when she'd tried to help clean up, telling her that Craig could help her stack the dishwasher because Pip needed 'to pack'. And Pip had wondered whether, once the two of them were alone, that Luke would be a little more friendly. A little less tense.

Apparently not.

She missed the fevered passion more than she cared to admit.

'Make yourself at home,' she said, feeling angry and miffed and confused and thinking she might as well start packing. It was just as well she was leaving. Even without having Luke tangled up in it all, things were getting way too complicated here, with the sudden revelation of the identity of her biological father and all the repercussions. Stupid! She'd known from day one she should avoid him.

Fool.

She pulled her case out from where she'd stashed it inside the wardrobe and unzipped it on the sofa, laying the half shells flat. She didn't dare put it on the bed. Even if he was in a bad mood, she wasn't mad enough to discourage him any more than he already seemed to be.

Because she ached for him. She'd thought they had one more night. And already she felt cheated. Because this wasn't the last night she'd imagined.

By the time she'd turned to gather the first load of clothes from the wardrobe, he was standing in the doorway, those wretched hands that she wanted to feel on her still jammed tight into his jean pockets.

She stopped and looked at his bleak, hard face. The lips and mouth that had taken her to heaven were now set in a thin, hard line as the silence stretched between them. 'Maybe you should just spit it out, Luke, instead of hovering like a black cloud.'

He sighed. 'What are you doing, Pip?'

She laughed. 'I'm flying to the moon. What does it look like I'm doing?'

'So you're still going?'

'Of course I'm going. I'm booked, aren't I?' She pulled out one drawer and dropped the contents unceremoniously into a corner of the open shell of her case.

'People have cancelled fights before.'

'Only when they change their mind.'

'I thought you might.'

She raised an eyebrow. 'Why would I want to do that? I've got a job to get back to. I have an interview on Monday.'

'You've just discovered you've got a sister and a niece and nephews and a brother-in-law!'

'And I'm excited about that. Of course, I am. But I still have to go back. I live in New York, remember? I have commitments.'

'And you have friends here who seem to hold you in much higher esteem than you do them.'

'That's rubbish.'

'Is it? You walk out of people's lives for years and years and then swan back in and expect everyone to cheer and say how wonderful and clever you are, and as soon as you've fed your ego you take off and leave everyone scratching their heads. What's so good about some place halfway around the world that you can't stay five minutes with the people who love you?'

Her eyes narrowed. 'This job means a lot to me. Don't try to take that away from me. Don't try to make out my life over there is worth nothing.'

'And what's your family worth? For god's sake, Pip, look at the gift you've just been given. You thought you had no connection to this place. You thought you were all alone. Well, now you've got family in spades. Don't throw your family away, now that you've found them.'

'So I'll come back. I'll visit.'

'Will you? When? It took your grandmother dying to get you back this time. What will it take next time? Chloe getting married? Will it be that long before you decide to leave your oh-so-perfect life and oh-so-important job in New York City and come back?'

'This is rubbish. I don't have to listen to this. I'm leaving in the morning. End of story.'

'You know what your problem is, Pip? Your problem is that you don't see what's right in front of your face. You sneak around the edges. You hide in the corners. You turn your face away so you can stay in the dark. All so you don't see the big fat truth that's sitting there right in front of your face.'

'Really. How interesting. And what is this big fat truth, seeing I'm doing such a good job of avoiding looking at it.'

'You can't let yourself be happy.'

'What?'

'It's not that complicated a concept, is it?'

'Oh, I imagined you were going to come up with some kind of revelation.'

'Isn't it?'

'Hardly. I smile. I laugh. There you go, you're wrong.'

'Like I said, you don't let yourself be happy. You deliberately cut yourself off from any chance to be happy. You walked away from me. You distanced yourself from your friends. You ran away from the people who loved you once before and you're still running now.'

She put a hand to her head. 'Give me a break. So you were my boyfriend once. Long, long, ago.'

'More than a boyfriend. We were lovers. We were going to be married.' He cocked his head. 'I asked you to marry me and you said yes. Remember that night out at the stone mounds, Pip? Remember making love under the stars and you telling me you'd love me forever? Remember that?'

'Do you think I'm ever going to forget that night? How could I? But that was before.'

'Yeah. Before you concocted a reason to hate me, because you had to, to justify walking away.'

'This is such rubbish. If you want to weasel out of what you did back then, that's fine, but don't expect me to come along to your little pity party.'

'You make it sound like I committed some major bloody crime!'

'You betrayed me! When I needed you the most, when I was at my lowest, you betrayed me.'

'I never betrayed you! You needed to believe it though.'

'Really. And why would that be?'

'Because you've been carrying around fifteen years of guilt about what happened that night.'

'Thank you Dr Spock. If I need a shrink I'll go see one. A qualified one.'

'But yours is the worst kind of guilt. Because you've spent the last fifteen years thinking you should have been in that car with them.'

She blinked up at him. 'Like I said. If I need a shrink –'

'That's why you won't let yourself be happy. You don't believe you deserve to be happy. I didn't realise it until Sally was talking today. She's had guilt eating away at her for more than thirty years. You want to talk about betrayal – look at what she's been carrying around. You heard what she said - you reap what you sow - like she actually believes she doesn't deserve to be happy. And you're just the same. You've buried your heart in a . . . in one of those bloody stone castles we used to build out there in the paddocks. And if anyone dares to get close, you send down the arrows and spears or retreat inside and hide. It's all because you think you should be dead and buried with the rest of your family, because you would have been if you hadn't snuck off to be with me that night instead.'

'Hey, I lied to them! I told them I was too sick to go to that Christmas party! But I should have been with them and I would have been, if I hadn't been with you.'

'But you were with me and you survived! But the way you choose to live, you might as well be lying under that slab. Do you think your parents – your brother – would have wanted that for you? Or would they want you to be happy and to make the most of your life, and honour their lives by you living yours to the full? But no. You choose to lock yourself away in some numb, unemotional shadow-land half a world away from the people who love you, where nobody can touch you, where you tell yourself you can't make love, you have sex. Where you can't even allow yourself a boyfriend but have to engage some kind of fuck buddy –'

Crack!

Her palm connected with his cheek, leaving her hand stinging with the impact and a violent slash of red across his face.

He put one hand to his cheek, rubbing the place where her hand had left its mark. 'Too close to the truth for comfort?'

'How dare you?' She was rigid with fury. 'You know nothing about me or my life.'

'I know you were happy in my arms. I know we weren't just having sex these last two nights. We were making love. What does that tell you right there, Pip?'

'What? Are you saying I love you? That you love me? You must be mad!'

He gave an ironic laugh. 'Yeah, I think you're right. A man would have to be mad to love you. But now it's your turn for a little self-discovery. Go back to New York City, Pip. Go back, knowing you've sorted out half your life and you know who your father was. Go find that shrink and sort out the rest.'

'Oh, I'm going, all right. I'm going back to my life and my job and I'm going to get that promotion and it will be a cold day in hell before I see you again.'

'Works for me. One less opportunity for you to walk out again. Knew there had to be an upside. Have a nice life.'

And then he was gone, slamming the door behind him so hard the windows rattled for a good twenty seconds.

TRACEY WAS BOILING the kettle in the kitchen, about to give Sally a call, when she heard the roar of an engine. She glanced out the window in time to see Turbo jump into the ute over Luke, before the door swung shut and he roared off down the driveway.

Uh-oh.

'Craig?'

Her husband pulled his head out of the pantry, where he was foraging for biscuits. 'Yeah?'

'Luke just left. He didn't look happy.'

'O-oh.'

'What does o-oh mean? Did Luke say anything to you about Pip?'

'Kind of,' he said, as he wandered over next to Trace at the window, not that there was anything to see but disappearing tail lights now Luke had gone. 'I said it was too bad she was leaving and he said he was going to talk to her.'

'About staying?'

'I guess.'

'O-oh.'

'That's what I thought.'

THE SPA WAS deep and hot and filled with bubbles and Pip lay there with her head on a rolled up towel, willing herself to relax. But the whooshing water jets were no match for the churning in her mind. Who the hell did Luke think he was to be criticising her? Making out that she had some kind of problem.

If she had a problem, it was him.

Her life was fine just the way it was.

She had a great job that with a little bit of luck was about to get one whole lot better.

She had a great flatmate and an apartment only a street back from Central Park.

And there was Chad.

For a moment she tried to think about him fondly. Tried to tell herself that she'd missed him and was looking forward to seeing him again.

Tried to, and failed miserably.

Which was a shame, because he was a nice guy, when he wasn't pulling stunts with hire cars. Good-looking. Great job. Maybe not as broad across the chest as Luke – and maybe not as well-equipped elsewhere come to think – but greyhound trim and not a callous in sight.

Once she was home in New York, she figured, as she hauled herself out of the slippery water, she'd appreciate that a whole lot more. She'd appreciate Chad a whole lot more.

Things would soon get back to normal once she was home.

She'd get her hair straightened and under control and her life under control with it.

She could hardly wait.

CHAPTER 30

*P*ip beat the sun up the next morning and was already packing the Audi by six when the grey of pre-dawn peeled back to soft pastel pinks and the sun rose in a blaze of glory and turned the sky blue. It would be hotter than any day so far, but for now it was blissfully cool. Mad to think she'd need a thick coat by the time she got to New York.

Tracey padded out in her dressing gown and ugg boots, with baby Chloe in her arms. 'Someone wants to say goodbye to aunty Pip,' Trace said. Pip took the smiling bundle and gave her a hug, kissing her head and breathing in her sweet baby smell, before wrapping an arm around her friend – *her sister.*

'Thank you. For everything,' she said, as Chloe gurgled happily at the group hug. 'I am going to miss you guys so much. Say goodbye to my nephews and to Craig, okay?'

Tracey sniffed and nodded. 'When will we see you again?' Her voice broke, and Pip saw the moisture in her eyes and had to bite back on the sting of tears. God, she hated goodbyes.

'Oh, Trace. I don't know.'

'Maybe next time you should come for Christmas. It's such a shame you couldn't have stayed longer.'

She nodded. 'I know. This one was a bit rushed. I'm sorry.' She gave them both what she thought was a final hug, planted a raspberry on Chloe's cheek and earned herself a gummy smile. 'God, I love this girl.'

'Pip, are you okay?'

'What?'

'Did you fight with Luke? Did he ask you to stay?'

She looked up at the cloudless sky, and towards the brand new sun making its presence felt with its promise of heat. She'd spent the night tossing and turning, playing over Luke's words, trying to make sense of them, finding none.

She wasn't running away.

She had a good life in New York.

She was happy.

Really, she was.

'We had words, yeah.'

'Don't be too hard on him,' Trace said. 'He's a good man. And underneath all the pain he's endured, I know he still feels something for you.'

She licked her lips. 'Well, he's sure got a funny way of showing it.'

'And you feel nothing for him?'

'It was a mistake to rehash the past.' She looked at her watch. 'I really have to get going, Trace. I want to stop by the cemetery along the way, visit the folks and Gran one more time.'

Tracey smiled. 'Of course you do. I'm going to miss you, Sis.'

'Oh god, don't do that to me,' she said, wiping tears away but still with a smile. 'I have to drive.'

And Trace laughed. 'Okay, no more words, you go. Let us know when you're back safe and sound in New York.'

'You bet,' she said, with one final hug for them both. 'I will.'

THE MOONTA CEMETERY was deserted at this time of the morning, as one would expect, as Pip walked past the old bell towards the graves of her family. Her Gran's grave was now a mound of earth, covered with flower arrangements that were drying, but still beautiful. The stonesmiths had been left their instructions. By the time she returned, whenever that was, she expected the earth would be settled again, and resurfaced.

But for now she took out the tiny shards of pottery she'd collected from the stone mounds the day she'd gone out there with Luke. She'd been intending to put them in the casket, together with Gran's favourite book, *Not Only in Stone*, but the fragments were so cold and hard that she'd changed her mind.

The shards of pottery she now lay across the base of the headstone that was waiting for a new plaque.

The book was packed in her hand luggage. It was going home with her.

She said a final farewell and headed to her family's plot. She stood there as long as she could, just breathing in the dry air and reflecting on the people she'd grown up with.

Her mum, Deirdre, who'd made a mistake and somehow still ended up with a good man. They'd had nowhere near enough years, but it had been a good life, until that night.

Her brother, Trent, who'd been denied the opportunity to spread his wings and become a man.

And Gerald. The man who'd been her father since before

she could remember and longer. Who'd rescued her mum and loved Pip as if she'd been his own.

'Thank you, Dad. You were the best dad ever.'

And then, because there was a plane she had to catch to make her international connection in Sydney, she turned her back and headed back to the car park.

But it wasn't just that. It was Luke's cold hard words spinning through her consciousness.

You might as well be under that slab with them.

No. He was wrong. She had a good life – in New York City, of all places. Life didn't get much better than that.

The town of Paskeville caught her attention for a moment as she passed through. She looked across the park towards the old church, now a gallery-cafe, thinking, *that was where it all began.* She tried to think of her mum and Sally as young girls vying for the same young man's attention, a man who would wrong them both.

And then it was on to Kulpura with its turn-off to Melton, and another pang in the chest thinking about the road crash markers on the side of the road and the house that was no longer there, and as she drove down the Hummocks on the road to Port Wakefield, it was like her past was being put back into place, laid to rest in the pages of yesterday.

She breathed out one long grateful sigh.

It was going to be okay.

The traffic grew heavy as she neared the city, and for a while she fretted that she might not get to the airport in time to return her car and drop her luggage.

With a hammering heart and sick feeling in her gut, she made it.

She'd barely cleared security and grabbed a couple of gifts for Carmen when the announcement came that her flight was boarding.

And that was the beauty of business class, she thought, as she hit the fast lane and sank thankfully into her seat.

Soon she'd be gone.

Soon she'd be back where her life was. Where she belonged.

And just as soon that uneasy feeling in her gut – that roiling feeling of things not being right – would settle down and be banished forever.

She feigned interest in a magazine until she felt the plane push back from the terminal. And then she watched from her windows as it taxied out to the runway. There were those hills again, and Mt Lofty to her right, as they waited on the tarmac for the final clearance.

The engines whined and the plane started moving down the runway, taking her on this first leg back towards New York. Taking her home.

Yes, she decided. New York was now her home.

The plane picked up speed, the front wheel lifted off and she watched the bumpy line of the Adelaide Hills racing by until they fell away and were left far below.

And Pip sat back in her seat and closed her eyes and felt her battered heart ache in her chest, and knew that soon, it would be okay again.

CHAPTER 31

P S: Tell Callan it's snowing! she added to the text she sent Tracey to let her know she was safely home. Snow tickled her nose and stuck to her eyelashes as she dived into a cab for the ride from JFK Airport. And as they headed along the Long Island Expressway towards the Midtown Tunnel, Pip caught her breath at the first view of the skyline of Manhattan, all lit up and shining bright through its dusting of snow

The view never failed to move her. She remembered arriving that first time, coming over the slight rise and seeing the city of New York all laid out before her, and the sight had brought tears of wonder to her eyes, because she'd known that she'd arrived, this girl from a tiny dot of a town on the other side of the globe. Yorke Peninsula to New York – they were worlds apart, but she'd made the transition. She'd succeeded.

This day it almost brought tears of relief. But she was done with tears. She'd shed a lifetime of tears back in Australia and there would be no more. So she just smiled and drank in the view before they entered the tunnel under the East River.

The cab battled its way along the congested streets towards her apartment on the Upper East Side and Pip was excited to be back amongst the buildings and buzz and pace of the Big Apple.

Harry, her doorman, welcomed her home and she smiled. She was back here, in New York City, and she belonged.

Of course she was happy. Who wouldn't be?

So much for Mr Would-be-psychoanalyst.

Wouldn't let herself be happy, what rot.

Don't give up the day job, Luke.

Carmen threw open the door and pulled her into a hug. 'I have so missed you! Oh my god, you are so tan!' she said, and Pip laughed because her Californian roommate was wearing a beanie and mittens and leg warmers, and the mercury had just reached thirty six degrees in Adelaide according to the world weather report.

'You would so love Australia,' Pip said, and then checked herself because she loved it right here and wasn't about to talk anyone into leaving.

She pulled out her gifts of Haigh's chocolates and a trio pack of Clare Valley wines and Carmen squealed – but not half as much as when she gave her the coaster that Adam had written his number on. She grabbed her phone and texted straight away.

Pip blinked. 'What are you doing?'

'Just letting him know that you're home safely.' And then she grinned. 'Just being neighborly.' With that, Carmen donned a down coat, heavy boots and a thick scarf and went out for Chinese takeout from the little restaurant across the street while Pip unpacked.

By the time Carmen returned, Pip was done unpacking and they opened a bottle of the riesling and sat on the sofa and ate egg foo yung and grilled shrimp with chopsticks. 'I swear this is my last takeout,' Pip said. 'After what I ate this last week, it's a wonder they could fit me on the plane.'

'You look great,' Carmen said. 'Every other New Yorker has pasty skin, but you glow. I love the way your hair is flipping out like that.'

'I don't,' Pip said, on a sigh, putting down her empty container. 'Rikki's fixing that for me tomorrow.'

'So, tell me everything.'

Pip pulled out her phone and let her roommate flick through the photos while Carmen bombarded her with questions about the funeral. About the christening. About Adam.

She clucked over the photos of Chloe. 'Who's this?' she said, holding up her phone.

'Ah, that's Tracey. She's a friend – and my half-sister too, as it turns out.'

Carmen looked up. 'I didn't know you had a sister.'

'Neither did I.' And then Pip told her about the note and the church and a secret that had been hidden for more than three decades.

'That's awesome,' Carmen said, swiping through the photos. 'To find a sister you never knew you had, and she's one of your oldest friends. Wow, you must be so glad you went.'

Pip gave that some thought. There had been some worthwhile moments, sure. Seeing her gran and saying her goodbyes. Catching up with Tracey and Fi and their families and learning that she and Tracey were half-sisters.

Luke.

No. Not Luke. Luke had been a mistake from start to finish.

'It had its moments.'

'Ooh, hello handsome Adam,' said Carmen, finding the

shot of Adam with Pip and smiling down on it. 'And you say it was warm over there.'

'It's summer right now. But they do have winters too, so don't go thinking it's some kind of Shangri-la. It's farming country with small towns and about as far as you can get from this place.'

'Do they have snow?'

'No.'

'Sounding better and better. Hey, who's this?'

'Show me.' She looked. Peered closer. And felt ill. She'd snapped the picture of Tracey holding Chloe in her gorgeous christening gown and hadn't realised she'd captured one half of the barbecue. The half behind which Luke was standing. 'That's um,' she said, her mouth dry, 'Tracey again with Chloe at the christening.'

'No, not them. The guy behind them. The cute one in the grey suit who's looking at you. Is that Chloe's dad?'

And Pip's stomach roiled. He was staring at her. Right at her, his mouth a straight line, his brow knitted and his eyes – his eyes were empty.

Oh, Luke.

'No. That's Luke. He's . . . Chloe's godfather.'

'Wow. What do they put in the water over there? How did you manage to make it out alive? I mean, it's not as if he's as good-looking as Adam, but he's not bad.'

Pip blinked. 'You don't think?'

'No. I like my men tall, dark and dangerous. And you said Adam was a policeman – with a uniform and everything.'

'Oh yeah,' said Pip, more than happy to change the subject, 'and he's probably got a really big truncheon.'

'Yeah,' Carmen said, on a wistful sigh. 'Just the way I like them.'

Carmen's phone beeped. Beeped again. And again. 'Ooh,'

she said, swiping it up eagerly, checking the messages, her smile stretching wide across her face, her eyes bright.

'Who's that?'

'Adam.'

'Already?'

'He texted me on his break while I was getting the take-out. Said he'd get back to me at lunch. I guess it's lunchtime over there.'

'You are one fast worker!' Pip shook her head, picking up her empty containers and wine glass, not wanting to prick anyone's bubbles, but wondering at the futility of a girl from California via New York City having a relationship by phone with a cop from the Yorke Peninsula, however big the size of his truncheon. 'Well, it's bedtime here. At least for this little black duck.' She hugged her roommate and thanked her for dinner and said, 'Have a good night. I am going to sleep like the dead.'

And then she shivered as Luke's words came back to her: *Under that slab.*

No, not like the dead. Like the living who just happened to be dog-tired. Because whatever he said, she was very much alive.

Morning in New York City came with a storm that dumped another few inches of snow onto the city. It's pretty, she told herself, as she cracked a bleary eye out her window at the streets below, even if the yellow cabs sometimes made more progress going sideways than forwards. Or at any rate, she thought, turning away, it might be pretty if her head didn't feel like someone had been hollowing it out all night with a rusty spoon.

She'd woken far too many times during the night to feel

refreshed. Woken from far too many dreams of Luke. Picturing herself in his arms. Naked in the spa. In a shower with his hot mouth making magic, hard up against a door with her legs wound around his hips . . .

Oh god, get over it!

Because her sleeplessness wasn't all down to him. It was the noise of the city. How had she not noticed its unrelenting pulse before? When every siren, every blast of a horn or shout from a drunk out past his bedtime permeated her consciousness? When the flashing light over the diner halfway down the street seemed to be aimed right at her window? How was anyone supposed to sleep through all that?

She made coffee in an empty kitchen – Carmen was out on her morning run through Central Park. Saturday. She'd normally be at the gym by this time. She really should be at the gym now.

But she didn't feel like it.

She caught a glance of herself in the hallway mirror on the way back to bed and wanted to cry. There were bags under her eyes and more kinks in her hair than ever.

She looked like somebody else.

She looked like a stranger.

Thank god she'd managed to book in to see Rikki this afternoon. She might even drag herself to the gym first.

She needed to get this slack body under control.

As well as her wayward hair.

And she needed to get this life of hers under control.

Later.

For now she sank back in bed with her coffee and the sound of sirens careening down the slippery streets below. Yeah, she told herself, it was good to be back.

She was happy.

Her phone buzzed and a name zinged electricity down her spine.

Luke.

Which was such a stupid thing to think, she told herself a moment later as sanity re-established itself and she checked the screen. Oh yeah, that caller made so much more sense.

Welcome back. Get-together tomorrow night?

Not likely. Get-together was code for sex, and she was in no particular hurry to see Chad. She put the phone down. Closed her eyes.

Besides, it wasn't like she'd gone without before. She smiled to herself.

Oh, no.

Because suddenly those pictures of Luke were front and centre of her mind again. And not just pictures; movies, in glorious high-definition Sensurround. Of them in the spa, the shower, on the old leather sofa in the shed . . .

Her thighs clenched.

She picked up her phone, read the message again. Maybe it wasn't just her hair and her gym that she needed to get under control. Maybe it was her wayward thoughts. Maybe a night with Chad might be the best way to banish dreams of Luke? To put them into perspective.

Perspective would be good.

She texted him back.

Meet me here at eight.

CHAPTER 32

'Hey, babe,' Chad said, with a hug and a kiss to the cheek when she opened the door for him.

'Hey, Chad,' she said, forcing a smile, trying to convince herself she was happy to see him as she watched him brush the snow from his shoulders before peeling off his coat.

Give it time.

Her hair was now perfectly straight, the kinks banished and the colour refreshed thanks to Rikki's expertise. Her body was shattered from two body pump classes in a row, and she was hungry because she'd discovered – when she'd finally worked up enough enthusiasm to go to the gym – that she'd put on four entire pounds while away. And she hadn't eaten dinner; she wanted to look her absolute best in her I-mean-business suit for her interview tomorrow.

But just like her muscles might take a bit of convincing to work out who was boss, so would her mind. After all, Chad was one good-looking guy. With his dark eyes, high cheek-bones and full lips, if he hadn't been a wiz playing the markets, he could have modelled for Barneys New York.

It was no hardship looking at him. It had never been any

hardship going to bed with him. It wouldn't be again, she told herself, and she'd soon put paid any more dreams of Luke.

'Where's Carmen tonight?'

'In her room.' Skyping Adam. Now there was a cyber relationship that was progressing at a rate of knots.

'So it's just the two of us?'

'More or less. Can you I get you a drink,' she said, heading for the kitchen before he answered. Because she sure needed something to settle this suddenly fluttery stomach of hers.

He snagged her hand. 'Why don't we go straight to bed?'

She swallowed down hard as her stomach damned near flipped right out of her mouth. 'Already?'

'I've got an early start in the morning.'

Yeah. So did she, not to mention another run through the notes she'd prepared for the interview. But still . . .

'Besides,' he said, running the fingers of one hand down the side of her face, 'I've missed you.' She closed her eyes and felt . . . not a thing. Not a tingle. Not a buzz. Not the merest sigh from her heart.

Damn.

'That's sweet,' she said, when she opened her eyes, and she tried to remember missing Chad, but all she could remember was cursing him about the car. That, and what Luke had called him.

Don't go there.

Don't think about Luke and his accusations. Don't give them oxygen.

'So . . . bed?'

'Um,' she licked her lips, feeling trapped all of a sudden. 'I might just grab a cup of joe.'

'You don't need coffee.'

'No?'

'Come on,' he said, already peeling off his sweater. 'I made a killing on the market last week and I feel like celebrating.'

'Hey, congratulations! I know, maybe we should go out somewhere and celebrate in style?'

'Are you kidding? It's snowing.' He said it like she was crazy.

'I know! Do you have any idea how much I have missed it? How about we go for a walk?'

The hand undoing his shirt buttons stopped. 'Pip, it's freezing out there. Are you serious?'

She turned on the puppy eyes. 'Oh, come on, Chad. We don't have to go far. I just need some fresh air. To wake me up a bit. It's the jet lag catching up with me. You don't want me falling asleep on you, do you?'

He sighed, redid his buttons and pulled on his sweater. 'Believe me, once you get outside, you'll want to come right back in.' He swiped up his coat and she gathered up her coat, scarf, gloves and ear muffs and pulled on her rubber soled boots before he could change his mind.

'I know.'

But she didn't know. The only thing she knew was that she'd made a huge mistake inviting Chad over tonight. She could no more go to bed with him than fly to the moon. Still she managed a smile for him in the elevator. 'It'll be fun, you'll see,' although he just grumbled and turned his eyes to the ceiling and muttered something under his breath about a waste of time.

The cold air hit her face like an icy slap, so sharp it hurt to breathe it in, while flurries of snow swirled and danced around them before joining their colleagues on the pavement. 'It's bracing,' she lied, and wound the scarf around her nose and mouth. Chad just rolled his eyes and shoved his hands into his coat pockets.

'So how was it over there?' he asked, and Pip wondered

whether, if they'd gone straight to bed, he would ever have asked, or whether he'd just been intent on getting his rocks off. Not that she could judge him. She'd never been interested in his wider world either.

'It was good,' she said, her voice muffled by the scarf. 'I'm glad I got to say goodbye to my gran.' She didn't bother telling him about discovering Tracey was also her sister.

Emotionless shadow-land.

She swallowed.

'So how was the car?'

'It was great,' she lied.

'Pip,' he said, jiggling his shoulders as they waited on a corner for the lights to change. 'It's freezing out here. You awake yet?'

'Not quite. A little longer?'

'Fine,' he said on a sigh 'Just so long as you're happy.'

Happy. Now there was a concept.

Was she happy? Not right now with a man she didn't want and she didn't know what to do with, she wasn't.

Unsettled was what she was.

Discombobulated.

Like the foundations of her world were shuddering and creaking, the walls threatening to topple down.

She'd always thought she was happy.

But now . . .

The first waft of roasted meat from the park food truck hit her then. It smelled like lamb. Spiced lamb. And it reminded her of Tracey's roast lamb, the meat stuck with slivers of garlic and rosemary. Her stomach rumbled more the closer they got. And rumbled.

The two guys manning the truck in lumpy jackets and trapper hats rubbed their hands together and looked at them hopefully. Clearly they were doing it tough out on the streets tonight.

'Are you hungry?' she asked him.

'Are you nuts?' he said, when he saw where she was looking. 'You don't eat that shit.'

Well, so maybe she didn't normally, and especially not when she'd just discovered she'd put on four pounds, but still she turned her head and sniffed the aromatic air.

'Like, how many calories do you reckon are in that?' he asked.

'I don't know, but it smells like it might be worth it.' She looked at him hopefully. 'Should we give it a try?'

He shook his head. 'I'm not touching it.'

'Okay,' she said, and stepped up to the window. 'Give me your best.' Five bucks later she had a steaming container of lamb gyros and chicken on spicy rice with garlic and chili sauce. 'Oh my god,' she said, swooshing away the fallen snow to sit herself down on a nearby bench. 'This smells amazing.'

'What in god's name are you doing?' he said, standing there, the snow falling around his hunched shoulders, his hands deep in his pockets.

'Eating dinner.' She tasted the rice. Amazing. She tasted a piece of lamb. Out of this world. The chicken. Awesome. And all together, heaven on a plate. She didn't even mind that through her thick coat, the seat under her behind might as well have been made of ice.

'Oh, this is so good,' she said, giving a thumbs up to the pair in the truck who were watching them, as if they were more interesting than what was on the telly. She held up the tray to Chad. 'Here, try some before it gets cold.'

'I don't want any.'

'Oh goodie. All the more for me,' she said, and pulled it back. She might need to rethink her wardrobe selection for tomorrow's interview. She might need to choose a slightly less slim-fitting pair of trousers, but god, it was worth it as the combination of garlic and spiced meat and cool yoghurt filled her senses.

'What I want,' Chad stressed, 'is to go to bed. The sooner the better, before I turn into Frosty the Snowman and my dick shrivels into a peanut.'

Pip blinked. The guys in the truck guffawed. And Chad turned around and saw them watching and looked like he wanted to disappear down a steaming manhole into the subway.

'I need to talk to you about that,' she said, folding her tray up and dropping it in the trash, because she'd eaten enough and because it was her fault Chad was standing out here freezing his nuts off.

'About what?'

'Walk with me.' She took his elbow and walked back towards her building, wondering at a touch that was familiar, but at the same time cold. And not physically cold. Just . . . bereft of any real warmth. Empty. Meaningless.

Exactly how their sex had been, she realised. Meaningless.

Not like with Luke . . .

She shook her head, trying to shake those thoughts away. Because, for god's sake, this wasn't about Luke.

This was about Chad.

This was about the half-life she was living.

Strange, how it had taken until now for his words to make sense. But he'd been right. Because she'd stood there at the grave and known she didn't want to be under there with her family. She wanted to live. She owed it to her parents to live. Really live, not merely exist.

And damn Luke to hell and back, he'd been right about more than that. Because she owed it to be them to be happy for all the days that they would never see. All the sunrises. All the sunsets.

All the stars.

She turned her face to the heavy grey sky and smiled as snowflakes settled on her face, winter's frozen kiss.

And all the snow.

She smiled. She was alive, for whatever reason. Did it matter what she had done that had made it so? Would her parents rather her dead too?

God, no.

She'd been such a fool.

'Uh, earth calling Pip. Anybody home? About what?' he prompted, and they stopped and she blinked at him, feeling as if the filters were coming off her eyes.

The snow floated and danced around them. 'I'm sorry,' she said, looking into his face. 'I should never have asked you to come over tonight. Chad, I'm sorry, but I don't want to go to bed with you.'

'What?'

'There's no point coming back up. You might as well go home.'

'Because you're jet-lagged?'

And she smiled sadly and slowly shook her head. Claiming jet lag would be the easy way out. But then there would be other nights and other excuses needed. It was pointless pretending. 'No. I just don't want to have sex with you anymore. I don't feel anything for you. I like you. But not like that.'

His eyes looked half confused, half angry. 'But that's what we agreed, didn't we? It's just sex. It's got nothing to do with feelings. You knew that all along.'

And his words cut deep, because they were true. Because that had been their arrangement and she'd been the one, tonight, to find fault with it.

'I did,' she said. 'But I've changed my mind. I can't do that anymore.'

The snow continued to fall about them, snowflakes landing on Chad's hair and even on his eyelashes, and she knew how funny that felt, but he didn't look amused, because the confusion in his eyes had fallen away, leaving behind a simmering anger that should have melted the snow right then and there.

'What's wrong with you? You go away just fine and you come back weird. What happened to you over there anyway?'

Oh, so much.

Burying her gran.

Finding her father.

Discovering a sister.

Luke . . .

So much had happened and yet nothing had really changed. Because she was still here in New York City, wasn't she?

'I saw stars in the sky. How long is it since you've seen stars?'

He snorted. 'I don't believe this. I'm freezing my ass off here and you're talking about stars?'

She smiled. 'You're a good-looking man, Chad. Go find yourself a nice woman. Someone who deserves you. Someone who will love you.'

He shook his head, scattering snowflakes, 'I don't have time for –'

'Make time,' she said and squeezed his arm. 'Now go home. I don't know if you've noticed, but it's freezing out here.'

Harry the doorman nodded, rubbing his hands together as she entered her building, shedding snow in her wake. 'Cold one out tonight, miss.'

'It sure is,' she said, and smiled, because she didn't feel cold anymore. She felt warm inside. She felt good. Maybe even halfway to happy.

And Harry's crinkled face lit up like the sun had just come out. He put his hand to his cap, 'You have a nice evening, Miss Martin.'

She was still smiling as she let herself back into the apartment. Carmen was sitting on the sofa with her duvet wrapped around her and her laptop on her crossed legs. She took one look at Pip and said, 'Wow, what happened to you?'

'I ate middle east lamb and rice from that truck near the corner.'

'You ate carbs?'

'Yup' And Pip laughed as she peeled off her coat and pulled off her boots, thinking about all the carbs she'd eaten in the last few days and how the world hadn't ended. 'And I broke up with Chad.'

'Whoa. Why?'

She shrugged as she hung the coat back in the closet. 'Because it was pointless.'

'You don't look too cut up about it.'

'I'm not,' she said, flopping down on the sofa next to Carmen and hugging a cushion to her chest. 'That was part one of Operation Happiness. Ridding myself of excess baggage. Part two is winning this promotion tomorrow. I'm going to be so happy, you won't know what's hit you.'

'Awesome! So what's brought this on all of a sudden?'

'Oh, just something someone said to me back on the Peninsula about finding out about my father and stuff. Something about finally being able to move on and sort the rest of my life out.'

'Yeah? Who?'

'An old friend.' She plucked at the fringe on the cushion, wondering why it had taken so long to recognise the truth in Luke's words. But she was going to be happy from now on. She was determined to be happy, and winning that promotion was the key. Her folks would be so proud of her if they knew. 'So, how's Adam?'

Her roommate looked coy. 'He's cute. He's got the sexiest accent.'

Pip arched an eyebrow. 'And that's always the best basis for any relationship, right there.'

Carmen grinned. 'Hey, for what it's worth, I think you did the right thing. You deserve better than Chad.'

'Yeah? You never said as much.'

The other woman shrugged. 'People make choices. It's not my place to criticise. I just thought you needed someone really hot.'

'Like Adam, you mean.'

'Yeah.'

And Pip got up and swiped her friend with the cushion. 'You nut job! I'm going to study my notes for tomorrow,' she said as she leaned over to give Carmen a hug. 'And thank you. I'll see you in the morning.'

CHAPTER 33

Breathe, she told herself as the clock ticked over to ten. She was sitting outside the meeting room, waiting for the current interview to wind up and for the interviewers to be ready.

She was prepared. She knew her stuff. She was confident she satisfied all the performance criteria and then some. She had the support of her team and those in management above her.

And she'd slept. She'd dropped a sleeping pill and had six dreamless hours of sleep. Perfect.

She looked good too – her hair impeccably straight, the colour a blend of caramel and toasted marshmallow and cinnamon, thanks to Rikki. Her outfit looked immaculate. She'd even managed to squeeze into her best business suit, and hadn't that made her feel happy right there?

Oh yes.

So she sat, and waited, one leg crossed over the other, hands entwined around one knee, burying any hint of nervousness and exuding confidence.

All she had to do was get in there, take a deep breath, and show them what she knew.

She could do this.

The door opened and Edward J Stanwyck Jnr emerged from within, smiling like the cat that got the cream as he thanked them for their time and told them he looked forward to their call.

Jerk.

He was so not getting this job.

Not if she had anything to do with it.

She smiled brightly when he turned. 'Hello Edward.' He stopped and blinked. A blink that said a thousand words and not one of them involving cats or cream. Her smile widened.

Dead meat.

'Two minutes,' the clerk holding the iPad indicated, and she turned her smile on him before he disappeared back inside.

She stood up, smoothing invisible creases from her slim fitting trousers.

'Good luck,' Edward said to her quietly.

She smiled thinly back. She didn't believe in luck and she didn't need it. Because this job was all but in the bag.

Operation Happiness, come on down.

Too easy.

THE INTERVIEW WAS GOING WELL. She'd talked about her role and her achievements. Without false modesty. Without arrogance. Just laying it out straight. She had a good track record and she knew it.

Her New York boss was sitting back looking pleased with himself, the London VP was nodding and she was feeling quietly confident when he said, 'So in this new role, you'd be expected to participate in recruitment interviews for the bank. What are the attributes you would stress to people coming into the organisation that sets this business apart?'

She loved that question. She knew this stuff by heart.

'A passion for work,' she said. 'Because the hours can be long and the work tough and the days intensive.'

And right out of nowhere a picture of Luke popped into her thoughts, front and centre. Because his days were long and tough and intensive too, and you could tell he worked hard by the muscles in his arms and his chest and abs.

'Anything else?' the UK partner prompted.

'Of course,' she said, gathering her thoughts. 'They'll need dedication and a keen sense of responsibility and a pride in what they do, and a realisation that sometimes that might mean making sacrifices.' As she continued, she realised that every single quality she mentioned reminded her of Luke. And she wished there was a pill she could take so she didn't have to put up with him invading her thoughts in her waking hours too.

'Excellent. And tell us, why do you want this job?'

So Edward can't have it.

She launched into the spiel she'd prepared. Edward was so not getting a look in. She still remembered the way he'd dumped her, still remembered the cold disdain of his mother; the narrowing eyes of his father when she'd done nothing more than suggest that the US constitution was fatally flawed and that everybody in New York City was in favour of gay marriage.

She blinked, her words faltering as Luke's words came back to her.

You can't let yourself be happy.

And like a thunderclap, she realised what she'd done that weekend when Edward had taken her home for Thanksgiving.

She'd sabotaged a chance at happiness with him. Cut it dead in the water. She might just as well have walked into a National Rifle Association convention wearing a T-shirt saying guns are for sissies. Of course his nice upper crust parents from Mission Hills, Kansas, were appalled.

You can't let yourself be happy.

And she hadn't.

All along she'd cut herself off from any chance of happiness.

Starting with walking away from Luke.

Luke.

A band around her chest pulled so tight she could barely breathe.

Oh god, what had she done?

We weren't just having sex. We were making love. What does that tell you?

A man would have to be mad to love you.

She hadn't loved Edward at all. She'd been going through the motions, pretending to live, and been trapped by a man who'd thought she was sincere and was trying to do the right thing.

No wonder she'd set the boundaries ever since at 'just sex'.

But she'd been kidding herself with Luke. It had never been 'just sex' with him. No wonder she'd been so angry with him that last night. Not only had he dared to tell her what her problems were – rightly, as it turned out – but he'd denied her one more night of pleasure.

Because it had never been 'just sex' with him. What they'd been doing was making love.

Oh, Luke . . .

'Ms Martin?'

'I'm sorry.' And she backed up to where her answer had stalled and limped through the rest of her delivery.

The two men exchanged glances and Pip smiled weakly, her stomach churning, her palms suddenly damp.

'So, maybe in conclusion,' the UK partner said, 'tell us why you think you are the best candidate for this role.'

She looked up at them, saw their frowns and the concern and doubt in their eyes and knew it was but a fraction of what she was experiencing right now. Turmoil. Shock. And fear that she was already too late. She blinked her eyes. 'Actually, I don't think I am.'

'What?'

'Excuse me?'

She didn't understand it herself. Not completely. But while she was probably too late to make it up to Luke, there was a chance going begging to make up for the way she'd treated Edward.

'I think you should give the job to Edward Stanwyck.' She looked at their disbelieving faces. 'And now if you'll excuse me,' she said, as she stood on wobbly legs, feeling sick and uncertain, but at the same time, knowing it was the right thing to do, 'there's somewhere I really need to be.'

CHAPTER 34

'What's wrong? What happened at the interview?' demanded Carmen, bursting into Pip's room. She was on her lunch break, and had come home in response to Pip's urgent text. She stopped dead at the door when she saw the open case and her friend sorting a pile of clothes on the bed. 'What are you doing?'

'I'm packing.'

'But we don't leave until Christmas Eve.' Carmen's eyes narrowed as she checked out the clothes Pip was packing. 'And it's warmer than here but it's not exactly a heatwave in California right now.'

'I'm sorry, Carmen, but I can't come to California with you this time.'

'Then where are you going?'

'Back.'

'To Australia?'

She nodded as she rolled more clothes into the suitcase. 'I've got a flight booked tonight. There's a car coming in an hour to take me to JFK and I'll be back in Adelaide by lunchtime on Christmas Eve. I've paid up two months in advance on the rent, just in case I don't get back for a while, and I've left some money for utilities in an envelope in the kitchen.

Carmen put a hand to her arm, stilling her for just a moment. 'Pip, you're making no sense. What's going on? What happened at the interview?'

Pip looked at her. 'I told them to give the job to Edward Stanwyck.'

'You what? The jerk who dumped you?'

'He's a good candidate. And I don't really want the job.'

'Hang on. Last night you were all about Operation Happiness. Getting this promotion was part of that. Wasn't it?'

'I changed my mind. That job wasn't going to make me happy. I realised what I really want.'

'And what's that?'

'Luke.'

'Who?'

'The guy in the photo – the one you asked about.'

Carmen's eyes opened wide. 'You mean the hot guy who was looking right at you?'

'Yeah.' She smiled. Because he was. Smoking hot, and she could finally admit that now.

'Whoa! Okay, this is going to take a bit of time. So start from the beginning.'

So Pip started from the beginning, and told her how they'd grown up neighbours together, and how they'd used to make stone castles in the mounds between their properties, and how friendship had turned to love and sex, before tragedy had intervened fifteen long years ago.

Carmen listened and passed her things when she asked for them, and Pip told her how she'd withdrawn from everyone after the accident because of an overwhelming feeling of guilt that she'd let her family down, and how she'd used the mystery of her father's identity as the excuse to cut herself off from Luke, from her friends, from everyone. How she hadn't even realised she was doing it.

'Wow,' Carmen said, when Pip reached the end and dropped her bathroom bag into the space she'd left. 'Just wow. Does he know you're coming?'

'I can't tell him. Not over the phone.'

'Shouldn't you warn him?'

She shook her head. 'The last time we spoke, he told me I'd never get the chance to walk out again on him. I have to talk to him in person. Have to make him see I mean it.'

'He's the friend, isn't he? The one who told you to sort out your life.'

She nodded as she zipped up her bag. 'He's the one. The only thing is –' she looked at her friend, that tightness around her chest squeezing tighter, '– I don't know if it's already too late.'

CHAPTER 35

'So, you actually want the convertible this time?'

God, what were the chances? The luggage had take its own sweet time to appear, somehow she'd been selected for a random bag check, and now the same attendant at the Adelaide Airport car rental agency was on duty. 'Yes. The very same. The same one that I booked.'

'Only,' he said, flicking his pen against the rental papers, 'I noticed the name and wondered if it was a mistake again.'

'No, this time it's not a mistake.' She looked at the lines of people waiting, longer now on Christmas Eve than they'd been just a couple of weeks ago at the start of school holidays. 'So . . .?'

'Well, you're in luck, because we've actually still got the Audi. Here you go.'

'Thank you so much,' she said, accepting the keys and resisting the urge to give him a clip around the ears with them. It was supposed to be a joke. Supposed to make Luke smile.

Please let him smile.

Please let him be happy that I've come back.

She wrestled her bag into the trunk – boot, she reminded herself – and opened her door, staring blindly for a moment at the missing steering wheel.

Oh my god, she thought, clambering in the other side.

I'm stuck in Groundhog Day.

LUKE HAD his head under the bonnet of the ute and was topping up the oil and water when Turbo started barking madly. He was about to head off down to Stansbury to have Christmas with his folks before a spot of fishing. 'What is it, fella?' he said, looking up. Finally, he heard the approaching car.

He screwed up his eyes as a bolt of electricity jolted through him.

No.

Not possible. It had to be a coincidence. A horrible coincidence.

She was back in New York City right now. He'd almost convinced himself that he was seeing things when the flash car came closer and he spotted Pip through the windscreen.

Fuck!

Turbo was barking and going crazy as she pulled up a few feet away, and Luke told his dog to sit down and shut up.

And felt like he was going barking mad into the deal.

Why the hell was she back? What the hell was she doing here?

She climbed from the car. Stiffly. Awkwardly. Closed the big door behind her. 'Hi Luke.'

He wiped his hands on a grease rag but he didn't move, apart from that. 'Pip.'

'I came back.'

'I can see that.' What he didn't understand was why, but

he figured she'd tell him if he waited long enough. Until then, he'd try to focus his brain on why she was back and will his body to stop celebrating already. Mind you, with her in that cute little lacy shirt and skinny jeans, it wasn't going to be easy.

He gazed down long and hard at the Toyota's engine before he dared look up again. Yup, it would be really useful if he could just focus his brain.

Turbo sat, his tail twitching on the ground, looking from his owner to the visitor. And when the silence stretched too long and too far, and the only noise was the buzz of a blowfly buzzing by, he barked.

'Hey Turbo,' she said, and the kelpie shot out and made a fuss of her.

Traitor.

And because he was getting tired of waiting, he said, 'Thought you had some big important interview in New York City to get back to.'

'I did,' she said, scratching behind Turbo's ears.

'So what brings you back here then?'

She straightened. 'You.'

And something dropped like a brick in his gut.

He sucked in air to fill the hole it had left. 'How do you figure that?'

'All those things you told me. That I didn't think I deserved to be happy. That I ran away from the people who loved me. That I'd buried my heart under a stone castle.' She paused. 'You were right.'

He gave a brief nod and brushed a hand on his pants. 'Good. A man doesn't like to be wrong too many times in his life. Gets to be habit forming, otherwise.'

She blinked, like that wasn't the response she was expecting. Even Turbo angled his head to the side. Well, he didn't know what to say either. He wasn't too well versed in meaningful discussions on the hop, and this one had all the hall-marks. He just wasn't sure he wanted be part of it.

'Luke. I came to say I was sorry.'

'You came a hell of a long way to say that.'

She shook her head. 'I did, but there's more.'

He swallowed. This time he wasn't going anywhere near anything that looked like a question. Because that brick was wreaking havoc in his gut again and there was a buzzing in his ears that had nothing to do with blowflies.

'You said that we been making love – as opposed to merely having sex. Do you remember?'

Oh god. He put his hands wide on the radiator grille and took another eyeful of engine. Yup. Battery was still right there where it should be. All good.

'And you also said that a man would be mad to love me.'

Radiator present and correct.

'Were you that man? Is that what you were trying to tell me?'

He squeezed his eyes shut and pinched the bridge of his nose. 'Does it matter?' He turned then, and faced her. 'Does it really matter, Pip?'

And blue eyes searched anguished blue eyes. Anguished eyes filled with what looked like fear.

And he knew he couldn't save her.

'Well,' she started, looking suddenly tiny and shrunken next to the car, as if she was caving in on herself by the minute. 'You see, you were right. I built that stone castle around my heart to protect me - and somehow you managed to break through. And do you know what I found inside, when those walls came down? Do you know what was left?'

He gave the briefest, barest shake of his head.

She gave a tremulous smile that faded on a frown. 'That all this time, all through the years, no matter how far I went and what I did, you were there, locked away, deep down where I couldn't see you. It was you, all this time. I just didn't know it. I know I've caused you so much pain. I know I've hurt you too many times to expect forgiveness. But I just had to come and say, I'm so sorry. And that I love you, Luke. I think I always have.'

She sniffed and took a deep breath, and made another attempt at a smile.

'And don't blame me for this but it's your fault, because you got me started about thinking how I can be happy. Really happy. And I look at what I threw away before and wonder if it's too late to try and recapture any of that, because we did, didn't we? When we danced and when we made love. Didn't we recapture something of it?

'And I thought, maybe it's not too late. Maybe we can try again. Maybe we can pick up the pieces and finally move on. Luke,' she said, coming closer, putting a hand on his arm. 'Can we move on? Can we try again?'

He looked at the hand on his arm. Felt her warmth and felt his body already hungering for more. But he'd been here before, and look how that had ended. But she was still waiting for his answer and the least he could do was be polite. 'What do you mean, try again?'

Air hissed through her teeth. 'Marry me, Luke, and make me the happiest woman in the world?'

He didn't know what to say. 'What about your job?'

'I walked out of the interview. I realised I didn't want the promotion after all. I realised I wanted something more. Someone more.'

'So what will you do - if you end up out here, I mean?'

'I don't know. There are banks here. Get a job in a bank. Help Fi out in the shop, meanwhile – because she's going to need help. I don't care. I just want to be here. With you. So will you? Marry me?'

She stood there, waiting in the sun with the flies buzzing

past and the rumble of a car down the gravel road. Waiting for his answer.

He never for the life of him thought she'd come back. He'd said those words to punish her. And to remind himself of all the reasons *he* should be happy that she was leaving again. He'd said them to make her wonder, all the long way home. He'd hoped they'd make her sort herself out.

He'd never thought they'd bring her back.

He'd never imagined.

She was everything he'd ever wanted. She was all he'd ever wanted, ever since he'd known what wanting really meant. She was all of that and more.

But now, after being married once before, having been dumped on from a great height more than once before, he wanted other things. Like peace and quiet and a simple life where no one could dump on him ever again.

He sighed, and slapped away a fly that had landed on his shoulder. 'I don't know, Pip.'

Her voice was tiny when it came. 'What?'

'Strangely enough, I've had a gutful of women walking out on me. I'm not sure I want to go through all that again.'

She bit her lip. 'I appreciate that. I know I've got form. But I love you – I do – and I thought, from what you said, that maybe there was still a chance that you still loved me. That maybe after all these wasted years, we could spend the rest of our lives together. And it would be the rest of our lives, I promise. Luke?'

He threw the rag on the car. 'Honestly, Pip, I don't know. You freeze me out for so many years, then you put me in a box that says 'just sex', and now you're telling me that you love me. I don't know what to believe.'

'Luke, listen –'

'No, Pip, you listen,' he said, the confusion he'd felt at her arrival boiling over to anger that she thought she could just waltz back into his life again and everything would be hunky dory. 'Do you have any idea what it's like to see the person you love walk away – and not just once, but twice? Do you have any idea what it's like to have your heart ripped from your body while you're still breathing? I don't think you do. I don't think you have any concept.'

She swallowed. 'So that's your final answer,' she said. 'That's a no, then.'

He nodded. 'Yeah, I guess that's about the size of it. You might as well take your poncy car and go back to where you came from.'

'Okay.' She pressed her lips tightly together, and if it was supposed to be a smile it fell a mile short of the mark. 'I'd better get going then.'

He said nothing, so she just nodded and said, 'Goodbye' and climbed back into the car. He watched her go, turning left back towards the highway.

At his feet, Turbo watched the departing vehicle and whimpered.

'Damn straight,' he said to the dog with a nod. 'She sure got what was coming to her. And with both barrels.'

Turbo just looked at him and whimpered some more.

'It was the right thing to do,' he said, nodding some more, dropping the bonnet of the ute with a crunch and wiping his hands on his pants. 'Our life is pretty damned fine just the way it is, eh Turbo? Who needs a woman to go messing it up?'

Turbo whined louder, his head to one side as he pawed his master's leg.

'You're not wrong, mate. That'll teach her to fuck around with the man who loves her.'

He stopped. Blinked. Looked at the dog. Looked over at the road in the direction she'd gone.

The man who loves her.

'Oh. Fuck!'

He reached into his jeans for the car keys. 'Turbo,' he shouted. 'In!'

They shot out of the driveway and onto the gravel road, spraying dust and stones in their wake, trying to guess which way she'd head when she hit the highway. Right and back to Adelaide and a plane to New York? Or left, to Tracey's?

'Which way?' he said, as he reached the T-junction, peering left and right, searching for some sign of her car.

Turbo barked.

'Yep,' he said, turning left. 'That's what I thought too.'

SHE'D BEEN DREAMING about their meeting, building it up in her mind through all the long hours of travel, picturing the surprise and the smile on his face. Imagining him sweeping her into his arms because against all the odds, she'd come back.

Imagining him saying yes.

Not once had her fevered mind thrown up the possibility that he'd out and out say no.

Oh, she wasn't stupid. Expecting him to simply run to her and welcome her with open arms had been in the realms of high fantasy, and she hadn't expected him to forgive her that quickly. She'd expected conditions to be imposed, demands to be made. That she promise to never leave him again. That she promise to love him forever.

Laughing, smiling conditions, sprinkled in between kisses that tasted like sunshine before he said yes. Because he'd been going to say yes all along.

Never once had she imagined him flatly turning her down.

Oh god, what a nightmare. She'd walked away from her

job, and for what? This? She flicked the wipers on, and only when they scraped across the dry windscreen did she realise why she couldn't see. She pulled off onto the verge and cried her eyes out as her fragile heart, the heart that she'd buried for so long and which now lay newly exposed, shattered into tiny pieces.

TURBO BARKED, jumping up on all fours, pawing at the window.

'That's her all right,' Luke said, as the red car came into view. But why had she stopped?

He pulled up behind and ran to her door and saw her hunched over her steering wheel and howling, her shoulders shaking as she heaved great shuddering sobs. 'Pip!' he said, flinging open the door. She hadn't heard him coming. She looked up in surprise and after one look at her grief stricken face, his heart broke. He'd seen that face before, the night after her family's funeral when she'd stumbled across the sodden paddocks to tell him what she'd overheard. And now he was gutted that it had been him who'd taken her back to that place again.

'Oh, god, Pip, I'm sorry.' And he crouched down to cradle her in his arms. 'I'm so sorry.'

She was still stuck there, held captive by that damned seatbelt and he reached over to unclick it so he could pull her from the car and properly into his arms.

She clung to him as he pulled her up and out, still sobbing and trembling, gasping for air and shaking her head. 'No. I'm sorry. You've done nothing wrong. It was me. I was horrible. I deserved it. It's all my fault.'

'Shh,' he said, rocking her in his arms. 'I shouldn't have

made you cry. I don't ever want to make you cry again. I promise never to make you cry again.'

She hiccupped and blubbered as she shook her head against his shoulder.

He put his hands on either side of her damp face and lifted it, pushing damp tendrils of hair from her brow. 'Will you hold me to that?'

She frowned and shook her head, her teeth catching her bottom lip. 'But . . . but you don't –'

'Answer me. Will you hold me to that?'

'But that would mean –'

'Yeah, you're right. I'm so sorry Pip. Maybe if you'd warned me you were coming. Maybe if I'd known in advance and had time to prepare. I've spent the best part of the last week telling myself you did the right thing going back to New York City. I'd almost convinced myself that I didn't . . .'

She sniffed and swallowed and blinked beautiful blue liquid eyes up at him. 'Didn't what?'

'Love you. But I do love you, Pip. I always have, and I always will. You know the worst thing about my crappy marriage to Sharon? The one thing that was never going to make it work, whatever else happened?'

'No.'

'She wasn't you.' He shook his head as he rubbed her back, still rocking. 'Everyone was waiting for me to move on. And so I did. I always felt like I was settling. Because I couldn't have you.'

'I'm so sorry! I've stuffed up so many lives. I've made such a mess of everything.'

'Hey,' he lifted her chin with the fingers of one hand. 'Here's one mess we can fix right now. That question you had. Would you mind popping it again? Because I think I might have been too hasty.'

She took a deep breath, her eyes filling with fresh promise, like when the sun comes out on a rainy day. 'The big question, you mean?'

'Yeah,' he said, grinning. 'That's the one.'

She took a moment to wipe away the dampness from her cheeks, to get her breathing under control and push wayward hair behind her ears.

'I love you, Luke Trenorden,' she said at last. 'Will you marry me?'

And his heart suddenly felt so big in his chest it was a wonder it didn't explode right then and there. 'Yes, I surely will marry you.' He kissed her, and she tasted of warmth and hope and new beginnings. She tasted of the woman he loved and she felt like heaven in his arms.

He was in heaven, and he wanted to tell it to the world. Had to tell it to the world.

He lifted his lips from hers, turned his face towards the sky, and howled. Turbo joined in so there were two of them, howling under the harvest sun, with Pip laughing in his arms.

'I love you, Luke. You and your crazy dog.' And she pulled his head down to hers and kissed him again.

EPILOGUE

They were married in February, because they hadn't wanted to wait and because Fi had said they would have to delay things until after these babies of hers were born if they didn't do it quickly, since she didn't want to look like a whale in the photos. It suited them fine that they were joined as man and wife in the gardens at Tracey and Craig's home, the lawns surrounded by a border of rose bushes lush with deep pink blooms. Tables covered in snowy white table-cloths were scattered about the lawns, while hay bales under big umbrellas served as more informal seating for when guests wanted to sit and escape the sun.

Sally had agreed to give Pip away, walking her down the pergola covered path in her champagne coloured vintage beaded gown with her bouquet of roses. Behind them, Tracey and Fi and Carmen followed them in identical carnelian red gowns. As she approached the man she loved, standing with his back to her in his charcoal suit, Pip had never felt happier.

Until Craig said something to him and tapped him on the shoulder and he turned and saw her coming, and his eyes were filled with so much love that Pip felt her heart swell even more.

She'd never believed it possible that she could feel so happy.

She'd never believed she'd deserved to.

Luke had made her believe it.

Luke had made it possible.

And she smiled. Widely. This one meant for him and him alone. Because he'd saved her. From a half life spent in a shadow world. Oh, how much did she owe this man? How much did she love him?

SHE WAS A GODDESS.

Luke watched her glide towards him, loving the way she'd worn her hair up, but left some bits of it to curl around her long column of throat. He didn't know much about fashion, but that dress, with its low V-neck, and with the way it hugged her curves before falling to the ground in some kind of floaty stuff that swirled around her legs, confirmed it right there. She was nothing short of a goddess, and she was his.

And didn't that make him proud?

They exchanged their vows and kissed and everyone cheered, because this wedding had been so long wished for and so long in coming and was all the sweeter because of it.

And afterwards they feasted on the best produce that the Yorke Peninsula had to offer, washed down with Clare Valley wines, and Turbo appeared wearing a bow tie and looking like it was all about him.

Everyone, it seemed, was there, including Sheila Ferguson and Jean Cutting, and who were more than happy to gang up on him now.

'What a glorious wedding,' announced Sheila. 'Of course, we all knew it would happen sooner or later.'

'You two were so close as teenagers,' added Jean. 'We were all hoping you'd end up as more than friends. Funny how that's happened, isn't it?'

'Yeah,' he said, because it was easy to just agree with them, and because maybe they were right. 'It sure is funny how things turn out.' And he looked around to try to find his new wife.

Pip caught up with Sally after the service, noticing Sam Riordan leaving her side and heading for the drinks table.

'Thank you so much for giving me away,' she said. 'It was so special to me that you were the one to do it.'

'It was an honour, Pip. You're the daughters I never had, you and Fi both. I so want for you to be happy.'

The women hugged.

'I'm so glad you could see your way to forgive me, Pip, for everything.'

And Pip looked into her eyes and held her hands and said, 'I want you to be happy too.'

Sally shook her head, a frown creasing her brow. 'I'm not sure what you mean.'

Pip nodded in the direction of the drinks table, where Sam was chatting to the barman as he picked up a beer and a glass of champagne. 'You've been by yourself a long time. Sam seems like a nice man.'

Sally shook her head and laughed a little nervous laugh. 'Oh no, it's not like that.'

'Why not?'

'Because I'm happy by myself.'

Pip nodded. 'I thought I was too.'

'You?'

She smiled. 'Me. I was so bound up in guilt over not being with my family that night.'

'But you can hardly blame yourself for that.'

'No. And nor can you blame yourself for something Jacob Everett did more than thirty years ago. But all the people in the world can tell you that and all the people in the world can forgive you, and still it makes no difference. Because sometimes, the hardest person to forgive is yourself.'

'Oh.' Sally blinked a few times, and looked at Sam as he strode back across the lawns towards them, beaming. 'He's asked me to go for a counter lunch at the pub tomorrow. I was going to say no, but . . .' She blinked up at Pip. 'Do you think?'

'Be happy,' Pip said. 'You're allowed.'

And Sally went to meet Sam halfway, the makings of a tentative smile on her face, when Carmen reappeared, sipping on a glass of champagne, her hazel eyes sparkling, her sleek up do looking less sleek than it once had. 'Where've you been?' Pip asked suspiciously as Carmen swiped at lipstick that had ventured a little too far from her lips, as Adam adjusted his tie behind and reached for a beer from a passing tray.

'Nowhere special,' she said, looking innocent, even as Adam ran his hand down her back and settled on the curve of her butt.

Pip smiled. 'I knew you'd love that B&B.'

Carmen just smiled and intertwined her hand with Adam's.

From the speakers came the mellow tones of Norah Jones singing the opening lyrics of 'The Nearness of You' and Pip felt a wave of liquid heat roll down her spine. 'Excuse me, everyone,' Luke said as he sought her out, offering her his forearm, 'Mrs Trenorden, I do believe they're playing our song.'

She nodded as she took his arm, and smiled as his blue eyes smiled down at her, so full of love that she felt her own heart swell with it. 'Mr Trenorden, I do believe you're right.' She let him lead her to the small dance floor set up near one of the borders of flowering rose bushes, and he took her into his arms and held her achingly close and they swayed as Norah sung for them.

She breathed him in as they moved, inhaled the scent of skin and his lemon soap and the smell of Luke so deep that it filled her, drank in the feel of his big hand around hers, his arm snug around her back and his hard body against hers and knew she could never have too much of this man.

He was the rock who'd always been there for her.

He'd shown her forgiveness and he'd given her his love.

He'd brought her home.

And she would never leave this place without him by her side again.

As Norah sang her last sweet line, and the piano's final few chords trailed slowly away, Pip lifted her head from his shoulder and looked up at him. 'I love you, Luke Trenorden.'

His blue eyes whorled with warmth and love before he answered her with a kiss.

A kiss that spoke of love.

A kiss that spoke of happiness.

A kiss that promised forever.

ACKNOWLEDGMENTS

There are stories that call to you, that tug on your heart-strings and that beg to be written. Always on my Mind was just such a story.

There were three reasons for this. First, my father was ailing and going downhill quickly as he was moved into a nursing home. So much of his history was tangled up in the Copper Triangle region, a place where I had my own memories of school holidays spent at a family farm on the Yorke Peninsula. And then there was a kitchen dresser rescued from that farm, and that found its way all the way over to Canberra, and that, when I opened the doors, I was transported into the past, all because it smelled exactly of the kitchen way back there on the farm in a tiny dot of a town on the Yorke Peninsula. The kitchen of a farm house that no longer existed.

So many times I'd given writing workshops talking about how important the senses were and recounted the story about receiving the dresser and opening it up and being transported into the past. And given my father's increasing frailty, it was suddenly vitally important that I write that story, of a girl who comes home to find nothing left of her home but a few bits of furniture and she opens that dresser door and is hurtled back there, into her past, only unlike me, her past was a place filled with tragedy and betrayal.

I read the early chapters to Dad. I wrote at his bedside. he died before I had more than those first few chapters, months before the story had even sold. But I knew he was there at my shoulder, riding shotgun. I knew, because I felt him there, every step of the way.

To Fiona McArthur, who said to me way back then, when the first offer to publish this book came in, 'Clouds are like opportunities. You can just watch them float by.' - Thank you again. Here is another opportunity to get this story out, with a lovely new title and cover, and to an entirely new audience. Thank you for making me throw out a grappling hook into this one.

And last, but by no means least, thank you, dear reader, for picking up this book. Always on my Mind is a real book of the heart for me.

I hope it touches yours.

Trish xxx

ABOUT THE AUTHOR

Trish always fancied herself a writer, so she dutifully picked gherkins and washed dishes in a Chinese restaurant on her way to earning herself an economics degree and a qualification as a Chartered Accountant instead. Work took her to Canberra, where she promptly fell in love with a tall, dark and handsome hero who cut computer code, and marriage and four daughters followed, which gave Trish time to step back from her career and think about what she'd really like to do.

Writing fiction was at the top of the list. Since then, Trish has sold more than 38 books, to Harlequin Mira/Harper Collins and Tule Publishing, with sales in excess of seven million globally, her books printed in more than thirty languages in forty countries worldwide.

Four times nominated and two times winner of Romance Writers of Australia's Ruby Award (the Romantic Book of the Year) Trish is also a 2012 RITA finalist in the US.

You can find out more about Trish and upcoming books at her website at www. trishmorey.com, and you can email her at trish@trishmorey.com.

Trish loves to hear from her readers.

ALSO BY TRISH MOREY

Contemporary Romance/Women's Fiction

Cherry Season

One Summer Between Friends

The Trouble with Choices

Tule Publishing

Burning Love - Hot Aussie Knights Bk 4

Second Chance Bride - The Great Wedding Giveaway Bk 2

Harlequin Presents/Sexy/Modern

Prince's Virgin in Venice

Consequence of the Greek's Revenge

Shackled to the Sheikh - Desert Brothers Bk 4

Captive of Kadar - Desert Brothers Bk 3

Tycoon's Temptation - The Chatsfield Bk 5

A Price Worth Paying

Bartering Her Innocence

The Sheikh's Last Gamble - Desert Brothers Bk 2

Duty and the Beast - Desert Brother's Bk 1

Secrets of Castillo del Arco

Fiancee for One Night

The Storm Within, in A Royal Engagement

The Heir from Nowhere

His Prisoner in Paradise

Forbidden: The Sheikh's Virgin - Dark-Hearted Desert Men Bk 3

His Mistress for a Million

The Ruthless Greek's Virgin Princess

The Italian Billionaire's Bride

Forced Wife, Royal Love Child

Back in the Spaniard's Bed - in The Latin Lover

The Italian Boss's Mistress of Revenge

The Sheikh's Convenient Virgin

The Boss's Christmas Baby

The Spaniard's Blackmailed Bride

The Greek's Virgin

A Virgin for the Taking

For Revenge…Or Pleasure?

The Mancini Marriage Bargain - The Arranged Brides
Bk 2

Stolen by the Sheikh - The Arranged Brides Bk 1

The Italian Boss's Secret Child

The Italian's Virgin Bride

The Greek Boss's Demand

READ ON FOR AN EXCERPT FROM
CHERRY SEASON

CHERRY SEASON

San Antonio, Texas

The tattoo artist on the corner of Geronimo and Vine preferred listening to Meatloaf's 'Bat out of Hell' to conversation, but Lucy didn't mind. She was in no mood for small talk.

Every few seconds he'd pull the buzzing gun from her shoulder and wipe over her skin with a cloth before the needle would find its place again and the buzzing and the pressure would resume. It didn't hurt so much as irritate, but still Lucy bit down on her lip when the press of the needle started to burn.

Finally it was done. He swiped her skin clean and held up a mirror so she could see how it looked in the mirror in front.

She stared at the reflection. Saw the design she'd drawn herself now etched forever into the skin of her shoulder and felt tears spring unbidden from her eyes.

It was perfect.

'Did it hurt?' the tattooist asked, frowning as he handed her the Kleenex.

'Yeah,' she said over the lump in her throat, knowing they were talking about different things. 'It did.'

Adelaide Hills - 2 years later

His sisters were up to something.

Dan Faraday knew that for a fact. He'd known it ever since Hannah had suggested a birthday dinner. On a picking day, no less, when she would have known that any dinner couldn't possibly happen before nine.

The niggle at the base of his neck kept right on niggling as he stacked the last boxes of today's cherries in the coolroom. Oh, yeah, they were up to something all right. When you were an Adelaide Hills orchardist and your birthday fell slap bang in the middle of cherry season, there were much more important things to worry about than having a birthday party.

Like bringing in a crop for a start. The first decent looking cherry crop in three years, but the worry was that the birds would get to the fruit faster than it could be picked, or that the thunderclouds would roll in and the fruit would split and the most promising harvest in recent times would be ruined. Another bust year and the banks would stop circling like sharks and head in for the kill.

It was make or break time and Dan knew it.

The three sisters who'd grown up with him on the orchard should have known it too.

So what the hell were they up to?

He sighed and checked his reflection in the cracked mirror above the shed's washbasin, taking in the dust in his whiskers and the ring around his head where his hat had stuck his hair down all day. The dust was an easy fix. Hat head, not so much. He did the best he could to unflatten the ring of hair with his fingers but in the end there wasn't a hell of a lot he could do about it, and why worry anyway? It wasn't like he'd asked for this party. 'Occupational hazard,' he muttered as he flicked off the lights in the packing shed, calling for Molly out of habit, before realising with a thud that Molly was gone.

Bugger.

Outside, day was fast slipping away to night, the orchard sleeping under a blanket of wispy cloud. No possibility of rain and warm enough that there was no chance of frost according to the weather bureau. He slapped his dusty hat against his legs. Small mercies.

Laughter drifted up from the house where his family had gathered. Most of the time he was happy to have family show up – even more so when they helped him and Pop out. They'd all spent a couple of hours in the packing shed grading cherries earlier before Pop had taken off to collect Nan, and the girls had headed for the kitchen to get supper ready. But it had been a long day in a series of long days that had started two weeks ago and wouldn't let up until the season was over, one way or another.

Besides which, he just wasn't all that fussed with birthdays.

That was all.

They were all waiting for him inside, Nan and Pop together with his three sisters, twins Hannah and Beth, plus Sophie, their junior by a couple of years, along with Siena, Beth's eight-year-old daughter. All of them arranged around a table laden with platters of sandwiches and sausage rolls fresh from the oven, if his nose wasn't mistaken. In spite of his mood, his stomach rumbled.

'Finally!' squealed Siena, his niece's face lighting up as

Dan shoved his battered hat onto a hook beside the door. She launched herself at him, wrapped her arms about his waist and looked up at him with big brown eyes. 'I'm starving, Uncle Dan!'

'You're always starving,' said Beth, as she reached for a bottle of sparkling wine to top up everyone's glasses. 'How about you wish your uncle a happy birthday instead of thinking about your stomach for a while?'

'I already did!' Siena protested. 'And I can't help it if I'm hungry.'

'She did too,' Dan agreed, as he patted his niece on the back, because Siena had burst into the packing shed ahead of Beth when they'd arrived, brimming with the news that they had a big secret for his birthday, which was kind of the same thing, surely? And despite the uneasy feeling in his gut about whatever this surprise might be, he was still clinging to the hope that the big secret comprised a bag of mixed nuts and a bottle of port, like it usually did.

'Of course the girl's hungry,' said silver-haired Nan, greeting her grandson with a hug, a surprisingly strong one for a woman in her late seventies who barely came up to his shoulders. 'Siena's growing and she's got hollow legs. You were all the same at that age.' She planted a kiss on Dan's cheek and he caught a whiff of the Estée Lauder perfume he'd bought her for Mother's Day, the same perfume he bought her every year, and if he didn't know that she loved it so much, he'd think she was drinking the stuff. 'Happy birthday, Daniel.'

'Nan brought a cake,' said Hannah.

'A sponge cake,' Sophie said with a wink. 'Your favourite.'

'Yeah? Thanks Nan,' he said, giving her another squeeze and starting to relax. Maybe he'd been overreacting, maybe he was just cranky after a long day in the orchard, because

Nan made the best sponge cakes and whatever else was happening, if there was sponge cake involved, it couldn't be all bad.

He snatched up a sausage roll, still warm from the oven, then dipped it in a bowl of tomato sauce and almost swallowed it down whole because he was so hungry. And suddenly he found himself thinking that maybe getting together for dinner tonight hadn't been such a bad idea after all, and it wasn't just because for once he didn't have to rummage around in the freezer for something to heat up.

They hardly ever got together as a family these days. Sophie sometimes dropped by when she'd finished work at the local school, but between the cherry season, Beth's shifts with the ambos, and Hannah being on call more often than not at the vet clinic, it would probably be Christmas before they were all together again. The way Siena was shooting up, she'd be a good couple of inches taller by then.

Best of all, it was an excuse for his Nan's sponge cake . . .

'Bubbles for you, Dan?' asked Beth, offering him a glass filled to the brim.

He shook his head. 'Not that kind. I'll grab a beer. How about you, Pop?' he said, as he headed for the fridge. 'Can I get you a beer?'

'Pop?' he said, standing there a few moments later with the fridge door open, because if his Pop had answered, he hadn't heard it. But Pop was sitting to one side, staring down at his untouched plate. Dan frowned and pulled a couple of stubbies from the door.

'You right, Pop?' he asked, when he pulled up a chair alongside.

'Wha –?' Pop said in his gravelly voice, blinking as he looked up. And then he saw the beer and smiled. 'Oh, yeah. I'd better have a beer to celebrate my favourite grandson's birthday.'

Dan snorted. 'Only grandson, more like it,' he said as he unscrewed the lids on a couple of Coopers and handed one over before taking a long, satisfying swig of the other. 'Long day,' he said at last, figuring that Pop must have been dog tired before he'd gone home to pick up Nan and heading back again. He might be as strong as an ox and look a good deal younger than he was, but the old fellow was pushing eighty. Dan ought to remember that.

Pop grunted as he put his untouched plate back up on the table. 'They're all long this time of year.'

'You're not hungry?'

'Indigestion. Need a good burp, that's all.' He grinned and raised his beer in Dan's direction. 'This'll fix it. Happy birthday, lad.'

They clinked bottles and both drank deeply. Suddenly Pop gave a good, long burp.

'Clarence Faraday!' chided his wife, while Siena giggled and Clarry simply sighed as he patted his belly.

'Ah, that feels better.'

Even Dan found a smile, because Pop was right. After a long hot day in the orchard, nothing beat an ice cold beer. Unless it was a supper he hadn't had to prepare. He loaded up his plate and tucked in, happy to let his three sisters drive the conversation. Not that he had much of a chance of getting a word in edgewise anyway with them eager to pick up the discussion they'd left off when he'd come inside. Something about how much they all had to get done before Christmas, but which was rapidly escalating into a dispute over which one of them deserved a holiday the most.

Which was a laugh, he thought, reaching for another sausage roll, because as far as he was concerned, there was no contest. He couldn't remember the last holiday he'd had.

'People don't appreciate how hard it is,' said Sophie,

'chasing after other people's kids all day. Not to mention, dealing with some of the parents.'

'I hope you're not referring to Siena and me,' said Beth, quick to take umbrage.

'Of course not! If all the kids were like Siena, it'd be a cake walk. Trouble is, they're not.'

'You're not going to get much sympathy from me,' Hannah said, clearly unimpressed. 'I'm on call, two weekends out of three at the vet surgery, and you work normal hours and get ten weeks paid holidays a year.'

Sophie shrugged. 'We need those holidays. There's got to be some kind of compensation for educating other people's kids.'

'So what compensation do I get,' Beth intervened, 'for having patients throw up and worse over me?'

'You get the satisfaction of knowing you're saving lives,' nodded Sophie, as if that was compensation enough.

Dan sipped on his beer and left his sisters to it, content that at least they weren't ganging up on him for a change.

Three sisters. What were the chances? And while their Dad had hankered for another son, and Dan wouldn't have said no to a brother to share this orchard caper with, given that none of his sisters seemed keen, he wouldn't trade any of these three for quids.

'Oh, hey, while I think of it,' Sophie interrupted, 'I meant to tell you all about the quiz night coming up at the primary school in a few weeks.'

'You've got to be kidding me?' Beth said. 'At this time of year? There's plenty enough going on in November and December without squeezing another event into the calendar.'

'Not to mention a cherry crop to bring in,' growled Dan. Was nobody else worried about the cherries?

Sophie held up both hands. 'I know, I know. But this is a

fundraiser for Jamie Hanson. You know, that little year two boy who's been diagnosed with that rare cancer. His family has to raise one hundred thousand dollars for his treatment in Germany and they can't wait until February. We have to do it before school breaks up.'

'Oh, that poor child,' said Nan. 'Of course we'll go, won't we Clarry. We've never said no to a quiz night yet, and we're not going to start now just because it's a busy time of year – not when there's a little boy's health at stake.'

'Well, don't count on me being there,' said Dan. 'I'm flat out enough this time of year without finding other stuff to do.'

'It's to help Jamie,' protested Siena.

'A very good cause,' Beth conceded. 'I'll be there. So long as I'm not working late shift .'

'We'll all be there,' Nan said, nodding sagely. 'It wouldn't be a quiz night if the Faraday table didn't show up.'

'Excuse me, am I the only one who's actually worried about this year's crop?'

'Hey, the cherries look great,' Hannah said.

'We still have to get them in,' he grumbled, and went back to nursing his beer.

Pop moved out of his seat for a minute and Sophie sat herself down beside him, clinking her wine glass against the beer bottle in his hands. 'Meant to tell you, Mum dropped me an email today. She said she'd popped a card in the post but to wish you a happy birthday in case you hadn't had a chance to clear the mail lately.'

He smiled. Now there was a woman who understood the demands of cherry season. 'Good of her to think of me.' Although to be fair, he knew there was more to it than just being nice. Wendy had married his dad when Dan had been nine years old and while she'd always been a great mum to him, she'd never tried to pretend he hadn't had another before her, or made him feel like he didn't belong when the girls had come along. In fact, three years after John had died, it had been Wendy who'd moved out of the family home.

'You're thirty now,' she'd said to him, explaining her decision to move with Sophie to a small unit down in the suburbs now that the two older girls were settled in a flat close to uni. 'You don't need your step-mum cramping your style.' He'd missed her, but he couldn't blame her for wanting her own space given that Dad was gone.

'How is Wendy?' he asked.

'Good. She wanted me to warn you though, there's an invitation in with the card. She and Dirk are getting hitched. She would have called herself only she knew we were coming around tonight and you'd be busy. But she wanted you to hear it from us before someone else blabbed the news.'

'They're getting married?'

Sophie put a hand on his arm. 'You don't mind do you? It's ten years now since Dad passed away.'

'Oh no,' he said, snapping himself out of it, 'not at all.' After all, Wendy deserved to be happy and Dirk seemed like a nice guy and he'd been on the scene a while. 'It's . . . kind of nice. I'm happy for her. For both of them.'

She squeezed his arm and smiled. 'I told her you would be.'

'Thing is,' Dan said, 'how do you feel about it? You're the one who's going to be impacted the most, aren't you?'

Sophie shook her head, setting the ends of her short dark bob swaying. 'Mum's moving in with Dirk - she's practically living with him as it is - and leaving me the unit for now.' She grinned. 'Just in case,' she said. Not that there's any chance of it not working out, I reckon.'

'That's cool,' Dan said, liking the idea more and more. 'Tell her I'll be there with bells on.'

Sophie grinned. 'I'd like to see that.'

'Who's been sitting in my chair?' growled Pop, and Sophie jumped up.

'Just keeping it warm for you, Papa Bear,' she said, heading back to her sisters.

'Well that's all right then,' he said, handing his grandson another beer before he sat stiffly down. 'Cherry auction's coming up this week. I reckon those Bings are going to be hard to beat.'

'Yeah,' agreed Dan, knowing the cherries had never looked better. 'That's what I'm hoping.' To get the cherries noticed and a swag of orders to follow. It wasn't too much to hope for, was it? 'So long as Des next door keeps his bloody cherry slug to himself and the weather holds out, the season might actually turn out all right for a change.'

'Hey you guys, no talking shop!' Beth interrupted, offering around a plate of cheese and crackers. 'Besides, Dan, I need to ask you if you're still okay to pick up Siena after Cassie's party on Sunday?'

Dan helped himself to some crackers and a few wedges of cheese. 'Sure. Balhannah wasn't it?'

'Yeah, the Duncan place, you know the one, the big double storey on Mugga Road. Four o'clock pick up, okay? I should be back pretty close to five, so just drop her off home.'

He nodded. 'Sure you don't need me to take her as well?'

'No, she's having a sleepover with Cassie the night before. Gotta warn you though, it might take a bit to prise her away.' She glanced over her shoulder at her daughter, who was sitting on Nan's lap and telling her a longwinded story about something, before turning back and whispering apologetically, 'It's a pony party.'

Oh. 'Thanks for the warning,' he said. The last time he'd had to pick up his niece from a pony party, it had taken forty-five minutes and a whole lot of wailing before he'd managed to lure her away from the horses and her friends and into the car. Siena had cried all the way home. Lucky this time he had a plan B.

Across the table, Hannah clapped her hands. 'Eat up, everyone, or we'll never get to cake.'

'And Uncle Dan's surprise,' added Siena, sliding off Nan's lap.

If he hadn't already been looking forward to his Nan's sponge cake, he might have been suspicious right about then. He might have read something into Hannah's eagerness or the glare Beth shot her daughter. But his stomach was full and he was halfway through a rare second beer and despite the casual way his family made light of his concerns, he was feeling mellow.

Until Sophie stood and moved the plates out the way for Hannah to swing the cake into pride of place on the table, and he saw the candles on top.

Bloody hell!

The birthday cake was practically groaning under the weight of tall curly candles in every colour of the rainbow. The last time he'd had more than one candle on a cake, he'd been about Siena's age, and that was more than a quarter of a century ago. What the hell were they playing at?

He turned to his niece, trying to keep the grump from his voice, because if someone younger than ten years of age had thought of it, he could just about forgive them for it. 'Is this your idea, Siena?'

'It was mum's idea,' she said gleefully, the reflected flames dancing in the chocolate brown of his niece's eyes while she watched the twins working quickly to light all the candles, even as the first ones started to drip wax onto the cake before the last had been lit. 'Mum's and Hannah's.'

'Is that so,' he said, because with a sick feeling, he realised he'd been right. His sisters had been up to something and here was the proof.

'Thirty-seven years years old,' Hannah said, working a lighted match around her end of the candles. 'How does it feel to be so old?'

'Three years till the big four oh,' said her twin, gleefully joining in the harassment as she worked her side of the cake. 'That's almost middle-aged, bro!'

'You'll be on a pension soon,' predicted Sophie. 'Do you have any last requests?'

'Yeah,' he said. 'Mostly for my sisters to stop banging on about my age.' There was a good reason he wasn't fussed with birthdays. A damned good reason. 'You do realise age is just a number.'

'And now for the finishing touch,' said Hannah, oblivious to his deepening scowl. She held four sparklers to the match flame and then stuck them at the four points of the cake, the lighted sparklers showering the table in silver sparks. 'Ta da!' she said triumphantly.

Dan couldn't prevent the roll of his eyes. With sparks flying every which way, it looked like the fireworks going off at the Royal Adelaide Show.

Siena clapped her hands, and squealed her delight. 'Yay, Uncle Dan!'

His sisters, he noticed, couldn't stop grinning.

Even Nan put her hands over her smiling mouth and said, 'Oh my. Have you ever seen anything like it, Clarry?'

He never heard his Pop's reply, over Hannah's, 'Siena, quick, turn off the lights. Okay, everyone all together, one two three,

Happy birthday to you . . . '

They all joined in. His three sisters and his niece, his Nan doing soprano and his Pop bringing in a quaky baritone. If Molly had been here, she would have been howling along with the lot of them.

Oh no.

Please God, tell me they haven't got me a new puppy.

'Happy birthday to you.'

The sparks flew and the curly tapers melted and sagged against each other and the flames merged and shot higher still.

'Happy birthday, dear Da-an.

'Happy birthday to you.'

He looked at the growing blaze on top of the cake, felt the heat from the flame and followed the smoky heat trail to the smoke detector screwed on tight to the ceiling above and hard-wired to the monitoring service, and thought, uh-oh ...

'Han,' he said, trying to get her attention.

'Hip hip – hooray!'

'Han!' But Hannah, his biggest little sister who'd bossed him around unmercifully since she was two years old, wasn't letting go of the reins just yet.

'Hip hip – hooray!'

'Hannah!' he said, pointing up to the ceiling. 'The bloody smoke detector!'

She looked up and managed a slight frown, but she was on a mission and there was no stopping her now.

'Hip hip –'

The alarm in the corner started screaming. Siena shrieked in an even higher pitch, and everyone ducked their heads and covered their ears, even Dan. 'I told you!' he yelled across the table.

She shook her head. 'What?'

'The smoke detector!'

'So blow them out!'

He craned his head over the table. 'What?'

'Blow the candles out!'

He snorted. Fat chance of that, – already they had a blaze that would do the Olympic flame justice – and lunged instead for the fire blanket hanging near the hotplates. The siren inside was joined now by the whoop of the alarm outside, and he had the silver blanket pulled from the package and unfolded and ready to throw when Hannah grabbed hold of his arm. 'Don't you dare!'

'But –' He glanced over at his Nan who looked close to tears, her hands over her mouth as she turned her face into Pop's chest, though whether from the cacophony going on around them or the thought that her precious sponge cake might be flattened, he couldn't tell.

Aw, hell. He threw the blanket aside and grabbed Siena's arm instead. 'Siena,' he shouted,

'help me out here.' He wasn't sure if his niece had heard him but he started blowing, and Siena joined in on his right flank, because there was no turning off the alarm until this bloody bushfire on a plate was out. Between the two of them, they somehow managed to get it under control, leaving a stunted forest of deformed candles and twisted sparkler wires sending tendrils of acrid smoke coiling into the air.

He turned on the exhaust fan in the kitchen on his march to the alarm panel and was punching in the code when the phone rang. 'It's the security agency,' said Beth, with her hand over the receiver. 'They want to know if there's a problem.'

Like she had to ask? Yes, there's a bloody problem all right, thought Dan, but he didn't say that. Instead he sucked in air and took the phone, gave them the password and assured them that yes, everything was under control and no, there was no need for an appliance.

No thanks to the three musketeers here.

'That was exciting,' said Hannah, clearing off the remaining savoury food when Dan got back to the table, still shaking his head. Yeah, normally he wouldn't swap his sisters for quids, but if someone was offering right now, he'd be sorely tempted .

'My ears are ringing,' said Nan, who'd recovered and was busy pulling out candles and picking out the worst of the wax from the top of the cake. She began cutting it into thick wedges, while Beth was boiling the kettle and organising coffee and tea. Dan picked up what was left of his beer and looked at it and put it down again, wondering what had happened to feeling mellow.

'Well,' said Pop, sounding almost breathless, 'that was a real heart-starter. I must be getting too old for all this palaver.'

Dan frowned, because now that he looked at him, Pop didn't just look tired, he looked grey, and every bit of his eighty years old. It struck him that his Pop hadn't moved at all during the excitement, let alone tried to put the fire out or deal with the alarm. He'd assumed he had been holding onto Nan, but now he wondered if it wasn't the other way around. 'Are you sure you're okay?

'Course I'm okay,' he said, puffing out his chest. 'Fit as a mallee bull, if you must know. A piece of Joanie's cake and I'll be right as rain, won't I love?'

'If you say so, Clarry, it's never failed to work before. Now, who else for cake? Birthday boy first. Siena, you can hand them out.'

'Can we do presents now?' asked Siena, as she passed plates of cake to her uncle and then her pop.

Oh, God, Dan thought. So the birthday cake from hell hadn't been the surprise. Please just let it be mixed nuts and port.

'Of course, we can,' said her mum. 'Uncle Dan can't wait, and besides, we can't stay much longer. You've got to get up early for school tomorrow.'

'Aww, do I have to go to school?'

'Yes you do,' said Beth, nodding.

'But it's almost holidays.'

'And when it's holidays, you can stay home. Until then, you go to school.'

The girl tossed her head up to the ceiling, looking pained. 'But Mu-um.'

'No.'

'I know,' said Siena, her brown eyes already alive with an alternate plan. 'I could come help Uncle Dan pick cherries.'

'No.'

'Sure, you can,' said Dan, only to earn himself a what-the-fuck frown from his sister. He grinned at that, happy to have scored a point against one of his sisters, when he was down so many. 'But you have to be here ready to start work at six.'

The girl pouted. 'I don't have to get up that early for school.'

'Ah, in that case you're better off going to school.'

For a moment, she looked like she wanted to argue the case.

'I thought you wanted to do presents,' said Beth, and the girl huffed off to forage in a basket, back a scant twenty seconds later with two familiar shaped packages hugged to her chest. And judging by the grin on her face, her disappointment was all but forgotten.. 'Happy birthday, Uncle Dan.' She handed them over one at a time and he took them in each hand and then wrapped his arms around her in a big hug to say thanks.

And never before had he meant it so much.

He'd have recognised those packages anywhere. Still, he took his time unwrapping each present carefully, expressing surprise and delight when sure enough, first nuts and then port were revealed.

'Fantastic,' he said, and meant it. 'My favourites.' Siena's grin widened.

'Something simple from us both,' said his Nan, handing him an unmistakably shaped box that also contained no secrets. And still he could be excited when he opened a box of chocolates.

'That's great guys,' he said. 'It's really good of you all to be here tonight. I appreciate it.'

'Hey,' piped up Beth, 'not so fast. There's one more present.'

Sophie handed him the small flat package. 'Happy birthday, bro. This is from us all.' He smiled and kissed her cheek and weighed it up in his hands; too thin for chocolates, not near enough legs for a puppy, but there was something inside – maybe some DVDs? That'd be all right too.

He ripped off the gift wrap and stopped and stared at the plain black box inside, a box embossed with the golden letters of a website.

'What's this?' he said, turning it over in his hands. 'What's hea dot com?'

'Not hea. H-E-A dot com,' spelled out Beth.

He shrugged. 'So?' It still meant nothing to him.

Hannah licked her lips, looking sideways at her sisters. 'We thought you could use a helping hand – so we bought you a profile on Happy Ever After.' She waited a few seconds while she let that sink it. 'It's an online dating service, Dan.'

And Siena clapped her hands. 'Surprise!

'You bought me a what?'

'It's a subscription, Dan,' said Hannah, softly.

'Just for three months,' Beth added.

'To a dating agency,' Sophie offered, smiling hopefully but sounding decidedly tentative. 'A really good one. Maybe you even might find someone to take with you to Wendy's wedding.'

'And the quiz night,' said Siena.

He growled and slung the black box skidding across the table as if it were poison, and looked at his sisters.

'Is this some kind of joke?' But not one of their faces cracked a smile, so he turned to his Nan and Pop, expecting them to be just as offended and horrified as he was. Because, of course, anyone in their right mind would be. He snorted. 'Can you believe this?'

His nan looked nervously away and he watched her put her hand across her chest and cough. 'We're all just worried about you, Dan,' she said, as she rose and started stacking cake plates. 'It's not as if you're getting any younger.'

Well, sure. Of course they were worried about him. 'But a dating agency? Really?'

He looked searchingly to his pop, who apparently felt a similar sudden need to clear his throat and still looked none the better for doing it. 'None of us is getting any younger and nobody lives forever. Your sisters would just like to see you settled. We all would. What's wrong with giving it a try?'

It was the longest speech he'd ever heard his pop give that didn't concern the weather or the cherries, but right now that wasn't something to celebrate. He turned back to his sisters. 'You really think I need signing up to a dating agency like some loser who can't find himself a girlfriend?'

If he'd expected them to look sorry, he was wrong. Hannah wasn't about to make any excuses. 'Nobody said you were a loser, Dan. We just thought it might offer you a few more options.'

'Options.' He nodded slowly. Exaggeratedly. 'For finding a girlfriend.'

'Exactly!' she said. 'Because isn't that what you ultimately want? Someone to share your life with and have a family and maybe even a child or two to pass the orchard down to – given none of us are lining up for the task? You can hardly find a wife if you don't find a girlfriend first.'

'Give me a break! Don't you think I'm perfectly capable of going out and finding myself someone to share my life with?'

His sisters exchanged looks, and it was what they didn't say that was more telling.

'What?' he demanded, his hands spread wide. 'What does that look mean? That I've got no chance otherwise?'

Beth shrugged. 'Well, face it Dan. It's not like you've dated anyone for a long time. What is it - ten years - since Margot?'

No way it could be ten years, but right now he wasn't about to argue that point. He held his arms out. 'And did it occur to anyone here that it's cherry season and I might be just a bit busy to go out socialising?'

'We know that!' said Beth. 'But if you don't mind me asking, what have you done in between cherry seasons?'

'Well,' he said, 'there's apple and pear season right on its heels and then there's winter and stuff to do in the orchard, and then it's spring again. What do you think, I've been sitting on my hands here?'

'Nobody thinks that,' said Hannah. 'We know how hard you work, which is why we thought it might be easier to meet someone online, and work out whether you're compatible before you meet them in person.'

'But I don't need to meet women online before I figure I want to date them!'

'Because?'

'Because there's heaps of women around here that I could date if I just asked.'

'Like who?'

He shrugged. 'Like that woman from the school library. Helen, or whatever her name is. Her!'

'You mean Ellen Coburn?'

'Yeah, that's the one. She seemed nice enough when I saw her at Siena's school music concert that time.'

Sophie slowly shook her head. 'Ellen got married a year ago.'

'Oh. Well, what about that woman who works in the pub sometimes? The redhead. Or is she married too?'

'If you mean Heather Adams, then no,' said Beth. 'She's not married, not last I heard.'

'You see? So I don't need this kind of – help – if that's what you call it. I'll look her up at the cherry auction next week.'

The girls exchanged glances. 'Exactly how long is it since you've been to the pub, big bro?'

He blinked and rubbed his stubbled jaw. 'I dunno. Couple of months, I guess. Why do you ask?'

'Heather left for South America more than six months ago. She took one of those volunteer jobs teaching kids English.'

Dan cut the air with his hands. Whatever their point was, he didn't want to hear it. 'So maybe I just don't have time to go to the pub!'

'That's just it, Dan,' cooed Hannah, stroking his shoulder and looking all too understanding, and Dan got the distinct impression this is exactly the way she'd be in the surgery, soothing a frightened labrador before sticking a dirty great needle in its leg to send him to sleep before she lopped something off. 'We know you don't have the time, so why don't you give it a try? What have you got to lose?'

He shook off her hand. He didn't need to be soothed. He didn't want to go to sleep and wake up and find his sisters had lopped anything off – even if it was just his right to decide how and when he'd meet women.

'I haven't got time for any of this.'

'Ah, but that's the best thing,' said Beth. 'It won't take a minute of your time because we've already set up your profile for you.'

He coughed. 'Excuse me. My *what?*'

'Your profile. So women can see what a fabulous catch you are.'

He snorted.

'But you are, Dan. Thirty-seven years old and never been hitched. Clean living and fit and if you weren't a cherry farmer, you could just about be a male model for one of those RM Williams catalogues.'

'Bullshit!'

'Dan,' scolded Nan, 'there's a child present.'

'Bugger. Sorry,' Dan said, and cursed himself again, even as Siena looked up and said, 'I've heard worse than that at school, Nan. You should hear what some of the kids say at recess when they know Mrs Innstairs isn't listening. They say –'

Beth clapped a hand over her daughter's mumbling mouth. 'We don't want to hear it, young lady,' she warned. And then she turned to her brother, wearing a smile that he didn't trust one bit. 'It's perfect, Dan. You don't have to leave home, you don't have to do a thing,' said Beth. 'Except wait for all the matches to roll in.'

'There's probably half a dozen lined up panting already,' said Sophie. 'Hey, so why don't we log in now, and show you how it works?'

'Great idea,' said Hannah, picking up the black box and brushing off a few stray crumbs before she held it out to Dan. 'All the details are inside. We can check out your potential matches right now.'

'Yeah, do it!' said Beth. 'See how good this is. You're gonna love it, bro.'

'I want to see!' said Siena, squirming out from under her

mother's silencing hold, and the fact that an eight-year-old was interested in his love life – or lack of it – was the last straw as far as Dan was concerned.

'No! Nobody is going to see anything.' This was rubbish and he had to put a stop to it. 'I don't know why you're all so worried about my love life. I don't see any of you guys lining up to get married.'

'Hey,' said Beth, looping her arms over her daughter's shoulders and pulling her in tight. 'I would have been.'

'Aw, Beth . . .' Dan put a hand to his head. What a stupid, dumb arse thing to say. Beth had beem the only one of them that ever looked like getting married. 'I'm sorry. I didn't think.'

'Nobody's given you a chance to think tonight,' clucked his Nan, doing what she did best and mending bridges. She got up and gathered various bits of Tupperware together, finding a moment to give Beth's shoulder a squeeze. 'I think we should all let Dan explore his present in private and at his leisure, don't you, girls? Come on, Clarry. It's getting late.'

'Yeah, we have to go too,' said Beth, propelling Siena into action. There were murmurs of agreement from his other sisters and in a few moments the kitchen was filled with activity as everyone began collecting their bits and divvying up the leftovers, with the lion's share being left for Dan.

Outside by their car, Dan leaned down to give his Nan a kiss and a hug. 'Thanks for the cake, Nan. And the chocolates.'

'My pleasure. And Dan?'

'Yeah?'

'Have a think about what your sisters are trying to doing for you. This thing doesn't have to be all bad. You know we'd all like to see you happy.'

'Who says I'm not happy?'

'You're the grumpiest orchardist in the district,' his Nan said bluntly. 'At least, that's what I've heard.'

'So I'm busy!'

'But you don't have to be grumpy. Do us all a favour and check this thing out. Before it's too late and nobody wants you.'

He rolled his eyes but still managed to summon a smile. 'Yeah,' he lied, 'I'll think about it.'

They were all gone, the last of the dishes were in the dishwasher, and the house was silent except for the ticking of the old grandfather clock – the sound louder than it had ever been, it seemed to Dan, as it counted down the minutes and hours of his remaining life.

Bloody hell, he wasn't that old. But neither was he stupid. He hadn't appreciated being presented with a done deal, but he was a pragmatist. He'd always planned on getting married and having kids one day. God, he might already have been married if Margot hadn't taken one look at Wendy and Nan still tending the raspberry canes, and got cold feet. But then it's just as well she had, because the orchard life was no place for a woman who didn't contribute and who wanted to be looked after.

But Margot was years ago – more than ten, he suddenly realised – and he'd always expected the marriage thing to happen naturally without too much effort, kind of organically, by osmosis or something.

He picked up the little black box from where it lay unopened on the table, and tapped it against the fingers of his other hand. If his sisters were right and there were single women already lined up waiting, it couldn't be too hard to find a wife. It wasn't like he had nothing going for him, even if his sisters were laying it on a bit thick when they made it sound like he was God's gift to single women.

And after his experience with Margot, it wasn't like he

didn't know what kind of woman the orchard needed. In fact, if he thought about it, it wasn't that hard to hammer out a list of requirements.

Someone sensible and mature.

Someone responsible and not afraid of long days and hard work.

Someone ready to start a family, probably around thirty to thirty-five years old who'd be a good mum.

Looks desirable but not compulsory. He wasn't a fool; he wasn't expecting too much in that department. She didn't need to be drop-dead gorgeous by any means – but if she had good teeth (because he'd heard from some of his mates that orthodontic bills for their kids were a killer) that'd be a bonus.

He thought of the leftovers in the fridge. Oh yeah, and someone who could cook.

It wasn't like he was asking for the world, he rationalised. He just needed someone who could fit in to a primary producer's life and who understood the responsibility and commitment that went with it.

That was about the size of it.

He looked at the box in his hand and tossed it back on the table. No, his sisters were underestimating him as usual. He'd check it out later if it came to that.

Now that they'd flagged the issue and he'd nutted out exactly what he was looking for, the hard work was just about done.

A woman like that shouldn't be hard to find.

❀

Like to read on?

You can find Cherry Season here.

Lightning Source UK Ltd.
Milton Keynes UK
UKHW012026280121
377836UK00002B/88